A WINTERY DELIGHT

On the far side of the garden facing south with its back to a steep-sloped spur of Wicken's Down, stood the orangery. From up on the moor, Mariette had seen the vast expanses of glass glittering in the sun and wondered what it was. Close to, it was still more impressive.

Because of reflections, little of the interior was visible from the outside. "May we go in?" Mariette asked.

"Yes, I have brought the key. It's kept locked so that the door is not left ajar by accident. The place is heated, as you will feel." He took a key from his pocket and opened the French door.

Mariette went first. Dry heat; she pushed back her hood. A sweet, exotic fragrance.

Despite all the windows, after the glare of the snow outside Mariette's sight took a moment to adjust. Then she saw the trees, ranked along the back wall in huge terra cotta pots. Against the glossy dark-green leaves, the orange globes of the fruit seemed to glow, while clusters of snow-white blossoms sent forth their aromatic, sensuous perfume.

"Oh, beautiful! I did not know they bloom at the same time the fruit ripens." She looked up at Lord Malcolm to share her delight.

"This is the best time," he said in an odd voice. And then he kissed her . . .

ZEBRA'S REGENCY ROMANCES
DAZZLE AND DELIGHT

A BEGUILING INTRIGUE   (4441, $3.99)
by Olivia Sumner

Pretty as a picture Justine Riggs cared nothing for propriety. She dressed as a boy, sat on her horse like a jockey, and pondered the stars like a scientist. But when she tried to best the handsome Quenton Fletcher, Marquess of Devon, by proving that she was the better equestrian, he would try to prove Justine's antics were pure folly. The game he had in mind was seduction — never imagining that he might lose his heart in the process!

AN INCONVENIENT ENGAGEMENT   (4442, $3.99)
by Joy Reed

Rebecca Wentworth was furious when she saw her betrothed waltzing with another. So she decides to make him jealous by flirting with the handsomest man at the ball, John Collinwood, Earl of Stanford. The "wicked" nobleman knew exactly what the enticing miss was up to — and he was only too happy to play along. But as Rebecca gazed into his magnificent eyes, her errant fiancé was soon utterly forgotten!

SCANDAL'S LADY   (4472, $3.99)
by Mary Kingsley

Cassandra was shocked to learn that the new Earl of Lynton was her childhood friend, Nicholas St. John. After years at sea and mixed feelings Nicholas had come home to take the family title. And although Cassandra knew her place as a governess, she could not help the thrill that went through her each time he was near. Nicholas was pleased to find that his old friend Cassandra was his new next door neighbor, but after being near her, he wondered if mere friendship would be enough . . .

HIS LORDSHIP'S REWARD   (4473, $3.99)
by Carola Dunn

As the daughter of a seasoned soldier, Fanny Ingram was accustomed to the vagaries of military life and cared not a whit about matters of rank and social standing. So she certainly never foresaw her *tendre* for handsome Viscount Roworth of Kent with whom she was forced to share lodgings, while he carried out his clandestine activities on behalf of the British Army. And though good sense told Roworth to keep his distance, he couldn't stop from taking Fanny in his arms for a kiss that made all hearts equal!

Available wherever paperbacks are sold, or order direct from the Publisher. Send cover price plus 50¢ per copy for mailing and handling to Penguin USA, P.O. Box 999, c/o Dept. 17109, Bergenfield, NJ 07621. Residents of New York and Tennessee must include sales tax. DO NOT SEND CASH.

Carola Dunn

The Tudor Secret

ZEBRA BOOKS
KENSINGTON PUBLISHING CORP.

ZEBRA BOOKS are published by

Kensington Publishing Corp.
850 Third Avenue
New York, NY 10022

First Printing: December, 1995

Printed in the United States of America

Chapter 1

"Pique, repique, and capot."

In the pale January sunshine filtering through the tall windows of the inn's coffee room, the handsome young face opposite Lord Malcolm was aghast. "It can't be. Let me see."

Malcolm spread out the tricks he had taken and lounged back in his Windsor chair, languid hands linked across his natty waistcoat, striped in coquelicot and pearl-grey. He watched as Sir Ralph Riddlesworth feverishly scanned the cards. Drooping eyelids hid the glint of triumph at this unbelievable stroke of good fortune. A devilishly promising start to his mission!

"Another *partie*," begged the youthful baronet, blue eyes appealing. "I'll win it back. It's a family heirloom." He reached for the signet ring, a topaz incised with a sphinx seal.

Malcolm's hand shot out and grasped his wrist in a grip of iron. "Not so fast, my friend. You pledged the ring because you had already lost all your blunt."

"I'll borrow some," said Riddlesworth sullenly, massaging his wrist. "Everyone knows me here."

His gaze sceptical, Malcolm scanned their surroundings. The Golden Hind was one of the busiest inns in Plymouth, but at present the room was nearly empty. The mail had come and gone; the stagecoach from London was not expected for another hour. By the next window two respectable middle-aged females gossiped over a pot of tea, and a retired sea captain with a wooden leg drowsed over his ale in the inglenook. The waiter had played least in sight since bringing their bottle of claret, now scarcely half emptied, and a sealed pack of cards. No doubt he was resting tired feet before the next rush.

The fair young man—no more than one or two and twenty, some six years Malcolm's junior—looked discomfited. "The landlord will oblige me," he muttered.

"Ah, but I do not choose to wait while you make your arrangements," Malcolm drawled, "nor, in fact, do I choose to play any longer. My thanks for the entertainment. Now excuse me, if you please." The ring safely bestowed in the inside breast pocket of his burgundy-red coat, he rose, bowed, and moved towards the door.

Riddlesworth followed him, plucking at his sleeve, pleading in a low voice for a chance to win back his heirloom. He was taller and heavier than Malcolm, who felt like a kestrel pestered by a crow.

"Enough, my dear fellow, pray don't make a cake of yourself." Distastefully brushing his sleeve, he continued out into the lobby and called for the landlord.

"I shall stay here tonight, my good man," he announced loudly, "and drive on to Corycombe in the morning. Tell my groom we'll leave at nine."

From the corner of his eye, he saw Riddlesworth's dismal visage brighten. Well and good!

Half an hour later, the collar of his multi-caped topcoat turned up against a chill wind off the sea, Malcolm strolled through the streets towards the Hoe. The few passersby hurried, their wraps hugged close about them. As the dusk of the short winter's day closed down, lamps flickered to life in shop windows.

Passing a gold- and silversmith's establishment, Malcolm glanced at the display in the leaded-glass bow window. Casually, as if drawn by something seen there, he pushed open the door and entered.

A bell attached to the door tinkled to announce his arrival. From a back room, pushing aside a heavy crimson velvet curtain, a small, balding man emerged to stand behind the counter. He peered through thick-lensed, gold-rimmed spectacles at his visitor, and took in the glossy beaver, caped greatcoat, and gleaming white-topped boots.

"What can I do for you, sir?"

"You are the proprietor? The goldsmith?"

The little man bowed. "Ebenezer Willett, goldsmith, silversmith, jeweller, at your service, sir."

"You have been commended to me for your discretion. I have a confidential task for you, if you think yourself capable of it." Malcolm took out the ring and laid it on the counter. "I want a copy of this. Not the ring or the topaz, just the seal. It must make an impression exactly like the original."

Willett pushed the ring back towards him with the tip of one long, delicate finger. "Can't be done, sir."

"You don't do such fine work?"

The jeweller drew himself up. "The finest in Plymouth, in Devon, nay, in the West Country, though I say it myself!"

"Then it is impossible?"

"That I didn't say, sir. Since you ask, I won't be a party to forgery, not for a thousand pounds."

With a nod of approval, Malcolm drew his wallet from his pocket and extracted a folded parchment. This he unfolded and laid on the counter beside the ring. "My name is Malcolm Eden," he said softly. "I'm on government business. Here is my commission from the Admiralty, signed and sealed by the First Lord himself. It's no forgery, I assure you."

Holding the parchment beneath the oil lamp suspended from the low ceiling, Willett perused it carefully from start to finish, studying the impressive seal closely. Then he turned and subjected his customer's face to the same rigorous examination. One or both apparently satisfied him. He returned the credentials, picked up the ring, and held back the velvet curtain.

"You'd best come through, my lord, where we shan't be interrupted."

Malcolm ducked under the curtain. The workshop behind was brightly lit, especially the bench which held an assortment of jewellers' tools and work in progress. Willett took off his spectacles, fixed a glass in one eye, and studied the topaz in its heavy, ornate gold setting with increasing enthusiasm.

"Remarkable! Early sixteenth-century English work, unless I miss my guess. There are few Tudor pieces left which have not been reset, and fewer still of such quality."

"Can you copy it?" Malcolm asked impatiently, consulting his pocket-watch.

"Oh yes. Even the finest Tudor craftsmen were a trifle crude by modern standards. They had not the tools we have today. Besides, if you don't want the sphinx carved into a gem, it's a comparatively simple matter of making an impression and using it as a mould. Gold, silver, brass?"

"Brass will do. You can have it ready by tomorrow morning?"

Willett cast a glance at his crowded work bench. "Your business is urgent?"

"It is. You will be well paid to postpone your other work."

"It's not the money." His narrow chest swelled with injured dignity. "I'll do it for England and our brave boys in the Navy. You may call for your seals any time you please tomorrow morning, my lord."

"Excellent! Remember, don't breathe a word of this to anyone. Lives may depend upon your silence."

The jeweller nodded solemnly, already clearing a space on his bench. "Not a word," he promised.

Malcolm continued on his way to the Hoe, walking briskly, a gentleman out for an evening's exercise. Nothing too out of character there. He was known in Town as something of a dandy, a fop even, bored by everything but the cut of a coat, yet even a dandy needs to stretch his legs after two and a half days on the road.

The first stars twinkled in the darkening sky, vying with the lanterns on the masts of the countless vessels in the Sound. Drake's Island was a black mound rising from the pallid waters, Mount Edgcumbe a mere shadowy bulk. In the distance, the periodic flash of the Eddystone lighthouse warned ships off the cruel rocks. A solitary figure in naval uniform stood gazing out over the estuary. The empty left sleeve of his coat was pinned across his breast.

Malcolm paused briefly beside him. "Well met, Des. Can you come to Corycombe tomorrow evening?"

"Not tomorrow."

"The next night? Good. I've much to tell you." Malcolm walked on.

Any watcher, he hoped, would have seen a chance meeting between strangers, an exchange of words about the view, perhaps, or the weather. It was cold enough for comment, the air now holding a hint of frost unusual in this sheltered southwestern corner of the realm. Des must be freezing, the stump of the arm he had lost two years ago at Trafalgar probably ached like the very devil.

Nonetheless, though unaccustomed to conspiracy, the captain surely knew better than to abandon his contemplative pose too quickly. Resisting an impulse to glance back at his friend, Malcolm turned his steps towards the town and the welcome warmth of the Golden Hind.

"I'm having trouble with my badger," said Mr. Barwith broodingly as Mariette ladled chicken soup into his bowl.

"I'm sorry to hear that, Uncle George." Mariette regarded with affection the lined face beneath the old-fashioned tie-wig. Tucking a stray strand of raven hair behind her ear, she tasted her soup before asking, "What is the difficulty this time?"

"To tell the truth, it looks more like a pig," the elderly gentleman confided. "I wish you will come and look after dinner. Your advice is always excellent."

"I'll see what I can do. Now do eat your soup before it

grows cold. Cook has made a rabbit pie and you know how soggy the crust gets if it stands."

"Rabbit pie? Excellent! Your cousin has been out with a gun, I suppose, since you prefer inanimate targets."

As always, Mariette was taken by surprise by her unworldly, reclusive uncle's occasional flashes of perspicacity. "Yes," she said wryly, "but I shall enjoy the pie, which I daresay makes me a hypocrite, especially as I used to enjoy fishing."

"I too, my dear. I never cared for shooting." He broke off a piece of his roll and surreptitiously fed it to Ragamuffin, lurking under the table. "Where is Ralph?"

"He rode into Plymouth, to see his friends." And to gamble, as she was all too aware. She didn't think Uncle George knew, though, so she quickly changed the subject. "I have been rereading Hume's *History of England,* Uncle, as you suggested. I do understand it better this time, but there are still parts which puzzle me."

For the rest of the meal they discussed David Hume's version of English history, with its strong bias in favour of the Scots. As Uncle George finished off a dish of bottled plums and custard, he fell silent, his thoughts doubtless returning to his badger.

Ragamuffin at their heels, they repaired to the front hall. A spacious chamber never distinguished by any particular architectural merit, it was now home to a veritable menagerie of animal sculptures. Pride of place was taken by a huge chunk of Dartmoor granite destined to become a lion. From one end emerged an unidentifiable muzzle and two ears, from the other a rump and the beginnings of a tail. Mariette patted one prospective flank as she passed, winding her way between the smaller sandstone sculptures. She left footprints in the gritty dust on the floor, for Mrs. Finney was long since resigned to the pointlessness of the maids' efforts to clean around the creatures.

Mariette's favourite was a diminutive fox. The red Devonshire sandstone was the perfect colour; the poor beast couldn't help it if it had one leg shorter than the others, lacked a tail, and squinted. Ragamuffin, who seemed to consider it an insult to caninedom, growled at it as usual.

The badger was definitely porcine. "The legs are too long," she said judicially, studying it under Uncle George's anxious eye, "and it's too fat. Its face looks a bit squashed, I'm afraid."

He gave a sad nod. "Too short in the nose. As I feared. I can reduce the legs and girth, but it's impossible to lengthen the face without reducing the whole in proportion." Standing back, he squinted at his handiwork and suddenly smiled. "Rather a handsome pig, don't you think, my dear? After all, there is no reason I should not make a statue of a pig. A useful creature! Let me see, now."

He picked up hammer and chisel. The chink of metal on metal followed Mariette to her favourite sitting room at the back of the house.

Ragamuffin slumped on the worn hearthrug. The fire's flickering light brought a sheen to his thick coat, mahogany patched with white. Mariette kicked off her slippers and curled up on the shabby sofa with a Minerva Press novel, tucking her warm, dark-blue woollen skirts about her ankles. *Gentleman of the Road, or, The Lost Heir* made a change from Hume. Nonetheless she hoped Ralph would come home soon. Bell-Tor Manor kept country hours and the dark winter evenings dragged on endlessly. Any sort of diversion was to be welcomed, even a game of draughts or backgammon would while away the time.

It was not long before she heard hurried footsteps in the passage from the back door. She looked up as her cousin burst into the room, neckcloth awry, hair tousled.

"You've missed dinner again," she said, dispassionately surveying his dishevelment. "Did you dine in town?"

"No! Yes! What does it matter?" Ralph cried wildly. Tossing hat and gloves onto a chair, he flung himself into another, which creaked under the assault. He ignored Ragamuffin's enthusiastic welcome. "You've got to help me, Mariette!"

"What is it this time?" She bit back a sigh as he covered

his face with his hands. Ragamuffin, rebuffed, returned to the hearthrug and she reached down to scratch behind his floppy ears. "Have you lost the whole of your quarter's allowance already?"

"Worse," he groaned. "Where's Uncle George?"

"Working on his badger. You're safe for he'll be busy all evening. So you can tell me . . . Oh, Ralph!" At last she noticed his bare finger. "Your ring? You've wagered your ring again?"

"The fellow wouldn't take a vowel," he said sulkily. "There's no need to make it sound as if I'm constantly losing it, dammit. This is only the second time."

"Good gad, once was enough." The previous occasion was all too clear in her memory. "How *could* you do it again?"

"I was sure he couldn't go on winning. He must have cheated. Yes, that's it, he looked like the veriest fop but he was a regular Captain Sharp, devil take him!"

"You were playing with a stranger?"

"Don't fuss so. After all, you don't care for my friends. Mariette, you'll redeem it for me, won't you? I'll pay you back, honestly."

"I daresay, and I'll lend you the money, of course, but I'll be dashed if I'll do your dirty work this time! I've never been so humiliated in my life as when I redeemed the blasted thing from Lord Wareham for you. He treated me like a particularly insignificant, yet irritating earwig." Her face burned as a vision of the baron's handsome, contemptuous countenance rose before her inner eye. "Besides, your Captain Sharp has probably vanished by now."

"Oh no, it's the greatest bit of luck!" The eternal optimism of the born gamester revived. "He's driving to Corycombe in the morning. The landlord told me he's Lady Lilian's brother, Lord Malcolm Eden."

"Another lord! I don't want anything to do with him."

"But you know Lady Lilian."

"Only to say 'good day' and 'what lovely weather we're having' if I meet her in her barouche when I'm out riding.

And though she's always quite polite, she's never introduced me to her daughter or her companion. I know she's shocked that I wear buckskin breeches and ride astride."

"Well, it ain't proper."

"Jim says it's simply not safe to gallop on the moor riding sidesaddle," she pointed out with a touch of defiance, straightening her heavy skirts. Safety was more important than propriety, she told herself, as warmth was more important than fashion in the draughty old manor.

"I know, I know," said Ralph impatiently, "but dammit, the point is you do know her so you can easily call tomorrow."

"And ask to speak to a man I've never met? No."

"Please, Mariette," he wheedled. "The sphinx has been in my family for nearly three centuries. It's not just a piece of trumpery."

"You should have thought of that before you wagered it."

"If you get it back for me, I swear I'll never lose it again."

This time Mariette's sigh escaped her. She had only herself to blame if her cousin relied on her to extract him from every difficulty. Though scarce six months the elder, she had always mothered him, always smoothed his path and rescued him from the consequences of his heedlessness. No wonder he turned to her when he lost his precious heirloom.

She could not let him down, but she wasn't prepared to plead with a stranger, to humble herself to a high-and-mighty lord, to redeem the ring. There must be another way!

And then a daring solution struck her, a way to combine recovery of the signet with the adventure she craved, a brief escape from her humdrum life. "You said Lord Malcolm will drive from Plymouth to Corycombe tomorrow morning?" she asked.

"I heard him tell the landlord he'll leave the Golden Hind at nine." Relieved, he smiled. How handsome he was with his ruffled blond hair, bright blue eyes, willful mouth, and deceptively firm chin. She had no illusions about him, which

was surely a sound basis for marriage—one must be practical, as *maman* had often repeated.

In any case, she intended to marry him. Otherwise who
would take care of him? Besides, said a wistful, treacherous
voice in her head, she never met any other gentlemen and
had no prospect of ever meeting any.

"You have a plan?" Ralph asked eagerly. His hopeful air
reminded her of Ragamuffin begging for a walk.

"A simply splendid plan." A bubble of excitement rose in
her and she smiled. "I'll hold up Lord Malcolm's carriage."

His mouth dropped open and he stared at her. "B-but
. . . Good gad, you have run mad!"

"Fiddlesticks! I'll wear a mask and pretend I'm a highwayman. It's what Arnulfo did to retrieve the seal which
proved him heir to the throne of Waldania. In my book,"
she explained as he continued to gape at her.

"Oh, a *novel*," he said dismissively. "That's just make-be-
lieve."

"Well, it won't be a real robbery. I'll only take the ring,
which Lord Malcolm won by cheating so he's not likely to
raise a hue and cry over it."

"All the same, you won't catch me doing anything so
harebrained!"

Since Mariette had not expected him to raise a finger to
help himself or her, that was no surprise. It dawned on her
that he'd be suspected anyway if only the ring was stolen.
"Better if you don't come," she said. "You must ride down
to Plymton, or even into Plymouth, and go somewhere
where they know you and can swear you were not on the
road to Corycombe between nine and ten. Make it from
nine till eleven to be safe."

"But I'll have to get up at eight," he complained. "Oh,
very well. You had best take Jim Groom with you."

"No, it wouldn't be fair to involve a servant and he might
be suspected. No one will suspect a female. I'm tall enough
to pass as a smallish man, in a mask and cloak and with my
hair tucked up under a hat." Dropping her book on the sofa
beside her, she jumped up. "Come on, let's go and see what

you have in your wardrobe that I can wear. No, the gun-room first. I'll need a pistol to wave at him."

Ragamuffin bouncing after her, Mariette sped from the room, trailed by her reluctant cousin.

The morning air was icy. When Mariette left the manor, the sun had not yet cleared the ridge of Grevin Moor, though to the north the sprinkle of snow on high Bell Tor already glistened in its slanting rays. She was glad of the warmth of Ralph's outgrown greatcoat.

She glanced back at the house. Long and low, built of grey limestone with lintels and sills of granite and a slate roof, it seemed a part of the hillside. It showed no signs of life except for the smoke from the chimneys. No one called her back.

Before Ralph set off for Plymouth he had entered a final token protest, a feeble attempt to persuade her to approach Lord Malcolm in a more conventional manner. Uncle George, already absorbed in contemplation of his pig/badger, had smiled absently when she kissed his cheek and told him she was going out riding. Jim Groom, saddling Sparrow for her, had made his usual offer to go with her but was unsurprised by her refusal; his old bones ached so early in the morning.

Only Ragamuffin did not fall in with her plans. She had intended to leave him at home, for he was well-known in the district. A report of a dog of his unique ancestry and distinctive colouring accompanying the highwayman would point to her as surely as a compass needle points to the poles. However, when she looked for him to shut him in, she could not find him. She added a length of cord to her equipment.

As if the dog had read her mind he was waiting for her, grinning, outside the gate to the stable-yard. Too late to take him back.

He roamed ahead as she and Sparrow started up the rocky path behind the house. As soon as they left the shelter of the trees, the east wind hit them. The sure-footed gelding took the blast in his stride, never faltering. Mariette, cling-ing with both legs, was certain a sidesaddle rider would have been swept from his back on the instant.

Fortunately she had thought to put her highwayman's hat—an old *chapeau bras* rescued from the attic—in a sad-dlebag and to bring some extra hairpins. Though her own riding hat was firmly tied on with ribbons, her knot of hair escaped in no time and streamed in a matted mass about her shoulders. She'd never get a comb through it!

In the hollows between grey-green furze thickets and rusty banks of withered bracken, sheep huddled. Raga-muffin ignored them, intent on a rabbit trail. He followed it to the edge of Bell Brook, here a tumbling rill, then gave up in disgust and returned to Mariette and Sparrow. She was glad of his company.

The path forked. One branch twisted up the hillside to-wards the pile of massive stones topping Bell Tor. They took the other branch, slanting westward across the steep slope of Wicken's Down. Gorse and bracken gave way to the dark green of heather and sparse, ochre grasses. Here and there the bare bones of the moor showed through in slabs of grey rock.

At the top the wind blew fiercer than ever, and colder though the sun shone in the pale sky. The air was crystal clear but shoulders of the hill hid both valleys from Ma-riette. Sparrow picked his way down until Corycombe came into sight, still far below. Mariette drew rein to inspect the scene.

She knew it well. The square, red-brick house stood on the lower slope with its back to her, facing west. The road to it ran along Cory Brook, mostly hidden by a grey haze of leafless trees. Farther south, where the valley widened, brick-red Devon cattle grazed the meadows around the straggling village of Wickenton.

At one point the road emerged from the woods to cross a low spur of the moor, skirting an outcrop of rocks. That was the best spot for an ambush, Mariette decided. The rocks were tall enough to hide behind, and the ground was fairly level for several hundred yards, allowing a quick escape. She turned Sparrow's head downward again.

In the shelter of the outcrop she coiled her tangled hair and pinned it up. Concealing her face with a mask cut from a black silk stocking reluctantly surrendered by Ralph, she jammed the tricorne on her head and turned up the collar of her coat.

Ragamuffin watched, fascinated. As her face disappeared, he gave a questioning bark.

"Hush!" she said. "Come here." She took him behind a large clump of heather, tying him to the tough stalk with what she hoped was an easily released knot. "Down and stay!" she ordered.

He gave her a disgusted look and flopped to the ground.

Mariette found a spot where she could peek between two rocks and watch the road to the point where it dipped behind the trees. Now, out of the wind and after the exercise, she was quite warm. Nonetheless she shivered. She wasn't afraid, she assured herself, merely a trifle nervous. After all, she had never held up a coach before. Unconventional, perhaps, but vastly preferable to the alternative—wasn't it?

The image of Lord Wareham's sneering face flashed before her mind's eye. Playing highwayman was *infinitely* preferable to such a mortifying scene!

Sparrow pricked his ears and a moment later she heard the jingle of harness and rumble of wheels. Four splendid bays came into view. They moved faster than she had expected, because they pulled not a heavy coach but a smart sporting curricle, moss green picked out in yellow, driven by a man in a multicaped greatcoat. Another man sat beside him, and a third up behind. A roan mare trotted after, tied to the rear.

Swinging hurriedly into the saddle, Mariette urged Sparrow forward. The distance was too short to attain a gallop, so she did not exactly thunder down upon her victim as she had pictured herself. However, she waved her pistol at the driver and shouted in her deepest voice, "Stand and deliver!"

The effect was gratifying. She had to admire the way the driver smartly pulled up his team, keeping control as he came to a halt right beside her. By his dress he must be Lord Malcolm Eden, the others his valet, perhaps, and a groom. Her plans had concentrated on the villain who cheated Ralph of his ring and she had not reckoned on so many. Training her gun on his lordship, she hoped the servants would not risk injury to their master.

She dropped the reins on Sparrow's neck, thankful she had trained him to stand still. "Give me your purse," she ordered Lord Malcolm gruffly, "and any rings or other baubles you are wearing or carrying."

He stared at her, a frown creasing his brow. "You're not . . ."

"Hurry, or I'll shoot!"

Laying his whip across his lap, he reached into his pocket. "My purse." He set it in her outstretched hand.

"M'lord!" the groom protested.

"Quiet." Lord Malcolm's voice was steady, unalarmed.

One-handed, Mariette loosened the drawstring, her gaze and her gun fixed on him. With his teeth he pulled off his right glove and showed her his bare fingers.

She nodded.

Transferring the reins to his right hand, he removed the left glove. Bare fingers again.

As she felt in the purse, he raised his chin and turned to the small, neat man beside him. "Padgett, pray remove my tie-pin for our friend."

"Never mind." She had the signet ring. Pocketing it, she tossed the clinking purse into the curricle. "My thanks, my lord."

Laughter bubbled up at the sight of his puzzled face. With a half-choked chuckle she kicked Sparrow into motion. They swung away from the curricle and raced for the shelter of the rocks.

Ragamuffin rose behind his heather bush and woofed a greeting.

"Oh *damn!*" She had forgotten him.

Flinging herself from Sparrow's back, she swiftly un-hitched the cord to set the dog free. Her foot in the stirrup, she sprang upwards just as a voice behind her yelled, "Don't shoot, you fool!"

Crack! A fiery flail struck Mariette in the buttocks. She lost her balance, tottered, fell. Her foot slipped from the stirrup as the world whirled about her, then her head met solid rock and blackness closed in.

Chapter 2

"Numskull!" Malcolm raged. "I told you he was to be allowed to escape."

"But it warn't the same bloke," Jessup squawked, jumping down from his perch and hurrying forward to hold the bays. "I seen 'im at the inn, m'lord, the fella you . . ."

"He returned my purse, didn't he?" Malcolm vaulted from the curricle. "Never mind now. Padgett, come with me."

He set off at a run across the uneven ground. Dammit, this could ruin his plans! Though Jessup was right in that the highwayman was too small to be Ralph Riddlesworth, he was undoubtedly an accomplice. Now how the devil was Malcolm to return the ring to Riddlesworth without arousing his suspicions?

A volley of barking halted him in his tracks. A skewbald dog stood over the sprawled body, lips drawn back to reveal teeth far more fearsome than its middling size warranted.

Malcolm advanced slowly but steadily, speaking in a low, soothing voice. "Here, boy, is your master hurt? I didn't mean it to happen, I promise you. You must let me help him. Come on, there's a good chap. I cannot claim to be a friend but I don't want him to die any more than you do." Such an outcome would thoroughly dash his hopes! "Good boy."

The dog whined uncertainly, then backed off a few steps. Its anxious brown eyes watched Malcolm's every motion.

The horse, a dun gelding, had also moved off a short way and was cropping the meagre grass. He saw trickles of blood on its flank but his first care must be for its rider.

The highwayman lay on his back. His hat had flown off but face and head were hidden by a black silk mask except for closed eyes fringed by long black lashes. Malcolm had seen the shotgun blast take him from the rear, and the back of his head had hit the rock a glancing blow as he twisted and fell. Best to unbutton his top-coat and pull his arms from the sleeves before turning him over. He knelt down.

First he took the ring from the pocket where he had seen him put it—it would be too ridiculous to lose it among the heather. That was the best place for the pistol, though. He flung it away. Then he unfastened the buttons . . .

" 'Fore Gad, 'tis a woman!"

The horrified exclamation burst from him as Padgett reached his side after picking his fastidious way through the scrub. Together they stared down at the slim figure disclosed by the opened coat. The man's riding jacket she wore beneath could not conceal the swell of her breasts, rising and falling, thank heaven, and the slender waist. If that were not enough, close-fitting buckskin breeches revealed . . .

Malcolm tore his eyes away. "Let's get her mask off. Gently, now. She hit her head in falling."

The girl's face was chalk-white. A young, attractive face, not beautiful but with a good bone-structure which would age well, Malcolm noted in a brief glance. Through a tangle of thick ebony hair he felt the back of her head.

"Not bleeding, but there's already a lump and she'll have a devil of a headache, if not a concussion. Help me turn her over."

Streams of crimson blood seeped from countless small holes riddling the seat of her buckskins. Padgett gasped.

"I'll fetch some clean linen, my lord."

"Good man. Hurry."

The little valet sped away at a near trot, as close as possible to a run without irreparably injuring his dignity.

Jessup arrived, breathless. "I tied the bays to . . ." He

stopped abruptly and stared down, aghast. " 'Twere only the lightest birdshot, m'lord!" he groaned.

"Just as well," Malcolm said grimly. "See to her horse. Your birdshot nicked him, too, if I'm not mistaken."

As he spoke, he took out his pocket knife and reached for the waistband of the girl's breeches. The dog growled. Malcolm calmly continued, slitting the garment until he could pull it back to either side to examine the full extent of the damage. Whimpering, the dog came over and licked his mistress's still face.

Beneath the buckskins, linen drawers were sodden with blood. Again Malcolm cut. There was nothing sexually inviting about the rounded buttocks he laid bare, besmeared with red like a painter's palette. Blood still oozed from a score of tiny cuts, though he thought the flow must be slowing.

The trouble was, every cut contained a pellet of lead which would have to be dug out. He had to get her to Lilian's house and send for a doctor.

Padgett returned with an armful of neckcloths and a flask of cognac. Without comment, he helped Malcolm clean and bind the wounds as best they could. Malcolm wondered whether to tip a little of the brandy down the girl's throat, but he had a notion spirits were not a good idea in cases of concussion. She was still alarmingly inert except for an occasional tremor which he put down to the biting chill of the air.

He wrapped her in her greatcoat. With a soothing word to the dog, he hoisted her over his shoulder and started for the curricle. Despite his slight build and foppish façade he carried her easily, which would be no surprise to the trusted sparring partners he met in a private room at Gentleman Jackson's Bond Street saloon. The image he chose to present to the rest of the world was deceptive.

Jessup had led the girl's mount down to the stream to bathe his side. They returned to the curricle as Malcolm approached with his burden.

"She'll live, won't she, m'lord?" the groom asked apprehensively.

"I believe so. What of the horse?"

"He's all right." Jessup stroked the gelding's nose. "I dug out a couple o' bits of shot but he didn't give me no trouble. Reckon he won't even scar."

Malcolm's lips twitched involuntarily. He had not considered the possibility of the girl's being scarred, but if so at least it was not a part of her anatomy she'd ever want to display in public!

"You'd better ride for a doctor," he said. "I don't know if there is one in Plympton. If not, go on to Plymouth, and don't return without one. Take the gelding as he's already saddled."

"Yes, m'lord!" Jessup mounted and a moment later galloped back down the road.

And a moment too late Malcolm cursed his stupidity. How the devil was he to lift the girl into the curricle and drive on to Corycombe without the groom's aid? Padgett was by no means strong enough to be of much assistance.

In the end, he laid her on the seat and wriggled in under her so that she was stretched across his lap, bottom up, with her face turned towards the back of the seat. Padgett had to untie the bays and scramble up behind, not at all what he was accustomed to.

Malcolm started the team at a fast trot towards Corycombe. The dog loped alongside. As the curricle jounced over a pothole, the girl stirred and moaned. Glancing down, he thought he saw her eyelids flicker shut. A tiny frown of pain creased her brow and she held her body tense, but she gave no other sign of returning to consciousness.

He didn't blame her. In all respects, she was in an excessively embarrassing situation.

She was limp again by the time they pulled up in front of Lilian's house. Padgett clambered down and ascended the steps to the front door, which was opened by a stiffly correct butler as he reached for the knocker.

"Good morning, Mr. Blount." The proprieties must be observed even in extraordinary circumstances.

"Good morning, Mr. Padgett," the elderly butler returned. "Welcome back to Corycombe, my lord. Does your lordship care to . . . Good gracious me! Surely that cannot be Miss Mariette? But I should recognize Ragamuffin anywhere!"

The panting dog had his front paws on the footboard of the curricle, his tail wagging hopefully.

"I don't know her name," said Malcolm, impatiently. He had a story prepared, as much for the sake of his mission as for the girl. Catching his valet's eye, he lied, "We found the young lady by the road. She's had an accident—peppered by a poacher, I suspect."

Padgett's grave nod conveyed comprehension to his master. He'd stick to the story and make sure Jessup knew what to say, not that Jessup was likely to be eager to broadcast the truth.

The same nod conveyed to the butler agreement with the poacher theory. "Gracious me!" said Blount again, shocked. "What is the world coming to?"

"My groom has gone for a doctor," said Malcolm quickly. "I need help to lift her down and someone to see to the horses."

"At once, my lord."

As the butler turned to summon aid, Lilian's voice demanded, "Is my brother come, Blount?"

"Yes, my lady, but . . ."

"Malcolm!" she called, coming out onto the top step. Daintily diminutive in her habitual grey trimmed with white lace, a black shawl about her shoulders, she looked not a day older than five and twenty though she had passed that age by a decade. "My dear, how good to see you."

His fifteen-year-old niece hovered shyly behind her mother, peeking over her shoulder. "Mama, is not that Miss Bertrand's dog?"

But Lilian had already realized something was amiss. She hurried down the steps. Closer to, the lines engraved by grief were apparent, though no thread of grey showed in her fair hair. "Oh, the poor child!" she exclaimed. "What has happened?"

Malcolm gave his brief explanation as a hefty footman rushed from the house. Between them they carried her up to the Dutch chamber, prepared for Malcolm, and laid her face-down on the bed. Lilian came in, followed by her hatchet-faced companion, Miss Thorne.

"Thank you, Charles," she said to the footman. "That will be all for the present. Malcolm, Mrs. Wittering is setting the maids to make up the green chamber for you. Will you go and see what you can do to calm Emily for me? She has made quite a mystery heroine of Miss Bertrand and is in high fidgets."

"As soon as I've seen Miss Bertrand made comfortable."

Outrage made Miss Thorne's face still more hatchetlike.

"My dear," said Lilian, "what can you be thinking of? You cannot possibly remain while we undress the poor girl!"

Feeling himself a good deal to blame for the young woman's injuries—he should have made sure Jessup thoroughly understood his instructions—he was reluctant to abandon her now, even to Lilian's tender care. "I have already seen most of what there is to see," he protested.

"Then I advise you to put it out of your mind with all due celerity. Out!"

He had to admit the propriety of her command. Reluctantly turning to obey, he saw Ragamuffin sneak through the half-open door, his nose testing the air, his ears pricking as he caught his mistress's scent.

"Out!" Malcolm ordered, pointing at the door.

Ragamuffin's ears flattened and his tail wagged obsequiously but he didn't budge. When Malcolm approached, he tensed and bared his teeth.

"Let him stay," said Lilian. "I daresay his presence will be a comfort to Miss Bertrand when she wakes."

Malcolm gave the favoured animal a rueful look, but his

anxiety revived. "She has been unconscious an excessively long time. Do you think she is concussed?"

"We must hope she has merely swooned from the pain. Now, off with you and let us do what we can for her."

He went downstairs and found Miss Emily Farrar in the morning room. A slight, demure figure in pink, brown tresses neatly tied back with a ribbon, she perched on the very edge of an elegant green satin sofa. In one hand she held an embroidery hoop, in the other a needle, unthreaded. She dropped them, jumped up and pattered to meet him, forgetting the painful shyness which had handicapped her for the past year or two.

Malcolm held out both hands to her. "Well, and how is my favourite niece?" he enquired. "Prettier and more grown up than ever, I see."

"I am allowed to put my hair up in the evenings. But never mind me, Uncle. How is Miss Bertrand?" Her blue eyes, so like her mother's, eagerly searched his face. "Mama would not let me help."

"Nor me. I don't believe she is badly hurt. Who is she, Emmie? Come and sit down and tell me all about her."

He offered her his arm. Proud to be treated as a lady, not a child, she laid her hand on it. Solemnly escorting her to a chair, he seated her and took a chair opposite, avoiding the sofa where, he suspected, the discarded needle lurked. One ambush was sufficient to the day.

"Miss Bertrand?" he prodded.

"Is she not wonderful? I have seen her from my window galloping across the moors without a thought for rabbit-holes or bogs or what anyone will think."

Startled, Malcolm said cautiously, "You find it irksome to have to obey the rules of propriety?"

"No, not really," Emily admitted. "Well, sometimes a tri-fle tiresome. But, you see, I want to dance at Almack's when I make my come-out, and Mama says nothing so disgusts the lady patronesses as indecorous conduct. Miss Bertrand need not care for such things. She never had a come-out and now she is too old, and anyway, she would never have obtained vouchers."

"Who is she?"

"Old Mr. Barwith's niece. He is mad as a March . . . I mean," she hurriedly corrected herself, "not quite right in the head. He never hired a governess for Miss Bertrand when her mama died, which was when she was just a child so she never learned how to behave properly." Her voice dropped to a whisper. "Only think, she wears *unmentionables* and rides astride! Mama is sorry for her but we do not call at Bell-Tor Manor."

Malcolm felt a pang of pity for Miss Bertrand, left without guidance and ostracized even by his amiable sister.

"She does not go to church," Emily added primly.

Since he only attended services when staying at Ashminster with his parents, he found nothing to cavil at in this evidence of dereliction. However, Miss Bertrand had held up his carriage and stolen an item of particular interest, he reminded himself. What was her connection with Ralph Riddlesworth?

"Has she no other relatives or friends to advise her?" he asked.

"There is Sir Ralph. I suppose he is her cousin since he is Mr. Barwith's nephew, but she cannot look to him for advice. He is much the same age as she is, and Mama says he is a shocking here-and-thereian."

Trying to disguise his curiosity, Malcolm said casually, "You are acquainted with him?"

"Oh no, not really, only to bow to because he is such a close neighbour, and not always so much. Mama says there are situations in which it is not impolite to cut an acquaintance. We saw him in Plymouth, once, when we had been shopping and met the carriage at the Golden Hind. He was playing cards with some sailors and though Mama said they were officers by their uniforms, they did not look at all gentlemanly, so we did not acknowledge Sir Ralph."

"Very wise." So Riddlesworth gambled with naval officers, did he? Very interesting!

"Another time he was singing in the street," Emily went on, "and Mama said she feared he must be a trifle foxed. That means he had drunk too much wine," she explained in a hushed voice.

Malcolm hid a smile. "A common failing in young men, alas. He lives in Plymouth, I suppose?"

"No, at Bell-Tor Manor—it's just on the other side of Wicken's Down—with Mr. Barwith and Miss Bertrand. The servants say Miss Bertrand mothered Sir Ralph right from the first when he was orphaned and went to live at the Manor, although she was only a little girl. Was not that fine of her? Oh, Uncle, pray do not tell Mama I have gossiped with the servants!"

"I shan't," he promised, glad to find a chink in his rather priggish niece's armour.

"I do not in general," she assured him, "but Charles's sister Carrie is in service at the Manor and sometimes he tells me things because he knows how I admire Miss Bertrand."

Wondering if Lilian realized the extent of her daughter's fascination with the ramshackle Miss Bertrand, Malcolm silently confessed that he himself could not help but admire her. Her courage and spirit were as undeniable as her folly. He had expected Riddlesworth to play the highwayman, not a green girl. Why had she done it?

Misplaced loyalty? Well, loyalty was a virtue, even when lavished on an undeserving object. In her own unconventional way, Miss Bertrand was admirable.

Riddlesworth, however, was not, and the girl was now Malcolm's link to the young baronet.

He sprang to his feet as Lilian came in. "How is she?"

"Miss Bertrand regained her senses, I am happy to . . ."

"I must speak to her!"

His vehemence made her stare. "You cannot. As I was about to say, she regained her senses but she was in such pain that I gave her some laudanum. She is drowsy, in no state for conversation."

"Not conversation. I wanted to speak to her about . . . the poacher."

"Oh, I asked her if she had seen the poacher who shot her. She was a little confused but she said quite clearly she had not. I fear we shall never discover the culprit."

Malcolm sincerely hoped not. The less anyone found out about the incident the better for all concerned.

"She asked after her horse. I told her your groom had seen to it."

"He has," agreed her brother a trifle grimly. He still was not sure how to get out of this mess of Jessup's making.

"Emily," said Lilian, turning to her daughter, "pray go and practise your music, my love. Your uncle will excuse you."

"Yes, Mama."

She curtsied to Malcolm, who leaned forward and whispered in her ear, "Don't forget to retrieve your needle before someone sits on it."

With a grateful glance for the reminder, Emily went to the sofa and picked up her tambour. After a brief search and a pricked finger, she found the needle, held it up in triumph to her uncle, and left the room.

Lilian watched with indulgence. "She is a good girl, Malcolm, and still a child in so many ways. That is what worries me. Of course I am glad you found Miss Bertrand and it was our duty to take her in, but she is not at all a suitable acquaintance for Emily, I fear."

"That was obvious from her dress," he said curtly with the old, familiar feeling that nothing he did would ever win wholehearted approval from his family. The distant tinkle of a Clementi sonatina drove home the difference between his niece and the would-be highwayman. "I'm sorry to have imposed her upon you, but I saw no alternative."

"Indeed, there was none." She wrinkled her nose at him, a youthful grimace which reminded him that she was the most sympathetic of his siblings as well as the closest in age. "I promise I do not mean to carp at you in an odious elder-sisterish way. Nor do I mean to imply that Miss Bertrand is in any way immoral or . . . or *vicious*. I should have heard if she were, for such tales circulate fast in the country. But there is no denying she has not the least notion of decorum, or even of propriety."

"How should she when—according to Emily at least—she has had no one to teach her?"

"I don't hold her to blame, Malcolm! In fact, I blame myself to some degree. When first I learned she had no female companion but the servants, I felt I ought to suggest to Mr. Barwith that he hire a governess. I shall always regret that I did not speak."

"Why did you not?"

"I let Frederick persuade me interference would be impertinent, and of course in those days we were seldom here." She sighed. "When he died and I came to live here, first there was all the fuss with Mama and Papa over whether I should go home to Ashminster . . ."

"And since then you have been fully occupied in overseeing the estate and bringing up your daughter," he said gently. "Miss Bertrand must have been too old for a governess by then in any case. You are no more to blame than she is herself."

"Perhaps not. That is little comfort in my present predicament."

"Surely it will not be difficult to keep her and Emily apart? Emily strikes me as a biddable young lady. Tell her not to visit Miss Bertrand's bedside." He had no intention of being likewise banned from the girl's chamber. "When your patient is fit to leave her room, you may send her home."

By then he'd have worked out how to give back the signet ring without arousing her suspicions.

"Yes." Lilian sounded doubtful. "Only I am afraid she will be able to leave before she is fully healed and she will not get proper care at home."

"This Barwith sounds like a curst rum touch!"

"Oh no, merely excessively absentminded. It was generous of him to give Miss Bertrand a home. Emily told you he is her uncle? She is not actually related by blood, you know."

"She's not?"

"No, her parents were French. The father was a *comte* or a *viscomte,* I believe. He was guillotined during the Terror." She shuddered. "His wife escaped to London with the child and there met and married George Barwith's brother. Both died not long thereafter, alas. Miss Bertrand was eight or nine when she was orphaned a second time and came to live. . . . Yes, Blount?"

"The doctor has arrived, my lady."

"Thank you. I shall take him up at once."

Lilian hurried out, leaving Malcolm distinctly thoughtful. So Miss Bertrand's ancestry was French? That was a new twist to the mystery!

Chapter 3

Mariette drifted in and out of consciousness. Her head ached, her bottom ached, but her chief emotion was embarrassment. If she had to be shot, why could it not have been a nice, clean bullet through the head?

Lady Lilian had been gently disapproving, even though Lord Malcolm had apparently told her some story about a poacher. Why he should lie for her Mariette could not guess. She was going to have to thank him for that, which was much worse than having to explain why she had played the highwayman.

She could see now that it had been a harebrained notion. It had worked for Arnulfo, but Arnulfo was only a character in a book, as Ralph had pointed out. However, Waldania had seemed more real to her than the medieval England she read about in histories. Not that she had any difficulty distinguishing fact from fiction, though Uncle George was right: if two histories disagreed, as was not uncommon, one or both must have their "facts" wrong.

As for Mr. Hume, how he could set up to be a historian when, in his philosophical essays, he denied the possibility of knowledge of matters of fact. . . .

Distracted from her woes, Mariette succumbed to the laudanum drops, sinking into a well of darkness from which she emerged to a dazzle of pain. Her buttocks flamed. A piercing probe drove a lance of fire up her spine. Instinctively she twisted away.

"Keep still!" came Lady Lilian's sharp voice and a grip on Mariette's ankles tightened. Realizing her wrists were held, too, she forced her eyes to open a slit.

"Nearly done." An incongruously cheerful voice she recognized as Dr. Barley from Plymton.

"Try to keep still, Miss Bertrand." Lord Malcolm's concerned face hovered above her. It was he who grasped her wrists. "The shot must be taken out for fear of infection. The worst is over now."

Gratitude for his reassurance, mortification at his presence, shame for her own stupidity, all disappeared in a whirl of pain as another burning lance transfixed her. She welcomed the dark.

When she roused again, a streak of light from the setting sun peeped through a gap in the curtains, filling the spacious blue and white chamber with a rosy glow. It illuminated a pair of bony hands. They were knitting something long and mustard-coloured, draped across a black satin skirt which delineated equally bony knees—Lady Lilian's companion, who disapproved of Mariette still more stringently than did her ladyship.

To postpone Miss Thorne's attentions, Mariette lay still. She felt wishy-washy, anyway, and disinclined to move. Her head no longer ached, though it was muzzy from the laudanum, as if a couple of busy spiders had left it hung with cobwebs. Her backside throbbed unmercifully.

It was going to be a long time before she sat without wincing, or even lay on her back, and riding was impossible. She'd have to walk home, unless Lady Lilian offered to send her in a carriage.

Not in Lord Malcolm's curricle! The thought made her hot all over. If she had felt humiliated by Lord Wareham's contempt, it had been a thousand times worse to find herself sprawled across his lordship's lap, her cheek pillowed on his hard-muscled thigh. Yet more shaming, she had gathered from listening to Lady Lilian and Miss Thorne that he had cleaned and bandaged her wounds, as well as assisting at Dr. Barley's ministrations. How was she ever to face him?

She wanted to crawl away and hide and never see nor hear of him again.

But she owed him an explanation. Besides, she realized in dismay, he was bound to have taken back the sphinx signet from her pocket. After her disastrous effort to avoid the unpleasant business, she had no choice but to beg him to let her redeem Ralph's ring.

A groan escaped her.

Miss Thorne composedly set aside her knitting and approached the bed. "You are awake, Miss Bertrand? You are in some discomfort, I fear." Her acid tone conveyed, "which is precisely what you deserve."

An immediate impulse to contradict led Mariette to declare, "I'm more hungry than anything else, ma'am." It was almost true. In excited anticipation of her adventure, she had skimped on breakfast this morning.

"Humph!" With a sniff, Miss Thorne reached for the bell-pull at the head of the bed. "How you are to eat and drink without sitting up, I am sure I cannot guess."

"I'll manage," said Mariette, determined to consume every crumb and drop of whatever was set before her, if only to prove the harridan wrong.

The chamber door was behind her so she did not see it open. A warm, slow Devonshire voice, a woman's, said, "You rang, ma'am?"

"Bring bread and butter and tea for Miss Bertrand, Pennick. And light the lamp before you go."

"Yes'm." A middle-aged, rosy-cheeked woman in a light brown woollen dress came round the bed and smiled at Mariette. Jenny Pennick, Lady Lilian's abigail. She lit the lamp on the dressing table by the window. " 'Tis a good sign you're hungry, miss," she murmured as she passed back towards the door.

At least bread and butter should be quite easy to eat, though Mariette felt in need of something considerably more substantial. How she was to cope with tea she had no idea.

Miss Thorne returned to her chair and her knitting. She

made no attempt at further communication, so Mariette laboriously raised herself and turned her head to the right to face the door. The bump on her head, on the left side, was distinctly tender. However, her neck was beginning to grow stiff from too long in the same strained position.

The door opened and Lady Lilian came in. "My maid tells me you are hungry, Miss Bertrand," she said kindly. "You are feeling more the thing? I am so glad."

"There was no need for Pennick to disturb you, Lilian," grumbled Miss Thorne. "You have already done far more than anyone could expect. . . ."

"I told Jenny to inform me when our patient roused, Cousin Tabitha. I have drunk my tea and you must be ready for yours. Do go down and join Emily and Malcolm."

Poor Emily and Malcolm, thought Mariette. Though perhaps Cousin Tabitha approved of them.

At the door, Miss Thorne met Jenny Pennick bearing a tray. She glanced at it, sniffed loudly, and departed, closing the door behind her with a hint of a slam. As the door shut, the bed began to shake. Frightened, Mariette wondered if she was falling into a fit caused by the knock on the head. She clutched the pillow.

But Lady Lilian and Jenny were looking at the floor by the bed and smiling. Jenny giggled. A moment later Ragamuffin put his front feet on the bed and licked Mariette's face.

Tears filled Mariette's eyes as she hugged him with one arm. "Did the old witch drive you into hiding?" she whispered in his ear.

He licked her again, pulled his head free, and gathered his haunches for a leap.

"Down, boy!" Mariette yelped.

Jenny grabbed his collar. "Oh, no you don't, my fine fellow. The floor's the place for the likes o' you."

"Does he sleep on your bed at home?" asked Lady Lilian, caught between amusement and dismay.

"Sometimes."

"I had a cat when I was a girl. . . . Well, that is long past.

Jenny, let us see if between us we can raise Miss Bertrand a little with pillows so that she may swallow more easily. Oh dear, you are going to be uncomfortable whatever we do."

"That's much better, my lady," said Mariette gratefully. Twisted at the waist, half on her front, half on her side, her position was awkward but bearable for a short while.

"Thank you, Jenny, you may go. I shall help Miss Bertrand."

Jenny curtsied and departed. Spreading a snowy napkin on the bed, Lady Lilian set on it a covered plate and a fork. She removed the cover to reveal poached chicken breast cut in bite-size pieces, florets of cauliflower, tiny brussel sprouts, and slices of pickled beetroot.

"Oh! Miss Thorne ordered bread and butter. . . ."

"And Dr. Barley said you must build up your strength."

"Good. I'm hungry as a horse."

Her ladyship looked startled. Since she knew Mariette was hungry, presumably it was the phrase which was unacceptable, Mariette guessed despairingly. Lady Lilian was so kind, the last thing she intended was to vex her but she was liable to do so inadvertently every time she opened her mouth.

However, after a momentary pause, Lady Lilian said a trifle stiffly, "How fortunate the doctor did not prescribe an invalid regimen of broth and gruel. You lost a good deal of blood, Miss Bertrand, but your thick coat and leather . . . *inexpressibles* protected you from serious injury. Dr. Barley said you are prodigious healthy and will soon recover your strength. My cook regarded it as a challenge to create a plateful you can eat with only a fork and without dripping. Hmm, I am not sure the beetroot was a good notion."

"I'll be careful," Mariette promised, remembering she had on one of Miss Thorne's nightgowns, much to that lady's resentment, Lady Lilian's and her daughter's being too small. She picked up the fork and set to.

Ragamuffin watched every forkful travel from plate to mouth.

Lady Lilian smiled. "I shall see the poor fellow is fed later," she said.

The chicken was delicious and Mariette wondered what liquid had been used to poach it. She would have liked to ask for the recipe, but she was afraid of blundering into another *faux-pas*. Was talk of cookery beneath a well-bred lady? How could she guess?

She wasn't even sure what to call her. "My lady" sounded like a servant, but "Lady Lilian" seemed much too familiar. Safest to use "ma'am," she decided.

The last scrap of food disappeared and Lady Lilian removed the plate. "Now something to drink," she said. "Dr. Barley was most particular that liquids are even more important than nourishment in restoring the blood, so I hope you are thirsty."

"Yes, ma'am, but I can't see how the deuce I'm to drink without spilling it all over the place."

Lady Lilian winced but said gaily, "Oh, Malcolm came up with a solution to that problem. A nursery trick. He and Emily have been out to the stables to find hollow straws—clean ones, I assure you, and Cook has rinsed them besides. You put one end in the drink and the other in your mouth and simply sip it up. Here, try it."

"What a clever idea!" Taking the cup and straw she offered, Mariette sucked up a little of the lemon-flavoured barley water and giggled. "It's fun!"

"Nanny used to grow quite irritable when we tried it in the nursery. 'Disgraceful conduct for young ladies and gentlemen,' she always told us." Lady Lilian must have seen Mariette's dismay for she quickly added, "But ideal for an invalid. I must admit we used to misbehave dreadfully. We blew bubbles in our milk, and my brothers shot bread pellets at each other and made horrible squawking noises when they reached the bottom of their cups."

The childhood reminiscence made her seem much more approachable.

Suddenly very tired, Mariette said hesitantly, "I . . . you

don't mind if I stay here tonight, ma'am? I don't think I can quite manage to get home."

"Of course you cannot, child! No more laudanum for the present, I think, but let me move your pillows so that you can lie down and sleep for a while. There, is that better?"

"Oh, yes. I don't know how to thank you for . . . for taking me in and everything."

"It is no more than one neighbour owes to another. The best thanks will be to rest and recover quickly."

"I'll try. Please tell your brother I'm very grateful for all his help." She didn't quite dare ask to see Lord Malcolm.

"Certainly." Slightly flushed, Lady Lilian said tentatively, "I don't know how much you recall of Dr. Barley's visit. Jenny faints at the sight of blood so I thought it best that Malcolm rather than any other servant should assist. . . . You may be assured that he is a gentleman and has already put out of his mind any . . . any untoward circumstances."

Mariette's cheeks felt a far brighter red than Lady Lilian's. Her eyes lowered, she murmured, "Yes, ma'am."

"So you will not object to speaking to him? He still hopes you will remember something to identify the villain who shot you. The sooner the better, he says; later this evening if you feel well enough. It is hardly proper that he should visit you in your bedchamber, but I cannot dissuade him. Jenny or I will chaperon you, of course."

"If you think it unexceptionable, ma'am."

"Allowable, at least." She turned down the lamp. "Will your dog come with me? Ragamuffin, dinner!"

Ragamuffin sprang to his feet and pranced after her, tail waving.

She left Mariette puzzled and apprehensive. Lord Malcolm knew perfectly well who had shot her. Why should he insist on questioning her about an imaginary poacher? Why had he invented a poacher in the first place?

His servant was in no danger from the law for firing on a highwayman. Instead of dragging her off to the nearest magistrate, he had taken care of her and lied to his sister, who'd surely not have received her at Corycombe had she known the truth. Mariette had every reason to be grateful, but her gratitude was tinged with suspicion.

Did Lord Malcolm want something from her in return, and if so, what? Recalling her bared bottom, she buried her hot face in her pillow. Surely that bloody sight had not inflamed his animal passions!

But she knew nothing of men, except that they were lamentably self-centred. Experience and history taught the same lesson. Throughout the centuries, men had committed deeds both dire and heroic for the sake of honour, fame, power, and riches; the comfort and happiness of others came as afterthoughts, if at all. Look at Edward III and the burghers of Calais. He'd have executed them without a qualm if the queen had not pleaded for their lives.

Even Uncle George, who had given her a home and never refused any request, was too occupied with his sculpture to pay the least regard to whether she was content with her lot. Which she was, of course. What was the point of repining? *Maman* always said one must not demand the moon.

Still, had Uncle George bothered to read the note Lady Lilian said she had sent? Did he miss her? Had he even noticed she wasn't there?

Ralph would be on tenterhooks, but only because he didn't know whether she had retrieved his ring. Even Ragamuffin had abandoned her at a promise of food.

By the time Mariette drifted into exhausted sleep, her pillowcase was damp from tears she was too weak to hold back.

"And when you've finished your supper, miss, his lordship'd take it kindly if you'd spare him a word."

Restored by food and rest, Mariette felt more equal to facing her rescuer. "Thank you, Jenny. Please tell Lord Malcolm I'll be ready to see him in half an hour."

"Beg pardon, miss, but if you'd like me to comb your hair first, it'll be longer than half an hour. Seeing it's in a shocking tangle and you with a great lump on your head I'll have to watch out for."

Suddenly conscious that he had seen her not only indecently stripped but in a disgraceful state of dishevelment, Mariette said subduedly, "Yes, I'd like my hair combed if you don't mind. Tell his lordship however long you think necessary."

Despite Jenny's care, the combing was a painful process. However, Mariette insisted that she proceed. No one had combed her hair for her since *maman* died, nor told her her black locks were beautiful, as the kindly abigail did. She peered eagerly into the silver-backed handglass Jenny gave her, trying to see if it were true. As usual, she decided she'd rather be blonde, like Lady Lilian.

Jenny braided her hair and tied it back with a bit of white satin ribbon. The maid was adjusting a shawl of incredibly soft white wool around Mariette's uppermost shoulder when someone tapped on the door.

Wishing she were able to adopt a rather more elegant posture, Mariette called, "Come in."

She had first seen Lord Malcolm when she was robbing him, more concerned with his movements than his appearance. After that, she had viewed him through a blur of pain. He had carried her up the stairs as if she weighed no more than a feather bolster. Now she was surprised to find he was of little more than average height, his strength belied by a slight though well-knit frame.

He was elegantly dressed, she thought, though she had little basis for comparison. His midnight blue coat, brass-buttoned, fitted to perfection. His snowy cravat was elaborately knotted and the frill of his shirt, equally snowy, projected over a low-cut waistcoat of blue and silver brocade. He wore trousers rather than the breeches still more common in the country. They moulded his muscular legs like a second skin. . . .

Hastily she transferred her gaze to his face: short, light-brown hair, brushed forward in the modern style; a broad brow above blue-grey eyes; a hint of an aristocratic hook to the nose; a determined chin, which Mariette knew was not necessarily a sign of a determined character. Altogether a rather ordinary face—he was nowhere near as good-looking as Ralph, or the haughty Lord Wareham.

His expression was not a bit haughty. He looked just about as wary as she felt.

He bowed. "Miss Bertrand," he said, "allow me to introduce myself. I am Malcolm Eden."

His formality put her at her ease. He wasn't treating her like a thief, like a naughty child, like a lightskirt with whose anatomy he was intimately familiar. He behaved as if she were an ordinary, respectable guest in his sister's home.

"How do you do, my lord. I—Get down, Ragamuffin!" She had been too busy staring at Lord Malcolm to notice his arrival until, miffed at being ignored, he reared up on the bed and licked her nose.

Watching her pet the dog, Malcolm suddenly decided that, whatever else she might be, she was adorable.

Before he could follow up this alarming thought, Lilian's abigail curtsied to him and said, "Her ladyship told me to stay, my lord."

"Yes, of course. Why don't you sit over here, Miss Pennick, and I'll bring over a branch of candles so that you can see your needlework." He settled her in a corner by the Dutch-tiled fireplace, as far from the bed as possible.

For himself, he set a chair at a precisely calculated distance from the bed, far enough for propriety, close enough to talk quietly without being overheard. Though he paused a moment before seating himself, apparently Miss Bertrand was unaware that she ought to give him permission to sit down. She regarded him gravely but without fear, thank heaven. The last thing he needed was to figure as a threat.

"I must apologize . . . ," they both said at once.

Malcolm laughed. Her answering smile brought a sparkle to eyes the lucent brown of a clear pool in a moorland stream—and revealed an unexpected dimple. His captivation was completed.

Gammon!

He knew his susceptibility to feminine pulchritude and he had never let it interfere with his work. Now was not the moment to succumb. He rushed into speech.

"I believe, Miss Bertrand, as a gentleman it is my privilege to be the first to apologize, particularly as yours was by far the severer injury. May I hope that you will forgive me?"

She looked bewildered. "Forgive you? But it wasn't you who shot me, was it?" Her voice was low and sweet, remarkably refined considering her upbringing, and without a trace of a French accent.

"It was my servant."

"I heard you try to stop him. You cannot be blamed, and I hope you haven't punished him? He was justified in firing on a highwayman. Is Sparrow all right? My horse?"

"Yes, Jessup is taking good care of him. Jessup was most certainly at fault. It was perfectly obvious you were no ordinary highwayman," he said dryly, "though I admit I had not guessed you were a female. What on earth possessed you to do anything so absolutely shatterbrained?"

"I know it was idiotic," she said, flushing. "I'm very sorry I threatened you with a gun, though it wasn't loaded, and robbed you, though I did give your money back and didn't take the stick-pin or anything else. But I had to do *something.*"

"Why?"

"Because Ralph—he's my cousin—was quite in despair. You see, the ring has been in his family for generations. It's all he has left, as his papa was a shocking gamester and lost the Riddlesworth estate as well as his wife's fortune. And you need not look at me like that. I know Ralph likes to gamble. He can't help it, it's in his blood."

"Of course he can help it. If you ask me, he's simply spoiled."

"Oh no," she said with an earnest air, "quite the reverse. When his parents died and he came to live at Bell-Tor Manor he was only a little boy, yet as a baronet he had too much pride to ask Uncle George for things."

"Understandable, I suppose." Though unrealistic if George Barwith was as heedless as he was reputed to be.

"It is, isn't it? So when we grew out of our clothes I was always the one to ask for new ones, but that's all. Uncle George has been so generous giving us a home all these years that I don't like to ask for things we don't really need. Except horses," she added conscientiously.

"A necessity," Malcolm assured her.

"Oh, and my subscription to the circulating library, but I pay for that out of my allowance now. Ralph wanted an allowance so I asked Uncle George for him, and Uncle George offered me one too. Did I not say he is excessively generous? The subscription is quite expensive but I don't regret a penny."

"I daresay you borrow Gothic novels, like every other young lady of my acquaintance," he quizzed her in an effort to conceal his anger at both Barwith's and Riddlesworth's treatment of her.

"Yes, I don't need to borrow serious books because the Manor has an excellent library." She obviously had no idea the mamas of the young ladies of his acquaintance frowned on the reading of romances, even if that didn't stop their daughters.

"And it's from a novel, I wager, you took the notion of dressing as a highwayman and holding up my carriage!"

Blushing delightfully, she fidgeted with the fringe of her cashmere shawl. "Yes," she confessed. "It sounded quite easy."

"That doesn't explain why *you* were the one to do it."

"Well, it was no use whatsoever expecting Ralph to make any effort to recover his blasted signet, so I had to. One must be practical."

He stared at her for an astonished moment, then burst into laughter. "Practical! My dear Miss Bertrand, I've never heard of anything less practical than your utterly romantical scheme!"

"It would have worked," she argued with spirit, "if Ragamuffin hadn't insisted on coming with me. If I hadn't had to untie him I'd have got away without being shot."

"Before going to such lengths," he said gently, "you might have tried simply asking me for the ring."

She hesitated before saying, "I didn't think you'd be willing to let me redeem it."

Her answer struck him as evasive, the more so because she failed to meet his eye. Surely Riddlesworth's fondness for his heirloom was insufficient to explain so dangerous a ploy! Had she been as desperate as her cousin to retrieve the sphinx seal without revealing her identity? Malcolm did not want to believe it.

"I am quite willing to give it to you." He took the signet ring from his pocket and put it in the drawer of the bedside table. "Its . . . *sentimental* value is far greater than its actual worth, I feel sure."

"Thank you, sir, but I shall pay you whatever sum Ralph pledged it for."

"Unnecessary."

She looked at him askance. "It's a debt of honour. I can afford it. My allowance is far greater than I need." Biting her lip, she went on shyly, "You have been much kinder than I deserve, my lord. I haven't thanked you yet for . . . for not leaving me to bleed to death, and for not telling Lady Lilian of my disgraceful behaviour. . . ."

"What a catalogue of negative virtues!"

". . . And for thinking of the straw for me to drink through. That was a vastly clever notion."

"I considered myself vastly clever when first I came up with the notion as a child—only to be told my older brothers had done it years before." He sighed. "The story of my life." Now why in heaven's name should he confide in this headstrong, quixotic chit, when he had never revealed to his most intimate friends his driving need to prove himself his brothers' equal?

She echoed his sigh. "I always thought it would be nice to have an elder brother. Or a sister. But how pleased Ralph will be when I take his ring back to him tomorrow."

"My dear Miss Bertrand, you cannot leave tomorrow."

"Of course I can. I feel much better already and I don't want to impose on Lady Lilian any longer than I must."

"I assure you . . ." At the sound of footsteps he looked around and rose in relief, dislodging Ragamuffin's head from his feet, as his sister came in.

"Malcolm, what can you be about, wearing Miss Bertrand out with your talk?"

"I'm trying to convince your patient of the impossibility of her going home tomorrow. I shall let you persuade her. Good night, Miss Bertrand. Sleep well."

Bidding Lord Malcolm good night, Mariette watched him bestow a farewell pat on Ragamuffin and depart. He still puzzled her, but she had no chance just now to pore over what he had said.

"There is no question of your leaving tomorrow," Lady Lilian told her firmly. "Mr. Barwith has received my note saying you will remain at Corycombe for several days. Here, his groom has brought a letter for you."

Uncle George's brief note hoped she was comfortable and would not be away from home too long. He needed her advice as he was having trouble with the pig's tail. Tails, he was willing to admit, were not his strong suit.

There was a second note, from her cousin. He knew she'd make a mull of it, he wrote. Now Lord Malcolm was on his guard, the signet was gone for good.

Ralph must be frantic with worry. Whatever Lord Malcolm and Lady Lilian said, she had to take his ring to him.

Chapter 4

The small dose of laudanum Lady Lilian insisted on Mariette taking sent her quickly to sleep, but she woke after a few hours. A glimmer of light came from the oil lamp, turned low, and the pale luminescence of a full moon shone between the window curtains.

Somewhere in the house a clock chimed three.

Her conversation with Lord Malcolm ran through her head. He had asked a great many questions. She had answered, both because she felt guilty about holding him up at gunpoint and because it was a pleasure to talk to someone who was interested in her.

Who *seemed* interested in her, she corrected herself sadly. Come to think of it, in actual fact he had only wanted to know exactly why she held him up. That was reasonable. She had intended to explain anyway. The one thing she had kept from him was her humiliating experience with Lord Wareham.

She, on the other hand, had had no chance to satisfy her curiosity about the poacher story. Was kindness really enough to explain why he had lied to his sister for the sake of a total stranger? He hadn't even known she would care whether Lady Lilian knew of her exploit. There was something rum about that.

Something rum, also, in his willingness—even eagerness—to give her the ring.

Perhaps, as Ralph claimed, he had indeed won it by

cheating and now felt guilty. That could account for the poacher faradiddle, too. If Lady Lilian learned about Mariette playing highwayman, she would hear about the ring. Her brother was afraid she might find out he had cheated at cards.

Restlessly Mariette turned her head to face the other way as if by so doing she could change the facts. She did not want to believe Lord Malcolm was a cheat.

Was it possible for a lord to be a Captain Sharp? In novels, a man who marked the cards was always an unshaven ruffian in a low tavern or gambling hell, not a gentleman in a respectable inn like the Golden Hind. She wished she knew more of the real world outside history books.

Was it possible for a man who was a cheat to be kind? For Lord Malcolm was amiable in other ways even if he invented the poacher for his own benefit. With such delicacy had he avoided any hint of having seen her unclothed that she had quite forgotten to be embarrassed.

She couldn't help liking him, which was something she had never expected to say of a lord after meeting Lord Wareham. Lord Malcolm wasn't in the least toplofty, nor even as starchy as Lady Lilian.

Despite her ladyship's benevolence, Mariette was under no illusion. Lady Lilian considered her an ill-bred, indecorous hoyden. Miss Thorne considered her an encroaching nobody. And Lord Malcolm considered her a reckless, impractical idiot. For some reason that hurt worst of all.

She turned her head again. Lying on her stomach was becoming positively irksome. After sleeping all afternoon she'd never go back to sleep now. She wanted to get up and move about.

She wanted to go home.

Lady Lilian and Lord Malcolm had told her she must stay, but she wasn't accustomed to doing anyone's bidding. It wasn't as if they actually *wanted* her to stay. On the contrary, they'd be relieved if she left, and how glad Ralph would be to see her.

The household slept. If she left now, no one would try to stop her.

Cautiously she propped herself up on her arms as far as she could. Her bottom ached, but otherwise she felt quite all right. With a wriggle she contrived to inch out from under the covers and swing her legs over the edge of the bed. Though it hurt when she bent in the middle, as soon as she stood upright the pain lessened. The momentary dizziness was just from the laudanum and would wear off in no time.

Ragamuffin stuck his head out from under the bed and licked her bare feet.

"We're going home, boy," she told him.

He emerged, tail wagging.

Mariette shivered. The fire had died down to a bed of glowing coals and the room was chilly. Oh lord, she thought, what the deuce was she going to wear?

Her buckskin riding breeches had been peppered with holes, not to mention bloodsoaked. Even if they had been miraculously cleaned and mended, she wasn't at all sure she wanted to pull them on over her sore and swollen rear end. Nor did she fancy the prospect of sitting on Sparrow's back, supposing she managed to saddle him and mount.

However, she had never been one to let difficulties daunt her. If she couldn't ride, she'd walk and send Jim Groom to fetch Sparrow later. As for clothes, the enormous clothes press in the corner must contain *something* wearable.

Turning up the lamp, she investigated. In the wardrobe she found her riding boots, stockings, shirt, jacket, and top-coat. The shot holes in the coat had been beautifully darned—Jenny no doubt, bless her. There was also an elegant, pale-pink, quilted dressing-gown. Shivering again, Mariette decided to cram on all the clothes she could, even keeping Miss Thorne's nightgown underneath. She'd have it washed and ironed and send it back.

Bending to put on the stockings proved impossible. Without their woolly thickness she managed to slip her feet into her boots. Shirt, dressing-gown, jacket, coat went on over the nightgown. Fortunately the coat was on the large side for her as it had been chosen to disguise her sex. She buttoned it down the front, turned up the collar, and put the ring in the pocket, where she found her gloves.

Ragamuffin gave a soft, hopeful bark.

"Sshh! I'm coming."

He went to the door, and she cast a last glance around the room. The white cashmere shawl was neatly draped over the back of a chair. Mariette tied it in country-woman style over her head. She'd send it back before anyone could imagine she had stolen it, or the nightgown and dressing-gown.

She opened the door and they set off. Ragamuffin's toenails clicked on the polished boards of the passageway, but no one stirred. A side-door was easily unbarred.

They slipped out into the moonlit night.

"My lord!"

"Padgett? What is it?" Malcolm sat up, instantly alert.

"I beg pardon for waking your lordship at this hour, but I was sure you'd want to know. Miss Bertrand's dog turned up in the stables in a fine frenzy. Her ladyship's head groom had the good sense to send a housemaid up to miss's chamber, and she's not there, my lord."

"The devil she's not!" Malcolm flung back the covers, swung his feet to the floor, and ripped off his nightshirt. "Not there, and the dog not with her?"

"Precisely, my lord." Padgett was already pulling a shirt over Malcolm's head. "The maid woke Miss Pennick, her ladyship's abigail, and not being wishful to rouse her ladyship she came to me. A shrewd woman, my lord, and goodhearted with it. Riding breeches, I assume, my lord?"

"Yes." Malcolm grabbed the proffered buckskins. "Is Miss Bertrand's gelding gone?"

"I believe not, my lord. I ventured to send a message to the stables to saddle a mount for your lordship."

"Good man." He waved away a neckcloth, to the valet's unspoken distress, and thrust his arms into the sleeves of his coat. "Boots."

"Here, my lord."

Five minutes after being woken, Malcolm arrived in the stable yard at a run. Half a dozen grooms and stable boys stood around Jessup, who held the bridles of Malcolm's roan mare, Incognita, and a stolid Welsh cob. Ragamuffin stopped whining and scratching at the closed gate to the yard, discharged an ear-shattering salvo of barks, and dashed up to Malcolm.

"Open the gate," he ordered the nearest boy, swinging up onto Incognita's back.

"C'n I come, m'lord?" Jessup begged, foot in the stirrup.

"Yes." He was very much afraid once again he'd need help to lift the little fool. Anxiety gnawed at him.

"Will I send out searchers, m'lord?" asked the head groom.

"Not yet. I hope the dog will lead us aright. But you'd better warn all the menservants they may be needed."

The cob at her heels, Incognita cantered through the gateway. In one direction, the carriage drive led round the house to the front. Ragamuffin turned the opposite way, dashing ahead along a stony ridge which quickly began to rise.

"I'm that sorry, m'lord." Jessup's face was screwed up in anguished remorse. " 'Bout shooting the miss, I mean."

"You haven't told anyone?" Malcolm said sharply.

"Nay, m'lord," he protested, "you knows I c'n keep a still tongue in me head."

"True, or you'd not be working for me."

" 'Sides, I'd be dicked in the nob to admit I shot a young lady, let alone one as is well liked hereabouts."

"She is?"

"There's plenty here has relatives over to Bell-Tor Manor and they all says old Mr. Barwith's folks is right fond o' miss. Allus does her bit for them that's in trouble, and not above a friendly word for anybody. She's more of a real lady, they says, than some as turns up their noses and won't pass the time o' day with her. Which her la'ship does," he added hastily, and fell silent.

Malcolm found himself uncommonly pleased at this report, and more anxious than ever about Miss Bertrand's fate.

Through a stand of dawn-misty conifers Ragamuffin raced, the horses close behind. They emerged on the moor and the track petered out into a rough path zigzagging back and forth across the steep face of the hill. The dog cut across, dodged and leapt heather and gorse, ignoring a lapwing that broke cover and flapped away, flickering black and white.

Malcolm didn't dare follow across unknown ground. He kept Incognita at a canter up the path, though. A showy, high-stepping creature suited to a dandy, like her master she had powers of strength and speed not apparent to the casual eye. Jessup had to spur his cob to keep up.

Up and up they rode. Though the sun now shone on the rocks atop Bell Tor, it had not yet risen above Wicken's Down. The cold wind swept down from the high moors and Malcolm was sorry he had not paused to don a muffler. He prayed he was mistaken—they all were mistaken—in fearing the dog's behaviour meant Miss Bertrand was lying somewhere out here on the bare moor.

Ragamuffin was waiting on the path ahead, but with an impatient yelp he plunged into the brush again. The crest lay just ahead. Corycombe was a doll's house below. How the deuce had the girl come so far? Sheer pluck and determination, he decided, to say nothing of windmills in her head.

It wasn't the crest, just a shoulder. At least the slope levelled off for some distance. The path stopped winding and headed directly eastward. Ragamuffin stayed on it, nose to the ground now.

Suddenly he veered to the side, stopped beside a large clump of heather, and howled.

She lay huddled in the lee of the heather, her head pillowed on her hands. Her face was paper-white, her lips blue, and continuous tremors shook her whole body. Kneeling beside her, Malcolm instantly dismissed the notion he'd had to take the troublesome chit on to Bell-Tor Manor since she was so stubbornly resolved to go there. She needed heat, and the sooner the better.

The dog gave a short, sharp bark as if to say, "Well, I've done my part, now get on with it."

"Ragamuffin," she murmured and opened her eyes. "Lord Malcolm!" Her voice shook. The brown eyes closed again and two tears squeezed out from beneath the long black lashes. Tears of relief? Disappointment? Dismay?

"You're safe now."

He lifted her and carried her in his arms to where Jessup held the horses. The groom regarded the limp figure with alarm.

"Will she die, m'lord? I'd 'ave it on me conscience the rest o' me life."

"She will if we stand here gabbling. Let go the bridles. Incognita won't move and I expect your beast will stay with her."

He transferred Miss Bertram to Jessup's arms, took off his top-coat, and folded it into a pillow. Mounting the well-trained mare, he placed the pillow in front of him. Jessup passed the girl up. Malcolm needed both arms to hold her so that her lower back rather than her rump rested on the makeshift cushion.

Perhaps sheer embarrassment drove her to run off, he thought. Of all the places to be shot!

"You'll have to lead Incognita," he said to the groom. "Ride as fast as you consider safe. It's more important to get her to warmth than to avoid jolting." Shivering himself, he could only hope he was right.

As Jessup mounted the cob, Miss Bertrand whispered, "I'm sorry."

He smiled down into those great brown eyes. "Little goosecap," he said tenderly. She needed someone to protect her from the world, and from herself.

"I wanted to take Ralph his ring."

"I shall send a groom with it today, I promise."

At that moment, Malcolm knew for certain he wanted to win her indomitable loyalty for himself.

* * *

Twelve paces from one end of the drawing room to the other. Twelve paces back again. That damned Clementi sonatina was driving him mad, Emily practising the same passage over and over accompanied by the click of Miss Thorne's knitting needles. But if he went elsewhere, he'd either have less room to pace or he'd be wandering the corridors like an unhappy ghost. He could not sit still while the doctor was with Miss Bertrand.

"I fear you will wear a path in the carpet, Lord Malcolm," Miss Thorne reproved him without a pause in her endless knitting of endless lengths of mustard wool. Distracted for a moment, Malcolm pitied the poor recipients of her charitable diligence.

The Clementi stopped in the middle of a phrase. "Never mind, Uncle. The carpet is already sadly worn and Mama has been saying this age that she means to replace it."

"Your mama told you to practise your music, Emily," Miss Thorne said sharply.

"Yes, ma'am." Emily obediently turned back to the pianoforte.

"Sing us a song," Malcolm suggested in desperation.

Emily hunted through her sheet music. "Here, this is a pretty one." She struck a few preliminary chords and warbled soulfully:

" 'Come away, come away, death,

" 'And in sad cypress let me be laid;

" 'Fly away, . . . ' "

"For pity's sake, not that! Not now."

"But it is about a gentleman dying, not a lady. Only listen: 'I am slain by a fair cruel maid.' So it must be a man singing, must it not?"

"Pray do not argue, Emily," said Miss Thorne. "You will beg your uncle's pardon at once."

"That is not necessary." Malcolm ran his hand through his hair, a shocking gesture for one who claimed to be a dandy, and one which would have appalled his valet. "I'm sorry for snapping at you, Emmie. It's just that I am dev—extremely anxious about Miss Bertrand."

Emily clasped her hands. "She is not really going to die, is she?"

"We must pray that Miss Bertrand will recover," Miss Thorne pronounced, "but any young person who goes racketing about the countryside utterly heedless of propriety must expect to bear the consequences."

"Propriety be damned! She's suffering from exposure to the cold, not lack of propriety!"

Emily's shocked glee more than Miss Thorne's affronted sniff made him regret his own lapse from decorum. He was about to apologise for his language, if not the sentiment, when Lilian came in. Eagerly he went to meet her.

"What does he say?"

"He fears she may develop an inflammation of the lungs, Malcolm. She must be watched constantly lest she grow feverish or start to cough. For the present she is resting as comfortably as may be expected."

"Thank heaven your Miss Pennick had prepared a hot bath and warmed her bed before we got back, as well as sending for Dr. Barley."

"Pennick takes a great deal too much upon herself," Miss Thorne observed with another sniff.

"Jenny is a gem, Cousin Tabitha," Lilian contradicted, her voice gentle but her lips tightening. "I cannot think how I should go on without her."

"You are excessively indulgent, Lilian. It never answers."

Emily started up, obviously ready to take up cudgels, but she subsided at a glance from her mother. "Mama, may I help to watch Miss Bertrand?"

"No, my dear, but I am glad you offered. Malcolm, I must speak with you. Will you come to the morning room?"

The green, white, and gold room was bright with wintry sunshine. Lilian sank with slightly weary grace onto a chair by the fire. Malcolm stood for a moment looking down at her.

"You will not let that woman watch Miss Bertrand!" he

said angrily. "She's more likely to drive her into a decline than to aid her recovery."

"Cousin Tabitha? Do stop hovering over me like an avenging Fury, Malcolm, and sit down. No, I shall not ask her to help. She would only do so in a spirit of grudging martyrdom."

"I cannot imagine why you put up with her."

"When Frederick died, Mama insisted that I must have someone to lend me countenance. It came down to a choice of Tabitha Thorne—she is Frederick's cousin, you know, not ours . . ."

"Thank heaven!"

" . . . Or Aunt Wilhelmina."

"Good Lord, what a choice. I'm not sure I wouldn't prefer Aunt W., though."

"Once I had asked Cousin Tabitha to come and live at Corycombe, it became impossible to send her away. She has been saying for years that she only stays to oblige and her brother wants her to keep house for him, but when I suggest his claim is the greater. . . ." She sighed.

"You are too soft-hearted."

"That is what *she* says," Lilian pointed out crossly. "She reprimanded me as though I were still in the schoolroom for taking Miss Bertrand in. Now I shall have to endure a lecture on my folly in taking her back when she clearly wishes to go home. Malcolm, do you know why she ran off?"

"No." He could not speak of Miss Bertrand's desire to return the ring to her cousin without inviting a host of further questions impossible to answer.

"I pray it was not I who drove her away. She said one or two odd things—nothing so very dreadful, as I should know who have five brothers! But I fear I failed to hide my dismay. I behaved just like Cousin Tabitha, in fact! I shall never forgive myself if Miss Bertrand left because she felt unwelcome."

"You are incapable of behaving like Cousin Tabitha! I wager your dismay was nought but a fleeting expression, not a regular Bill of Attainder. It's more likely to be my fault.

Considering the . . . unfortunate circumstances of our first encounter, no doubt she was simply overwhelmed with embarrassment at the prospect of seeing me again." Malcolm made the suggestion to comfort Lilian, but he was suddenly horribly afraid it might be true.

"Fustian! Your *fault,* for saving her life? Twice now! Her chief emotion must be gratitude."

"Come now, Lilian, you must own she has cause for embarrassment. Any virtuous female of the slightest sensibility must be mortified to know a gentleman has made himself familiar with her . . ."

"Malcolm! My dear, spare my blushes. You are right, of course, and I do believe Miss Bertrand to be virtuous and not without sensibility. Yet she agreed to see you last night. You did not give her further cause for awkwardness?"

"Certainly not. She talked freely, argued with me in fact!" He smiled, remembering her spirited defence, her insistence on paying for the ring. "She must have had some other reason for running off in the middle of the night without a word. I daresay she was muddled by the laudanum. What on earth was that pink garment she had on under her coat?"

"Mrs. Wittering's best dressing gown."

"Mrs. Wittering's!" Malcolm tried to imagine the stout housekeeper in pink quilted satin instead of her usual black.

"Mine and Emmie's are too small and I will not ask Cousin Tabitha after the fuss she made over lending a nightgown, let alone helping me dress the girl in it." Lilian frowned in thought. "Mrs. Wittering lent her dressing gown gladly so perhaps she will not mind sitting with Miss Bertrand sometimes, though it is hardly part of her duties. I offered to send to the Manor for Miss Bertrand's abigail but the poor girl has none."

"You will be short-handed with neither Miss Thorne nor Emily to help. I shall take my turn."

"My dear brother, even without considering—in your own words—the unfortunate circumstances of your first encounter, absolutely not!"

"I hope to marry her, Lilian," Malcolm said quietly.

Lilian's jaw dropped. "B-but you hardly know her!"

"I know her well enough to admire her courage, her spirit, her . . ." He must not speak of her loyalty to her cousin. "Her beauty. Well enough to know my mind."

"Oh, Mama is constantly writing to tell me you are in love again," Lilian recalled with obvious relief.

"I can't deny I have often admired a pretty face, but never to the point of wishing to see it over breakfast every morning for the rest of my life!"

"You don't believe you have compromised her, do you, Malcolm? Because of the unfortunate way you met?"

"No! Padgett will not talk. Jessup saw nothing. Dr. Barley is bound by professional discretion and you told me Jenny Pennick and Miss Thorne will keep their mouths closed."

"Whatever her faults, Cousin Tabitha is no tattlemonger. Surely Miss Bertrand is unlikely to broadcast her misfortune. Yes, I daresay you are safe. You are not obliged to marry her."

"It's not a matter of obligation. I *wish* to marry her."

"Indeed, Malcolm, she is not at all a suitable bride for an Eden."

"Her birth is good enough," he argued. "You said yourself her father was a count or viscount. Etiquette can be learned. As for lack of fortune, that is no one's business but my own. My income may be modest but I can afford to support a wife who considers a library subscription to be an extravagance!"

"No, does she? Poor child! All the same, Mama and Father will be appalled when they hear . . ."

"Don't tell the family. They will only brush it off as my latest diverting start," he said bitterly.

As a child ten years younger than his nearest brother, he had grown accustomed perforce to seeing his every attempt at emulation greeted with indulgent amusement. He had done well at Harrow, but not quite as well as Reggie academically or Peter at sports. Reggie was now a Dean at Canterbury, Peter a Brigadier, James ambassador to some obscure Balkan kingdom; in the Church, the Army, or the Diplomatic Service, Malcolm would always be a poor second. And Radford, of course, was heir to a marquisate, to their father's title and lands—admittedly an honour to which Malcolm did not aspire.

His present occupation was not one about which he was able to boast to the family, which was one of its attractions. Whatever he did they would not take it seriously. He could marry a royal princess and he'd still be the runt of the litter, so why should he not please himself?

Miss Bertrand was the wife for him. Miss Bertrand? "Dash it, I don't know her christian name! Blount said Miss . . . Marie?"

"Mariette," Lilian corrected him distractedly.

"Mariette." He savoured the word, then looked up at the ceiling. "Mariette," he said softly, "you must get well quickly, for I mean to woo and win you!"

Chapter 5

"Captain Aldrich, my lady." Blount stood aside and the captain stepped into the drawing room. He wore unobtrusive riding clothes, not his uniform, Malcolm noted with approval. The captain's visit to Corycombe was not exactly a secret but there was no sense drawing attention to it.

Malcolm went to meet him and shook his hand. "Good to see you again, Des. Lilian, allow me to present Captain Desmond Aldrich. I fagged for Des at Harrow and he's never let me forget it."

Hearing Lilian's sharply indrawn breath, Malcolm wondered if he should have warned her about the captain's empty sleeve. However, she rose with her usual graceful composure and held out her hand.

"Welcome to Corycombe, Captain Aldrich."

"My lady." Des flushed slightly as he bowed over her hand. "Your pardon for intruding, ma'am. I asked for your brother but the butler . . ."

"Blount was instructed to show you in here, captain. You are just in time to join us for dinner."

His flush deepened. "I thought I had come early enough to complete our business and be gone before you dined. I'm not dressed for company."

"We keep country hours, sir. We expected you to dine with us, though Malcolm was uncertain just when you would arrive. And if I have no quarrel to your dress, I am sure Cousin Tabitha and Emily do not. May I present you to Miss Thorne? And this is my daughter."

Miss Thorne's expression made it plain that she strongly objected to the captain's dress, and probably to his presence. Her nod was frigid.

Emmie made a most presentable curtsy. "How do you do, sir," she said breathlessly. Far too shy and too well-brought-up to enquire about his missing arm, she was nonetheless obviously dying to ask. Her uncle diagnosed an incipient case of hero worship.

"Miss Thorne, Miss Farrar." Even as he bowed, Des stared at Emily. He turned to Lilian. "Your *daughter?*"

It was Lilian's turn to blush. "Yes, captain."

"Impossible!" he said with conviction.

Though Des was Malcolm's elder by a mere four years, his life at sea had weathered his thin face and he looked older than the youthful Lady Lilian. With a becoming pink in her cheeks, she appeared younger than ever. Malcolm suspected the sailor's blunt disbelief pleased her more than any number of polished compliments. His sincerity was unmistakable.

Blount came back to announce dinner. Lilian beckoned to him and spoke briefly in an undertone. "Certainly, my lady," he said and departed with rather more haste than was quite proper in a very proper butler of his age and dignity.

The captain gallantly offered Lilian his only arm, Malcolm gave his two to Miss Thorne and Emily, and they proceeded to the dining room. In such a small company conversation was general. The inevitable topic was Miss Bertrand's "accident."

"The lady has my deepest sympathy," Des said when he heard the story—with the tactful omission of the precise part of her anatomy which had been peppered. "A painful business!"

Too curious to be shy, Emily seized the opening. "Does it hurt dreadfully to be shot, sir?" she asked.

"Emmie, dear!" her mother expostulated.

"That's all right, ma'am." Des touched Lilian's arm reassuringly, then, as he realized what he had done, he hurriedly withdrew his hand and turned to Emily. "Yes, Miss Farrar, it hurts dreadfully."

Soup forgotten, she leaned forward, eyes wide. "Was it the French who shot you?"

"I believe so, though truth to tell I didn't much care whether the cannonball was French or Spanish."

"You fought at Trafalgar?" Lilian was almost as wide-eyed as her daughter.

"I had that honour."

"You must have known Lord Nelson, then?"

"Not personally, ma'am," said Des regretfully. "I met him several times but only as one of many captains. Admiral Collingwood was my immediate superior."

Despite this disclaimer, Lilian and Emily wanted to know all he could tell them about the hero of Trafalgar. Even Miss Thorne put in a question or two. And in spite of his modesty, some of the glamour of that glorious victory clung to Captain Aldrich.

While they talked, Blount and the footman, Charles, removed the soup. Malcolm noticed every dish served thereafter was cut up so as to be easily eaten without a knife. So that was what Lilian had whispered to the butler! Mariette's difficulties must have given her the notion. She really was a dear, even if her exaggerated notion of his consequence led her to the featherheaded opinion that Mariette was not good enough for him.

The dishes in the second course had been prepared in the same way. Des ate hungrily without apparent awareness of the pains taken to accommodate him, but Malcolm had seen him struggle to cope with a slice of beef during his convalescence, too proud to ask for help. He was sure his friend appreciated Lilian's thoughtfulness, compounded by her silence on the subject.

Her curiosity about Lord Nelson satisfied, Emily asked, "Are you still in the Navy, sir?"

"Yes, Miss Farrar. Just when I was about to be invalided, I was offered a position ashore instead, under Rear-Admiral

Gault at Devonport. I was lucky enough to have a friend put in a good word for me."

He looked at Malcolm, who said hastily, "Your grandfather, Emmie."

"At your uncle's behest," Des told her.

"The least I could do for the man whose boots I used to black!"

"Did you really, Uncle Malcolm? Is that what you meant when you said you fagged for Captain Aldrich? What else did he make you do?"

"That is enough, Emily," said Lilian. "We shall leave the gentlemen to their port and their business." She led Miss Thorne and Emily out.

The captain's gaze followed her every step of the way.

As soon as Blount had set out the port and brandy and closed the door behind him, Des sighed and said, "When you wrote that you were staying with your elder sister, I pictured a stout, matronly woman like my own elder sister."

"Lilian must have come as quite a surprise, then."

"That she did! Before I forget—not that I'm likely to—will you convey my thanks to her ladyship for . . . for the meal?"

Pouring brandy, Malcolm nodded his understanding. "Of course, old lad. Here, try this. It crossed the Channel long before Boney set himself up."

Des visibly tore his mind from Lilian's kindness, and her charms. "Thanks." He warmed the glass in his hand, sniffed, and sipped. "First rate. It still comes across, you know. Navy, Coast Guard, Excise, between the lot of us we've never been able to stop the smuggling."

"I know," Malcolm said grimly.

"Are smugglers concerned in this mysterious affair which brings you down to Devon?"

"They have a role in it."

"And is Miss Bertrand involved, by any chance?"

"Only on the periphery. How the deuce did you guess?"

"Your expression when she was talked about. I remember

the look from our schooldays. You were concealing something."

"Not a parcel of goodies from home," Malcolm said, grinning.

"I still remember those fruitcakes. All right, what's going on, and where do I come into it?"

Malcolm reached into his inside pocket for his letter of commission, unfolded it, and laid the parchment before the captain. Des read it in silence, then looked up.

"The First Lord! I thought my position wasn't all your father's doing. You have some influence at the Admiralty."

"Not much. I'm just an errand boy. This is the first mission entrusted to me." He drew his chair closer and lowered his voice. "It starts, believe it or not, with a smuggler who has a patriotic conscience."

"A contradiction in terms, if ever I heard one."

"Not quite. True, the fellow don't cavil at cheating the Customs and Excise, nor at trafficking with the French. But when he was asked to carry a letter, he opened it and read it and didn't like what he saw. He turned it over to a local Justice of the Peace—who turns a blind eye in exchange for his share of smuggled brandy and a bit of lace for his lady, I daresay—and the Justice sent it up to the Admiralty."

"Naval secrets?"

Malcolm nodded. "It ended up on my superior's desk. There wasn't much to be done at that point. We assumed no more letters would be entrusted to the man since the one failed to get through."

"You didn't question this smuggler?"

"We don't know who he is. The Justice, William Penhallow, refused to say more than that it is a Cornishman, on the grounds that if the fellow ceased to trust him we'd hear no more."

"Reasonable, I suppose," Des admitted.

"Effective, at all events. There have been three more letters."

"You don't know where he gets them, I take it."

"He swears to Penhallow he doesn't know the man who

gives them to him, only that he's a buyer of run goods and by his voice he's a Devon man. They all sound the same to me."

"Oh no, if I've learned anything living down here it's that you can tell which side of the Tamar a man comes from by his speech. Still, that's not much help."

"No. Apart from anything else, the man is probably no more than a messenger and may know neither the contents of the letter nor who provides the information. Fortunately we have another clue. The letters are all marked with a curious seal, presumably to verify their provenance to the recipient. A seal in the form of a sphinx."

"A sphinx! Unusual indeed, but how the deuce do we go about tracking down its owner?"

"Oh, I've already done that," Malcolm said nonchalantly.

"Already? You only reached Plymouth yesterday, didn't you? Good gad, you Whitehall men work fast!"

"I'd like you to think I'm incredibly clever, but it was quite fortuitous," Malcolm confessed, taking the goldsmith's work from his pocket and pushing it across the table. "I decided a copy might come in useful."

Des examined it. "Cut line, Malcolm," he said in disgust. "You'd have me believe within a few hours of arriving you not only discovered the owner quite by chance but took possession of the seal for long enough to have a copy made? You're gammoning me."

"Not I." He grinned. "Merely indulging in a little mystification to whet your curiosity."

"You have. Start at the beginning."

"I was in the coffee room at the Golden Hind, whiling away the hours before I met you. A young man approached me and asked if I cared for a game of piquet. I had nothing better to do. If he saw me as a pigeon worth plucking, well, I cut my eyeteeth long ago."

"A mixed metaphor which would have earned you a couple from old Venables. You won the seal from him?"

"Yes, he lost all his rhino and pledged his signet, a rather attractive Tudor ring."

With a frown, Des pointed out, "If he uses it to pass secrets to France, surely he'd not risk losing it."

"I've learned more of him since. He's a young scapegrace, and a dedicated gambler. The ring is a valued heirloom which he was desolated to lose, but that didn't stop him wagering it on the turn of a card."

"He's betraying his country for the sake of the money, then. Who is he?"

"Sir Ralph Riddlesworth."

"Young Riddlesworth! You're right, he's a gambler. I've often seen him at cards or dice with our officers and generally losing. I wouldn't have guessed he had the wit or the nerve to make a spy."

"It's not difficult to appear stupider than one really is," said Malcolm wryly, "as I can attest from personal experience."

Des laughed. "Though I know you to be far from stupid, my friend, I admit I never guessed you had much on your mind beyond the latest way to tie a neckcloth."

"Good gad, man, the set of a coat and the pattern of a waistcoat are just as important!"

"That's a pretty one you have on." He pretended to raise a quizzing glass to Malcolm's grass-green waistcoat, embroidered with primroses. Then he turned serious again. "I'd give a monkey to know which of our fellows is the gabster, and whether on purpose or through careless talk."

"If it's careless talk, it may be more than one. I'll show you the letters—I brought copies—and you can tell me how much of the information is known to whom. All they need do is chat among themselves where Riddlesworth can overhear."

"True. Are you going to arrest him?"

"Not yet. There must be others involved and I'm hoping he'll lead us to them. Until then, I mean to use the copy of the seal to feed false information to the French through Penhallow and his smuggler."

"Capital! What's more, we can deliberately feed false information to Riddlesworth through the officers he gambles with. When it turns up in the letters your pet smuggler hands over, you'll have evidence against him."

"That's a good notion, Des. I'll leave it to you to choose which officers to use."

The captain reddened and said gruffly, "How can you be sure I'm not the one blowing the gaff? I work closely with Admiral Gault and probably know as much as anyone about the movement of ships."

Malcolm chose his words with care. "I don't believe a man who gave an arm to Boney would willingly give him anything else. More to the point, I know you, Des, better than I know my own brothers. There's no one I'd sooner trust. Now, have some more brandy and let's get down to details of how we're going to manage the business."

"Wait a bit. How does the young lady shot by the poacher come into it?"

Malcolm took a swallow of brandy. He'd trust Des with his life—but not quite yet with the fact that he had been struck amidships by Cupid's darts, grappled and boarded by a chit with black hair and bewitching brown eyes.

"There was no poacher," he said nonchalantly. "Miss Bertrand held up my carriage, dressed as a highwayman. Jessup shot her, although I'd warned him to expect something of the sort and not to fire."

"You'd *what?*"

"I made sure Riddlesworth knew my movements. I was fairly sure he'd either come to Corycombe to redeem the ring or relieve me of it on the way."

"Of course, you had to return it to him somehow. But the *girl* held you up?"

"She is Riddlesworth's cousin. They were brought up together by an uncle and she has made a habit of extricating her cousin from the briars, I gather. At least, strictly speaking they are not related. Her parents were French and . . ."

"French! And she was the one who retrieved the signet, or tried to. I wager Miss Bertrand is in it over head and ears!"

Malcolm sought desperately for a credible, dispassionate reason to deny the possibility. He found none.

For three days Mariette slept, woke to eat, and slept again. On the second day Dr. Barley pronounced her out of danger, but she felt weak as a newborn lamb and disinclined to argue with his prescription of bedrest.

To her relief, prompted by Lady Lilian he agreed that her midnight departure was to be blamed on the muddling effect of laudanum. It might even be true. In retrospect, her attempt to walk home seemed even more caperwitted than the highwayman lark. If only she had known beforehand how different Lord Malcolm was from Lord Wareham, she'd simply have gone to him and paid him for Ralph's confounded ring.

From the moment she opened her eyes and saw him bending over her, up there on the moor, she had known she was safe. Once more she owed him her life. How could she ever have believed he cheated at cards, she reproached herself. That was just one of Ralph's wild excuses.

Ralph must have received his ring by now, for he hadn't written to her again. Nor had Uncle George. Lady Lilian said Jim Groom rode over every day to enquire after her, but that was quite likely his own idea, or Mrs. Finney's. Certainly it was the housekeeper's idea to send Mariette her own two nightgowns, her brown flannel dressing-gown, three dresses, cotton stockings, chemises, and a pair of slippers.

It wasn't that Uncle George and Ralph didn't miss her, she told herself. It wasn't that they didn't care. It just never dawned on them that she'd like to hear from them.

She still had not received a word from either when she woke on the fourth morning feeling so much better she couldn't bear the thought of lying in bed all day.

"I shall get up today," she said to Jenny when the abigail came in with her breakfast.

"You're likely weaker than you think, miss," Jenny said

dubiously, setting the tray on the bedside table and drawing back the curtains to reveal an overcast sky.

"I'll never grow any stronger if I don't move about," Mariette pointed out, fending off Ragamuffin's morning greeting. "Get down, boy. You'll upset the tray. At least I could lie on a sofa for a change."

"We'll see what her ladyship says, miss. Here you are, now. A nice bit of grilled gammon cut up in cubes so's you can manage it, and your tea's milky and not too hot. His lordship's found some fresh straws for you."

"He's still here?" A surge of gladness took her by surprise. "I was afraid he'd leave before I could thank him."

"Be here a while yet, from what I hear. My lady's that happy to have him visit. It's a lonely life she leads, the poor dear."

"But she has Miss Farrar and Miss Thorne, and the neighbours call."

"That Miss Thorne's no sort of companion, if you ask me, and Miss Emily's still a child. As for neighbours, there's some I could name she'd be better off without."

"Who?"

"I'm sure it's not for me to say, miss. Well, I mustn't stand here gossiping. I'll take the dog down and let him out, shall I? Alice'll be in for your tray in a bit."

When the housemaid had removed the tray, Mariette rearranged her pillows and rolled over onto her back. The effort left her limp. Walking might be a trifle beyond her, she conceded. However, though she suspected it would be a while before her bottom was ready to sit upon, the discomfort of lying still did not amount to pain. She could perfectly well recline upon a sofa.

She lay studying the ceiling. It was worthy of study, being festooned with plaster garlands and cherubs, but by the time she had counted the cherubs twice she was growing bored. Before she was driven to experiment further with her strength, Lady Lilian came to see her.

"Jenny told me you are much improved," she said with a

smile, "but I did not know you were already lying on your back."

"I turned over by myself. May I go down to lie on a sofa, ma'am? I'm quite well enough."

"Good gracious, no!" Lady Lilian sounded shocked. "That is, I cannot think it wise. If you are tired of your bed, as I can well imagine, I shall have a chaise longue brought in here."

"It's not that it isn't an exceedingly comfortable bed, ma'am," Mariette hastened to assure her.

"But you are more than ready for a change. Perfectly understandable."

Shortly after she left, Mrs. Wittering arrived followed by Charles and Alice with an elegant chaise longue, all white and gilt. "From my lady's dressing room, miss," the housekeeper reported as, under her supervision, the maid and footman set it by the fireplace. "Miss Pennick'll be along in a minute to help you to it."

Even with Jenny's help, the short distance from bed to chaise exhausted Mariette. She lay quite happily for some time admiring the blue-and-white Dutch tiles around the fireplace and watching the flames flicker. She was just beginning to wish for a book when she heard a soft tap upon the chamber door and called eagerly, "Come in!"

Miss Farrar slipped into the room, holding the door to let Ragamuffin in, then closing it quickly and quietly behind him. Mariette was conscious of a faint disappointment—not that she had really expected Lord Malcolm. Any visitor was welcome. She smiled at the girl.

"Jenny told me you had left your bed," Miss Farrar said in a breathless whisper, approaching the chaise on tiptoe.

She was wearing a delightful gown of pale pink Circassian cloth with a straight, narrow skirt. Though it was quite plain, with two rows of darker pink velvet ribbon at the hem and the wrists and a wider ribbon for a sash at the high waist, Mariette was envious. She always wore dark colours because they were more practical and lasted longer and she hated to present Uncle George with bills. What was more, she sewed her own clothes, and she'd be the first to admit she was no expert seamstress.

"I feel much better," she said. "Do sit down. How pretty you look, Miss Farrar."

"Do you really think so?" The girl blushed as she took the chair on the other side of the fireplace. "I think you are beautiful, and prodigiously brave. Uncle Malcolm says he's never known a female so courageous."

Mariette stared. All he had called her to her face was a romantical shatterbrain! "He told you that?"

"He told Cousin Tabitha, when she chided him for bringing you here."

"Oh dear, did she?"

"I beg your pardon, I should not have mentioned it, but truly you must not mind what Cousin Tabitha says. She is always pinching at someone. Why, she even finds fault with Mama. Oh, Miss Bertrand, pray don't tell Mama I came to see you!"

"I won't," Mariette promised, dismayed. "Are you forbidden to visit me?"

"Not precisely, only Mama said I must not disturb you. Am I disturbing you?" she enquired diffidently.

"Not a bit. I'm very happy to see you, but perhaps you ought not to come if Lady Lilian doesn't want you to." She recalled how her ladyship had always avoided introducing her daughter. She had never minded much before, knowing she was not a fit model for a gently bred young lady, but now it hurt.

That was why her hostess had been shocked when she asked to go below stairs. Regardless of her health, she was not welcome in the Corycombe drawing room. Had not Lady Lilian said the best thanks for her hospitality would be to recover—and be able to go away—quickly? Miss Thorne was right. Callers would be thrown into a tweak if required to acknowledge her existence, and Miss Farrar might be tainted by her acquaintance.

Her attempt to go home was not so caperwitted after all.

Miss Farrar was regarding her with anxiety. "All of a

sudden you look horridly tired," she said. "I had better go, but I shall come again, if you do not mind? Just for a few minutes now and then, until you are quite well. You must be sadly dull all alone up here."

"A little. Perhaps you could find a book for me to read? You can give it to Jenny . . ."

"I shall bring you one myself," Miss Farrar declared stoutly, and Mariette hadn't the heart to argue.

Already she was a bad influence, leading the girl to disobey her mother. Which might not be such a bad thing, she decided hopefully. Miss Farrar had sounded completely incredulous when she said Miss Thorne was wont to criticize Lady Lilian. Surely a fifteen-year-old ought to have more independence of mind than to believe her mother perfect.

On this consoling thought, Mariette dozed off. Drowsing, she was distantly aware of someone entering the room. She forced her eyelids up just in time to see a masculine back in a beautifully tailored dark red coat moving towards the door, watched with disappointment by Ragamuffin.

"Don't go!"

Lord Malcolm swung round, revealing a waistcoat striped in poppy-red and pale grey. "Mar—My dear Miss Bertrand! I trust Ragamuffin and I between us did not wake you?"

"Oh no! I was no more than half asleep. I have slept my fill these last few days."

"My niece informed me you're in need of entertainment. She consulted me as to what books you might like to read and knowing your tastes I suggested novels." A teasing gleam in his eye, he held up several volumes. "I offered to bring them up as she has been set to her needlework."

"How kind of you, sir," she retorted with spirit. "I hope they're full of highwaymen?"

He gave an exaggerated sigh as he placed them on the occasional table beside the chaise. "I'm sorry to disappoint you, but I fear not. Emily's reading is more prosaic. Maria Edgeworth and Fanny Burney tend to write about ordinary, everyday people and events. I daresay you'll find 'em sadly flat and commonplace."

"On the contrary," Mariette said wryly, "what you consider ordinary, everyday life is anything but commonplace to me. I expect . . . I expect Lady Lilian doesn't permit Miss Farrar to read romances."

"I believe not."

"She wasn't supposed to come and see me. You won't betray her, will you?"

"I'm not such an unprincipled wretch! At least," he amended with a grin, "I shan't give Emmie away if you won't give me away. I'm not supposed to be here either. As I was therefore unable to provide a chaperon, I had best be going. I just wanted to see for myself how you go on. You really are much better, aren't you?"

"Oh yes."

"Quite bobbish, I'd say. Now, not a word to m'sister, mind." A conspiratorial wink, a finger to his lips, and he tiptoed out, leaving Mariette laughing.

He closed the door before she realized she hadn't thanked him. Still, even if Lady Lilian disapproved of his visits to her chamber, perhaps he'd find an excuse to come again.

She picked up the first volume of *Cecilia* with a contented sigh. There was something deliciously intimate about a shared secret.

Chapter 6

"Lord Wareham has called, my lady."

"Oh bother!" said Lilian. "Yes, show him in, Blount, and tell Cook there will be one extra for luncheon. One cannot deny the neighbours," she said resignedly to Malcolm, "and Lord Wareham rides several miles to call, but he always seems to arrive just in time for a meal so one must invite him to stay."

"Like Des Aldrich."

Malcolm noted with interest the pink rising in Lilian's cheeks. "That was quite different. The captain is your friend and was expected. I wonder whether he will call again. Is your business with him finished?"

"No, but I've arranged to meet him in Plymouth."

"Malcolm, he will think he is not welcome here! You must tell him—Oh, good morning, Lord Wareham."

The baron bowed over her hand, holding it, in Malcolm's opinion, a trifle longer than was quite proper. He had met Wareham on a previous visit and had not greatly cared for him. A tall, broad-shouldered, handsome man of about forty, he seemed rather too conscious of his good looks. He wore neat riding dress, as befitted a country gentleman. The contemptuous glance he bestowed upon Malcolm's vividly striped waistcoat did not endear him.

"How d'ye do, Eden," he said, after a dismissive nod in response to Emily's curtsy and Miss Thorne's greeting. "What has dragged you away from the fleshpots?"

"Just rusticating," Malcolm drawled. "A week or two in a backwater makes the bright lights shine the brighter, don't y'know."

"We have our moments of excitement in our little backwater, do we not, Lady Lilian? I hear Barwith's chit was shot by a poacher on your land. Dashed generous of you to take the girl in."

"Miss Bertrand was too badly hurt to travel any farther than necessary," Lilian informed him coolly.

Wareham was patently uninterested in Miss Bertrand's well-being. "I trust the man will be caught and will hang," he said.

"Not likely now." Feigning a complete lack of interest, Malcolm ostentatiously covered a yawn.

"Of course, the landless need not worry about poachers," the baron said with a sneer. "Lady Lilian will agree with me that the rascals should be hanged or transported, every one."

Lilian shook her head. "The man who shot Miss Bertrand was not a poacher," she said with certainty.

Malcolm blenched. Had Mariette confessed the truth about the highwayman incident? He should have warned her to keep mum. But surely Lilian would have spoken about it to him, sooner than to a mere acquaintance!

"How so, ma'am?" Wareham enquired.

"There are no poachers on my land because I allow my people to take what game and fish they will. After all, I do not shoot, and they often make me presents from their catch."

"My dear lady, most unwise and a shockingly bad example! It goes to show that the gentle sex should not bother their pretty heads with business. The ladies need us men to take care of them, don't they, Eden?"

Malcolm knew that, with the aid of an excellent bailiff any gentleman would have been glad to employ, Lilian ran her estate most competently. He thought of Mariette, growing up in a male household, so greatly in need of female guidance.

"No," he said blandly.

Lilian gave him a grateful look. Emily, modestly silent as befitted a schoolroom miss but avidly following every word, clapped her hands—and flushed, abashed, as her mother frowned at her.

"Well, *most* men are better qualified to run the world," Wareham conceded, his laugh condescending. "A Town beau must be expected to find himself at a loss faced with the problems of a landowner."

"No doubt," Malcolm agreed with a languid, indifferent wave of the hand, fuming inside. Supercilious coxcomb! And what the devil did he mean by calling Lilian "my dear lady" and referring to Mariette as "Barwith's chit" when she had a perfectly good name?

Malcolm had the greatest difficulty remaining polite and maintaining his insouciant façade throughout luncheon.

After luncheon, Mariette alternately dozed and read. She enjoyed Fanny Burney's lively style and didn't regret in the least the absence of highwaymen, ghosts, mad monks, and wicked noblemen with ghastly secrets. Nonetheless, she was glad to hear a tap on the door and delighted when Lord Malcolm sneaked in.

He was wearing riding clothes and his brown hair was ruffled. After a joyful welcome, Ragamuffin sniffed at his boots with great interest. "Do I stink of the stables?" Lord Malcolm asked him, laughing. "I'll take him for a walk in a little while, shall I? He's admirably loyal, but I'm sure he'd be the better for some exercise."

"That would be very kind, sir, but you've already been out, haven't you?"

He looked annoyed. "My dear girl, I'm not such a poor fish I cannot manage a stroll because I've just been for a ride."

"I beg your pardon," said Mariette, taken aback. "I didn't mean to imply . . ."

"No, I beg yours," he said ruefully, sitting down. "I'm

afraid one of Lilian's visitors this morning put my nose out of joint, but it's the outside of enough to take it out on you. I thought my gallop on the moor had blown away the megrims."

"It's wonderfully refreshing, isn't it? You can ride for miles and never meet anyone but sheep and the wild ponies." No one to see her riding astride in breeches, she wanted to point out. "Much better than in the valleys or down towards the coast."

"Or Hyde Park at the fashionable hour. You'll understand that when I came back after the freedom of the moors and was told the vicar and his wife were ensconced in the drawing room, I simply couldn't face them!"

Mariette laughed. "It wasn't the vicar who had you on the high ropes this morning, then."

"No, Lord Wareham. Do you know him?"

"I've met him," she said with caution. She didn't want him to know the meeting had been utterly humiliating. "I doubt he'd recognize me."

"The man must be blind then," he said with a warmth which flustered her.

"What did he do to provoke you?" she asked in haste, then hoped she was not being impertinently inquisitive.

"He called me a Town beau!"

"Are you not?"

Lord Malcolm opened his mouth, then closed it again, looking disconcerted. "Well, yes, I suppose so," he said sheepishly, "but he said it as if it were synonymous with a useless fribble, as if a man's mind could be judged by his waistcoat."

"I like your waistcoats. You must have great fun choosing them."

He grinned at her. "I do."

"Perhaps Lord Wareham is just envious. I daresay there is nothing so smart to be found in Plymouth. He does have a rather . . . rather *toplofty* manner. Is he a friend of Lady Lilian's?"

"Not exactly a friend." He frowned. "I'm not sure he's not a suitor."

"A suitor!" Mariette exclaimed, dismayed. Lady Lilian was too good for that arrogant wretch.

"My sister is a wealthy woman. Corycombe is not entailed so my brother-in-law left it to her free and clear, and she has a considerable fortune bequeathed by a relative, also. Not that I have any grounds but my own dislike to suppose Wareham is after her fortune! For all I know, he sincerely admires her and genuinely believes she needs a man to run her life."

"I'm sure he must admire her. Who can help it? And even though she runs her own life quite successfully, perhaps she will marry him for companionship. Jenny says she is lonely."

"Lonely? She has Emmie, and Miss Thorne for what she's worth. I hope she won't accept the fellow only for the sake. . . . Dash it, I shouldn't be discussing Lilian with you. Nothing is so tedious as the affairs of someone one barely knows. How are you enjoying Fanny Burney's work? Or Madame d'Arblay as one ought to say since she married that Frenchman."

Before Mariette could respond, either to disclaim tedium or to give her opinion of *Cecilia,* once again there came a tap on the door.

Lord Malcolm pulled a comical face. "If that is Lilian, I'm going to be properly raked over the coals."

"You could hide under the bed. Ragamuffin finds it quite cosy. Come in," she called in answer to a second tap.

Miss Farrar entered. "I just came to see . . . Oh, Uncle Malcolm, I did not know you were here."

"He's promised not to give you away, and no, you are not disturbing me, Miss Farrar."

"How did you escape from the worthy vicar, Emmie?" Lord Malcolm asked.

She giggled. "You are naughty, Uncle! I did not escape, Mama sent me away because they started to talk about something I was not allowed to hear. I came to ask if you like the books I chose, Miss Bertrand, or shall I find something else?"

"I'm enjoying this one prodigiously," Mariette assured her. "Thank you for lending it to me."

They talked about *Cecilia.* Several times Lord Malcolm had to intervene to stop his niece from divulging the end of story, and they were all laughing at his teasing when Lady Lilian walked in.

Lord Malcolm leapt to his feet with a guilty look. Emily—as she had invited Mariette to call her—clapped her hands to her mouth. Mariette suddenly felt immeasurably tired.

Lady Lilian's expression changed from vexed to chagrined. "I have no wish to figure as an ogre," she said.

"Oh no, Mama, you are not an ogre!" Emily ran to her and hugged her.

"Emily has been acting as chaperon," Lord Malcolm said hopefully.

"I did not disturb Mariette, Mama. Uncle Malcolm was here already."

"Was he indeed!"

"Very briefly." His voice was contrite but Mariette thought his eyes were laughing. "At that point, the dog was our chaperon."

"Well, I only hope you may not have set back Miss Bertrand's recovery by a week."

"Truly they have not," Mariette assured her.

"I am glad to hear it. Nevertheless, off you go now, both of you, and let her rest."

"Yes, Mama."

"Yes, ma'am." He was definitely laughing. "Come along, Ragamuffin. I'll return him to you safe and sound, Miss Bertrand."

He made his escape before his sister had a chance to forbid him to do anything of the sort.

She turned to Mariette. "I am sure you must be tired, Miss Bertrand."

"A little, but none the worse for my visitors, I promise

you. I'm sorry, I know he shouldn't have been here without a chaperon, but I couldn't order him to go." Actually it had not crossed her mind to try. "He's a lord, after all."

"My dear, a lord is merely a mortal." Her ladyship sounded amused. "More to the point, Malcolm is a young man and you are a young woman. For your own sake, you must not let him encroach."

"He didn't try to . . . to flirt with me." Though Mariette wasn't very sure what flirting involved. Extravagant compliments? All he had said was that Lord Wareham must be blind to have forgotten her, and he was just teasing.

"I should hope not! He is a gentleman, after all." Lady Lilian sighed. "But gentlemen are often heedless and I am responsible for your well-being while you are in my house. Still, I daresay there will be no harm in your permitting him to visit you, properly chaperoned, as long as you are out of your bed. Ragamuffin is not an adequate chaperon!"

"No, ma'am. Is . . . is Miss Farrar?"

"Emily?" She looked disconcerted. "I had not intended . . ." Hesitating, she sighed again. "Well, yes, I suppose she is. Now it is time you went back to bed. It is your first day up, after all. I shall send Jenny to help you."

Mariette willingly retired to bed. She was not to lose her two new friends after all, not at once, anyway. Two new friends! It was almost worth being shot.

As it was a windy day even in the valley, Malcolm took Ragamuffin down to Cory Brook and let him roam. Emily went with them, chattering about Mariette as they strolled through the leafless woods, along a streamside path. He scarcely listened, though his thoughts were on the same subject.

Mariette's comments on the book had been intelligent and astute. She was not slow-witted. Her mistakes were due to ignorance, to inexperience, not to stupidity. Of course he had guessed that from the first, or he would not have fallen in love with her. He didn't want to marry a woman without a rational thought in her pretty head.

She was kindhearted, too, and not only towards her scapegrace cousin. With what concern she had spoken of Lilian's loneliness, when her own was ten times greater! And she had made excuses for Wareham: he was just envious, his manner rather toplofty.

Yet she had seemed dismayed when Malcolm suggested Wareham was courting Lilian, he recalled. Devil take it, never say she was jealous! Did she admire the coxcomb? He was tall, handsome, and very likely the only gentleman—besides her uncle and cousin—with whom she was acquainted.

Malcolm tried to remember what she had said about meeting Wareham. She'd been evasive, he thought. On the other hand, she doubted the fellow would recognize her.

Gammon! How could any normal male forget her? Malcolm dwelled lovingly on glossy black hair, lustrous brown eyes, kissable lips, a slender but well-rounded figure with a neat little—no, he had promised Lilian to put *that* attribute out of his mind. Still, there was plenty for a man to admire, though he'd take his oath Mariette's modesty was genuine. No doubt neither her uncle nor her cousin had ever told her she was lovely, damn their eyes.

"Uncle Malcolm, I don't believe you have listened to a word I have said!" Emily reproached him.

"Of course I have. You've been talking about Miss Bertrand."

"That was an age ago. I asked whether you will stand up with me at Almack's when I make my come-out."

"Good gad, that's not for years yet."

"Only two years. I shall be sixteen in March. Though I must admit two years sometimes seems like forever."

"I may be too old and decrepit by then to dance."

"Oh, fustian! I know you are much younger than Mama."

"Or Almack's may burn down."

"Do stop teasing, Uncle. Will you?"

"If you have room for me on your dance card."

"Do you think I shall take?"

"How can you doubt it?" If pretty face and sweet nature failed, her fortune would make her popular, but there was no need for her to know that yet.

"Shall I tell you what I should like? I should like to invite Mariette to go with us to London and share my come-out, even if she is too old. It would be wonderful to have a friend with me. I do believe I should not be shy at all."

Startled, Malcolm asked, "Have you no other friends who will be in Town for the Season?"

"No one I really know well," Emily said wistfully.

"You scarcely know Mariette!"

"But I like her *immensely* already. Do not you?"

"Yes." He smiled. "Oh, yes, I do indeed. But Emmie, if I were you I should not mention this to your mama until a good deal nearer the time. Give her time to become better acquainted with Mariette." No need to worry Lilian since he had every intention of marrying Mariette long before Emily's Season!

He would take her to London himself. The trouble was, she was by no means up to snuff. Thrown willy-nilly into Society she'd feel like a fish out of water, and he was not at all certain of his competence to teach her. . . .

"Take care, Uncle!" Emily squealed as he tripped over a root and stumbled to the very edge of the stream.

Catching at a sapling, he managed not to measure his length in the shallow but undoubtedly icy water. Pellucid brown, Cory Brook chattered over its pebble bed, swirling round rocks and gurgling under overhanging banks. Just ahead it foamed over a stone shelf into a pool.

A charming pool, doubtless clear and still and a haven for fish—when not being used as a swimming bath by Ragamuffin. He paddled vigorously about, lapping the water as he went.

"He will drown!" screeched Emily. "Oh, save him, save him!"

"Nonsense," Malcolm snorted. "He's happy as a lark."

His niece, he decided, had led a much too sheltered life. A friendship with Mariette could do her nothing but good.

Ragamuffin sighted a floating stick, swam to it, grabbed it, and headed for the bank. Scrambling out, he brought it to lay at Malcolm's feet. His tail wagged and he looked up hopefully. Then, inevitably, he shook himself.

Malcolm had reflexively stepped back, so Emily took the full force of the shower.

"Oh," she wailed, "my pelisse! It is ruined."

"Nonsense, it's only water."

"Why did he *do* that?"

"Because he didn't bring a towel with him."

Tired of waiting, Ragamuffin picked up the stick again and laid it at Emily's feet.

"What does he want?"

"He wants you to throw it, so that he can bring it back to you."

"Really? Me?" Emily looked pleased. "But it is dirty. My gloves will be ruined."

"Take 'em off," said her uncle.

"A lady always wears gloves out of doors."

"For pity's sake, Emmie, stop being a lady just for a few minutes. No one would believe your mother was a bit of a tomboy."

"Mama?" Her eyes were round with wonder.

"Only a bit! Inevitable with four elder brothers. Swear you won't tell her I told you."

"I swear."

Ragamuffin gave a short, demanding bark. Emily stripped off her gloves, stuffed them in her pocket, and picked up her stick. At first her throws were feeble but the dog was patient and she improved. Finally she threw the stick into the pool, deliberately, and laughed when Ragamuffin shook all over her again.

When they returned towards the house, her hands were grubby, her pelisse was damp, her bonnet was awry, and beneath it her hair was tousled. But her cheeks were pink, her blue eyes glowed, and she was smiling.

They took the dog to the stables to be thoroughly dried by Jessup before he was allowed indoors. While Malcolm spoke to the groom, Emily scampered ahead into the house.

When Malcolm followed, he met Lilian in the front hall. She stood gazing up the stairs, a faint smile on her lips.

"I have not seen Emmie so happy since she was a little girl," she said, turning to him. "What have you been doing?"

"Throwing a stick for Ragamuffin. Lilian, it's not my place to interfere, and I know it must be difficult bringing up a daughter without her father, but don't overrestrain her."

"Do I?"

"She didn't want to take her gloves off because a lady always wears gloves outdoors! You are an independent person yourself, or you would have gone back to Ashminster years ago. You were the one who taught me to fish, and to climb trees, and to play cricket. The others were all too grown-up to bother. Don't you remember when we climbed that apple tree in the orchard and gorged on green apples till we were sick as dogs?"

"I had rather forget that particular occasion! You may be right about Emmie, Malcolm. I shall have to think about it. But I suspect this is all an attempt to persuade me to let her make friends with Miss Bertrand."

"I rather fear you are too late to stop it. She tells me she likes her immensely."

"Malcolm, did you by any chance intend to present me with an accomplished fact?"

He grinned. "All's fair in love and war."

"You encouraged Emily to defy me?"

"Lord, no! I had nothing to do with Emily's presence. That was her own notion. You told her not to disturb Mariette, I collect, an insufficiently precise prohibition. Are you going to issue another more precise dictate?"

"I should," said Lilian, exasperated. "But I have already told Miss Bertrand—and it is most improper for you to call her Mariette!—that Emily is sufficient chaperon when you visit her."

"Bless you, m'dear." He kissed her cheek.

"I take it you still hold to your ridiculous resolve to marry her?"

"I do. Lilian, I have a favour to ask. I want her to be perfectly comfortable in our world. When she is stronger, when she has been downstairs a few days, will you offer to teach her how to go on in Society?"

She smiled wryly. "I seem to recall the reason why I taught you to fish and climb trees was that you could always twist me around your little finger. All right, Malcolm, I will think about it, but if I do offer, don't be surprised if she resents it."

"She won't," he said with confidence. "I'm sure she's aware of the deficiencies in her upbringing and she's far too intelligent to turn down the opportunity to learn."

"My dear," said Lilian, "she really has bewitched you, has she not? I hope she appreciates what she has won."

"I'll make her," Malcolm said, and silently prayed that the abominable but handsome Wareham would not turn out to be his rival.

Chapter 7

Stiff, wobbly-kneed, but triumphant, Mariette clung to the finial globe at the top of the staircase. She had walked all the way from her chamber, leaning on Lord Malcolm's arm only for the last few yards.

"My dear," said Lady Lilian, "when I said you might spend a few hours in the morning room as soon as you were strong enough to walk to the stairs, I did not mean you should set out at once!"

Lord Malcolm laughed. "You might as well show a red rag to a bull as present Miss Bertrand with a challenge."

"I simply wanted to get out of that room!" said Mariette, adding quickly, "It is a very pretty chamber, Lady Lilian, and very comfortable, but I am looking forward to a change."

"You will like the morning room," Emily assured her. "It is the prettiest room in the house. I shall go and make sure there are plenty of cushions on the sofa for you." She started down the stairs.

"Send Charles to carry Mariette down, Emily," said her mother.

"Charles!" Lord Malcolm exclaimed. "You don't think I shall entrust Miss Bertrand to a footman, do you?" He swept her up into his arms and followed Emily. Ragamuffin bounded past them and waited at the bottom, tail waving.

Mariette laid her head on Lord Malcolm's shoulder. She felt utterly safe, protected against the world by the strength

of his arms. She had forgotten that her step-papa used to
carry her up to bed like this sometimes, when she was sleepy.
Maman would come after, saying anxiously, "Be careful,"
as Lady Lilian did now.

"Really, Malcolm!" her ladyship continued crossly as
they reached the bottom of the stairs. "Let Charles carry her
the rest of the way."

Her tone, more than her words, warned Mariette she
ought to have been embarrassed and indignant to be held so
close by a gentleman. Though she could not imagine why a
servant's aid was acceptable, she was naturally at once over-
come by embarrassment, if not indignation. She stiffened.

Lord Malcolm instantly set her on her feet. "I beg your
pardon, Miss Bertrand," he said, but his smiling eyes told
her he was not in the least contrite, which redoubled her embarrassment. "I knew you were eager to reach the morning
room as soon as possible."

"Thank you, sir," she said, her cheeks hot. "I shall walk
the rest of the way."

"May I offer Miss Bertrand my arm, Lilian?" he enquired
meekly.

"Yes, you wretch. Do try to behave yourself!"

He grinned. "Within reason," he conceded.

It was exceeding odd, thought Mariette, how the feel of
his arm beneath her hand now disturbed instead of soothed
her. She shivered.

Lord Malcolm put his hand over hers. "You are cold.
Charles! Bring a rug to the morning room and build up the
fire. Footmen do have their uses," he said to Mariette, "but
Lilian is out in her reckoning if she supposes I shall trust
him to carry you on the stairs."

She tried to hide her agitation and speak calmly. "If Lady
Lilian thinks it wrong, sir, I cannot allow you to carry me."

He patted her hand. "Don't worry, I shall sort it out with
her before you go up again."

Altogether confused and uncertain of what she wanted,
Mariette was glad to collapse onto the sofa. Emily bustled
about her, stuffing cushions in here and there.

Lord Malcolm and Lady Lilian vanished, but Miss Thorne sat nearby, rigidly erect, her mouth pursed, knitting another—or the same—mustard-coloured garment. Mariette had not seen the woman since her original awakening in this house. She felt she ought to thank her for the loan of the nightgown, but perhaps the mention of such a garment was improper. She began to wish she had not been so determined to leave the refuge of her chamber.

"There," said Emily, "are you quite comfortable?"

"Yes, thank you." She smiled at the obliging girl. In the last few days she had grown very fond of her. Emboldened by Emily's solicitude, she ventured, "Good morning, Miss Thorne." Surely the woman could not object to a simple greeting.

"Good morning, Miss Bertrand. How fortunate that you are recovering so rapidly."

"Is it not splendid, ma'am?" said Emily.

"Humph. No doubt Miss Bertrand will be able to leave Corycombe in a day or two. I am sure she cannot wish to stay where she is not . . . quite at home."

"As to that, ma'am, I must rely upon Dr. Barley's and Lady Lilian's advice."

"I hope you will stay more than a day or two, Mariette," cried Emily in dismay.

"Emily," snapped Miss Thorne, "I am sure you ought not to address Miss Bertrand by her Christian name."

"She said I may, ma'am."

"Your mama cannot possibly approve."

"Mama says it is for Mariette to decide. We are good friends now, you know."

Miss Thorne sniffed.

The footman came in with a rug, which Emily tucked around Mariette's legs. "Your groom's here, miss," he announced, "which, hearing as you're down, he was wondering could he have a word with you."

"Jim? Oh yes!" said Mariette, hoping for messages from Uncle George and Ralph. "Pray show him in."

"A groom in the morning room?" Miss Thorne quivered with outrage. "Unthinkable!"

At that moment Lady Lilian came into the room. "Mariette, your groom is asking to see you. Do you feel up to it?"

"Yes, I shall come at once." She pushed back the rug.

"Heavens, no, stay there. You have walked quite enough for the present. Charles, pray go and bring him here."

"Into the morning room, Lilian?" Miss Thorne gasped.

"Blount says the man is perfectly respectable and respectful, Cousin Tabitha, and Mariette must be anxious for news of home. Perhaps you prefer to remove to the drawing room."

"I certainly do! This is not at all what I am accustomed to." She swept out, trailing mustard wool.

"Oh dear," said Lady Lilian, "what a staid life we must live if a groom in the morning room causes such a flutter."

"I'm sorry," Mariette said, unhappily aware that once again she had done the wrong thing. "Jim is such an old friend—I did not think . . ."

"*I* am not in a flutter," Lady Lilian assured her dryly, "and it is after all my morning room."

"Your groom is your friend?" Emily asked with interest.

"Yes, he's a dear." She refused to repudiate friendship for the sake of etiquette. "It was he who suggested I ask Uncle George for ponies for me and Ralph, and he taught us to ride."

"Is that why you don't use a sidesaddle?"

"We started out bareback, because there were no pony-size saddles. When we grew too big for the ponies, there were old saddles in the stables we could use, but no sidesaddles."

"Mama, I should like to learn to ride. Sidesaddle, of course," Emily added hastily.

"As a girl I enjoyed riding," Lady Lilian mused. "Your papa was so afraid I might fall, I gave it up and we never had you taught. Well, my dear, I can see no reason why you should not. But at present it is time you went to practise your music."

"Yes, Mama. *Thank* you, Mama!" Emily kissed her mother, swooped down to kiss Mariette, and went off with a joyful beam.

"I'm afraid I am causing all sorts of turmoil in your household, Lady Lilian," Mariette apologized.

"Perhaps a certain amount of turmoil is no bad thing."

"An excellent thing, in moderation." Lord Malcolm came in, followed by Jim, who was greeted with delight by Ragamuffin. "Keeps the rust off," Lord Malcolm went on. "What particular turmoil are we discussing?"

"Emily wants to learn to ride."

"Did you not tell me once Frederick would not let you ride because he considered sidesaddles unsafe?"

"Aye, pesky things they be," Jim interjected, nodding his grey head. "Not fit for more'n a bit of a trot. Begging your pardon, my lady."

Lady Lilian, a trifle disconcerted, said firmly "Emily will learn to ride with a sidesaddle or not at all."

"Miss'll do right enough wi' your head groom, my lady. A steady sort o' fellow, and me own nevvie."

"Is he, indeed! Well, Mariette, I shall leave you to talk to your man. I suggest you ask him to bring you more clothes since you are well enough to come down. Do not tire yourself. Are you coming, Malcolm?"

"No." He gave his sister a lazy smile. "No, Jim shall be our chaperon."

Jim turned pink, twisted his hat in his gnarled hands, and muttered something indistinguishable. Lady Lilian cast a glance of reproof at her brother but departed without him.

"Do sit down, Jim," said Mariette.

"It ain't fitting, miss." He gazed round at all the elegant chairs, painted white and gilt and upholstered in spring-green satin, then down at his grubby leather breeches.

"My neck will get stiff if I have to look up at you."

"Here you are, Jim." Lord Malcolm brought a plain cane-bottomed chair from the marquetry writing table in the window and set it where Mariette could see the groom without turning her head. He went to stand by the fireplace, leaning against the white and gold mantelpiece. Ragamuffin flopped on the hearthrug at his feet.

"I thank 'ee kindly, m'lord." Creaking a bit at the knees, the old man lowered himself onto the chair. "Well, Miss Mariette, you're better seemingly. The master'll be glad to hear it."

"How is Uncle George?"

"Same nor ever, miss, same nor ever. I did hear as he's been working on that there big lump o' granite us brung down off the moor twenty year sin'."

"Oh dear!"

"Why do you say 'oh dear'?" Lord Malcolm enquired with interest.

"Because Uncle George only chips at the granite when he is troubled, which is rarely. Sandstone is much easier to work with, so it doesn't matter as much when a statue goes wrong. They all do, you see," she admitted. "I wonder what has disturbed him."

"Your accident and your absence, perhaps," he said a trifle acidly.

Mariette brightened. "Do you think so? Perhaps he's a bit lonely. Has Ralph been much at home, Jim?"

"Nay, miss, Master Ralph's off down to Plymouth most every day." He spoke with deep disapproval. Jim had his own notions of what was right and proper. "There's some nights he don't come home till morning, the losel."

"He is young, Jim," she excused him, swallowing her dismay, and her hurt that he had not come to visit her. She did not want Lord Malcolm to think ill of Ralph, for if he despised her cousin, how could he help but despise her, too? "There's not much for him to do at home. How is Mrs. Finney? Will you ask her to pack up the rest of my clothes for me?"

It was all very well for Lady Lilian to tell her she needed more clothes at Corycombe but she already had almost everything she possessed except a few summer frocks.

At least it seemed her ladyship was not going to send her home in a day or two. She was no longer in any hurry to go home, though she could hardly tell that to Lord Malcolm after all the trouble she had caused him. He did not appear to resent her prolonged stay. In fact he grew more charming every day.

He raised his eyebrows, a slight smile on his lips, and she realized she was staring.

"I have just noticed your waistcoat," she excused herself, quelling a blush. "It is magnificent!" And it was: pale blue silk embroidered with snowflakes.

His smile broadened to a grin. "I hoped it would amuse you," he said modestly.

Jim snorted. Mariette hastily turned back to him and enquired after the rest of the servants and the tenants.

All were well—and anxious for news of her—except: "I were down to Bell Valley Farm yesterday, Miss Mariette, fetching the milk. Tom Wilkes wants to cut some trees in Moorside Copse. Weakened by that wind t'other day they was, and he's afeard they'll fall."

"Has he talked to Mr. Taffert?"

"You know how it is, Miss Mariette, folks don't care to take their questions to Mr. Taffert. Not as he's a bad chap in his way, but a furriner and curt-like, and they don't feel comf'table."

"Mr. Taffert is your uncle's bailiff?" Lord Malcolm asked.

"Yes, an excellent man, and I get on very well with him but as Jim says he's rather stiff and taciturn, and he's not a local man. From Okehampton, I believe, north of the moor. Many of the tenants prefer to approach him through me when they want or need something."

"They don't go direct to Mr. Barwith?"

"Oh, Uncle George just agrees to whatever they ask and tells them to go to his bailiff! If they come to me, I can explain the difficulty to Mr. Taffert, then he goes to the tenant and gives his answer. It may sound odd and cumbersome but it works, doesn't it, Jim?"

"Aye, m'lord, and everybody happy. What'll I tell Tom Wilkes, Miss Mariette?"

"I shall write to Mr. Taffert and you must take him the letter." With caution, Mariette started to lever herself upright.

Lord Malcolm crossed the space between them in two strides and pushed her down with a hand on her shoulder. "Don't sit up."

"I can manage, just for a few minutes. My . . . I am much better, truly, and I cannot write lying down."

"No need. You shall dictate to me."

"Dictate?" she said uncertainly.

"You tell me what you want to say and I shall write it." He moved one of the satin-covered chairs to the writing table and took out writing materials. "I am said to have a legible hand, if not a neat one, though my spelling leaves something to be desired. Only don't speak too fast, if you please."

This last request sent Jim into a paroxysm of silent, knee-slapping laughter. Far from being offended, Lord Malcolm grinned and asked, "What's the joke?"

"That's just what us was allus telling Miss Mariette when first she come to the manor, m'lord. Gabble away she did, wi' bits o' Frog talk thrown in. Us couldn't hardly make head nor tail of it."

"How *did* you learn to speak English so well, Miss Bertrand?"

"I had an English governess in France. *Maman* and I lived with her in London until *maman* married my steppapa. *Maman* was always very particular about a correct accent, so after . . . after they died and I came to Devon, I always asked Uncle George if I didn't know how to pronounce a word I found in a book."

"Do you remember your French?"

"Not very much." She was puzzled by his look of relief. "I was only six when we came to England. I hardly remember my father at all. He was usually away in Paris, and much too grand when he came home to pay any attention to a little girl."

"Mr. Taffert, he'll want a letter in English," Jim hinted, so they turned to business.

Pausing at the top of the stairs, Mariette struggled against the urge to tug on the bodice of her gown. Altered by Jenny's clever needle, it fitted much more snugly than she was accustomed to. She felt exposed.

Lady Lilian had wanted to give her a new gown. All her clothes were most unsuitable now she was well enough to sit in the drawing room, well enough to meet callers. Mariette had not pointed out that she was well enough to go home. How could she bear to be parted from Lord . . . from her new friends?

Nor did she protest that she didn't want to meet the neighbours, none of whom had ever seen fit to call at Bell-Tor Manor. If her kind hostess wished to present her to them, she would just have to do her best, keep her mouth closed and endure whatever scorn her gaucherie brought down upon her.

So, though she could not possibly accept any new clothes, she allowed Jenny to alter her old, drab, heavy woollen gowns. The abigail even sewed on a bit of lace and some ribbons taken from dresses Emily had outgrown. Putting on the navy blue, now trimmed with a light blue satin bow at the waist and lace around the high neckline, Mariette had felt quite smart. However, with Lord Malcolm standing below in the hall, handsome and elegant and looking up at her, she had an awful urge to tug on the breast-hugging bodice.

Her hesitation alarmed him. "What is wrong?" He started up the stairs, two at a time. "Pray lean on my arm."

She was tempted. "No, I must do it myself. I am quite all right, only a little stiff."

"Hold onto the banister."

Obeying, she glanced back at the hovering abigail.

"Thank you, Jenny, I shan't need your help. I expect Lord Malcolm will catch me if I fall over my own feet."

"With pleasure," he assured her, a glint in his eye.

Was he flirting with her, or just teasing? Mariette was not sure. She moved very carefully down the stairs.

At the bottom, he gravely congratulated her and insisted that she lean on his arm to cross the hall.

The drawing room was an impressive apartment. Corycombe was no larger than Bell-Tor Manor but it was modern and well cared for. The rooms were beautifully proportioned and elegantly decorated, and the woodwork gleamed. Sinking onto a sofa provided with extra cushions by the attentive Emily, Mariette gazed around.

The predominant colour was a smoky blue-grey, reminding Mariette of Lord Malcolm's eyes. Gold braid and fringes on crimson curtains and cushions picked up the tones of the portrait over the fireplace, a young gentleman in ceremonial robes.

"That is Papa," Emily informed Mariett, "in his finery for the opening of Parliament. He was Viscount Farrar of Dorland. My uncle is Lord Farrar now and lives at Dorland. It is a very grand house but I like Corycombe better. Your papa was a French lord, was he not?"

"Yes, though it is immaterial as there are no lords in France anymore."

"Oh, but there are," said Lord Malcolm casually. "Since he crowned himself emperor, Bonaparte has created a new nobility and restored some of the old to their ranks and estates."

"Has he?" Mariette said, surprised. "I know he is emperor—the servants and tenants talk and Ralph sometimes brings home a newspaper—but Uncle George doesn't take one and the books in our library are all at least twenty years old."

Emily clapped her hands. "How splendid, Mariette, perhaps you can recover your papa's estate!"

"Hardly! Recollect that we are at war with France and

Boney is our enemy! I would not accept a brass farthing from the monster."

"Oh yes," said Emily, disappointed.

Lord Malcolm smiled warmly at Mariette, so warmly she was suddenly much too hot. Fortunately Miss Thorne came in and her glance of icy disapproval instantly cooled Mariette's burning cheeks.

"Did you ask her ladyship whether she wishes to admit you to her drawing room, Miss Bertrand?" she asked suspiciously.

They all spoke at once.

"Mama *invited* Mariette."

"It was Lilian's suggestion."

"I assure you, ma'am, I've no desire to encroach."

"Humph!" sniffed Miss Thorne and took her mustard knitting from her tapestry-work knitting bag. "I suppose Lilian knows what she is about."

That day the only callers were the vicar of St. Bride's in Wickenton and his wife. A benign but somewhat lethargic elderly couple, they were not inclined to be critical, especially as Mariette was from a different parish.

She carefully observed Lady Lilian's and Emily's every word and action, and kept her mouth shut except when directly addressed. Enquiries about her health were easily answered—she had no intention of disclosing the site of her injuries!—and comments on Lady Lilian's Christian charity were equally easy to respond to. She managed not to put either herself or her kind hostess to the blush.

The next day was more difficult. Word had spread that Mariette was on show and a constant stream of visitors came to view her.

Again she took refuge in reticence. Most were polite enough and did not pester her with questions, Lady Lilian having made it clear that she was convalescent. Nonetheless she heartily sympathized with the caged wild beasts her step-papa once took her to see at the Tower of London.

Most trying were Sir Nesbit and Lady Bolger and their offspring. Miss Bolger, a muffin-faced girl a year or two older than Emily, stared at Mariette with alarm in her prominent eyes, as if afraid she might bite. Young Mr. Bolger knew Ralph and loudly pronounced him a rattling good fellow, an out-and-outer up to every rig and row. He continued in this vein until his father, still more loudly, announced that if his son and heir followed Riddlesworth's example he'd find himself at Point Nonplus in no time.

"Ramshackle puppy!" he snorted.

Lady Bolger was worst. A noted gossipmonger, she was determined to wring from Mariette every detail of her past, her life at Bell-Tor Manor, and her future prospects. Lord Malcolm sat beside Mariette and did his best to shield her unobtrusively, but it was Lady Lilian who saved her. She asked about Miss Bolger's coming London Season, a topic still more interesting to the young lady's hopeful mama.

After that, Mariette only had to endure an occasional query about her own lack of a Season and snide commiseration on her being practically on the shelf. The Bolgers did not stay long, although they had come some distance. Sir Nesbit failed to interest Lord Malcolm in the local hunt, and his daughter's Court and coming-out ball gowns he decried, loudly, as feminine fripperies beneath his notice. Bored, he removed his family after half an hour.

"Thank heaven!" said Lady Lilian as the door closed behind them. "Another five minutes and I should have had to offer tea. Emmie, when we come to preparing for your season, pray do not let me prose on and on about your gowns like that! Mariette, are you quite exhausted?"

"Only of sitting still and minding my tongue, Lady Lilian. I should like to walk a little."

"Take my arm," said Lord Malcolm at once, helping her to stand. "Play us a march, Emmie."

Laughing, Emily went to the piano and looked through her music. Mariette and Lord Malcolm strolled to one end of the long room, admired a landscape hanging there, and strolled back. As they passed Miss Thorne she muttered something disagreeable about wearing a path in the carpet.

Lord Malcolm pressed Mariette's hand and she made no response, but Lady Lilian had overheard.

"My dear Cousin Tabitha," she said, more sharply than Mariette had yet heard her speak, "carpets are made to be walked on."

"I am only trying to preserve your beautiful possessions, Lilian," said Miss Thorne with an injured sniff.

Mariette looked down at the carpet, patterned with an intricate design in blue-grey and crimson, which she had not particularly noted before. "It is a splendid carpet," she said in an undertone to Lord Malcolm. She could not be overheard as Emily started to thump away at a march. "I am surprised Miss Thorne appreciates beauty when she chooses such a revolting colour for her knitting."

"She knits for the Poor Basket," he said sardonically. "The poor do not deserve attractive colours. They must be kept in their place."

"Is that what she thinks?"

"I don't know," he admitted, slightly shamefaced. "Perhaps she likes mustard-yellow and believes the recipients do too."

They reached the window at the end of the drawing room and stood looking down the valley. The sky was hazy and a brisk breeze from the southwest rippled through the bare woods. Mariette's mind was elsewhere.

"I should not care to model my behaviour on Miss Thorne's," she said hesitantly. "I daresay she is always decorous and ladylike and proper, but I cannot like her disposition. Nor would I choose Lady Bolger as a patterncard."

"Good Lord no! Dreadful female."

"I expect it is a great impertinence in me to presume to criticize when I have not the least notion how to go on, but . . ."

"Not at all. You show excellent judgment. But . . . ?"

"But I am so very lucky to have made Lady Lilian's acquaintance first, to be able to compare the others to her. She is a perfect lady, is she not?"

"Come now, Miss Bertrand, you cannot expect a brother

to admit to his sister's perfection! You see, I remember her teaching me to climb trees."

"She did?" Astonished, Mariette glanced back to view Lady Lilian with an entirely new eye. "That only adds to her perfection—but I know how to climb trees."

He grinned. "I was sure you must, and without a teacher no doubt. However, in other matters I will agree you cannot do better than to learn from her."

The music stopped. "You are not walking," cried Emily.

"Play something a little less vigorous," proposed her uncle. "Miss Bertrand is not quite well enough to join the army after all."

Not quite well enough to join the army, perhaps, Mariette thought, but for several days she had been quite well enough to go home. Uncle George's aged trap would be uncomfortable, but not unbearable with a cushion on the seat, if she were not offered the use of a carriage. She must not take advantage of Lady Lilian's generosity much longer.

Just one more day she would give herself to learn what she could by observing her ladyship. One more day to be cosseted by Emily and Jenny. One more day to lean on Lord Malcolm's arm, to bask in the warmth of his smile.

Did she dare hope he might call at Bell-Tor Manor?

Chapter 8

After helping Mariette upstairs, a frustrating process as he'd much rather have carried her, Malcolm sought out his sister. Remorseless, he invaded her sanctum, a small room, part study and part sitting room. She used it to keep her accounts, write letters, consult with bailiff, housekeeper, and butler, and also to escape her household. No one entered without an appointment or an invitation.

No one except a disrespectful younger brother with a matter of pressing importance on his mind.

"Lilian, are you going to offer to teach Mariette?"

She glared at him over gold-rimmed spectacles. "This is my *private* room."

"Good, no one will interrupt us. Good gad, Lilian, I didn't know you wore spectacles."

"Only for close work," she said defensively, laying down her pen and taking them off with a self-conscious air. "Since you arrived I have had no time for reading or embroidery. Pray do not tell . . . anyone."

"Oho, vain, are we? You need not fret, Des won't care a groat."

Lilian blushed. "I was not thinking of Captain Aldrich. You did make sure he understands he is expected to dinner tomorrow?"

"He'll be here. Mariette will be well enough to dine with us, too, I believe. When do you mean to offer to teach her?"

"I have not said I will."

"She won't be offended, Lilian, truly. Have you not noticed how bashful she is with visitors? She is afraid of making mistakes. You must be aware how closely she observes you and Emily."

"Indeed! I find myself thinking twice before I say a word or move a finger."

"She told me today she thinks you quite perfect."

"Perfect!" Lilian groaned. "Oh, Malcolm, what a dreadful responsibility."

"I had a notion that would disturb you." He grinned. "So I revealed your tree-climbing youth."

"You wretch!"

"Not the green-apple episode, not yet."

"You would not!"

"Not if you agree to teach her," Malcolm said blandly and shamelessly.

"Odious wretch! I shall speak to her tomorrow. As a matter of fact, I had already decided to offer to help her. I like her."

"Bless you, Lilian! She is a darling, isn't she? Do you think she might come to care for me enough to marry me?"

"You do mean to *ask* her, do you? I feared you intended to wed her out of hand."

"Now who is the wretch? I shall go down on my knees to her." He glanced down at his immaculate trousers. "If necessary. Will she have me?"

"How can I tell? It is far too early for you to press her. Wait at least until she is more at home in the world, for she has her pride and will not like to accept you while she feels herself your inferior."

"Inferior! She is perfection," said Malcolm dreamily, then shook his head and smiled. "No, not perfection, just a darling. Very well, I shall wait—for a little while."

The following morning brought no callers but shortly after luncheon Blount announced Lord Wareham.

At once Mariette was certain that, however adequately

she had dealt with previous visitors, she was bound to make a mull of things. The baron had only to look at her with his supercilious eyebrows raised and she would disgrace herself.

She threw a panicked glance at Lord Malcolm. He was regarding her seriously, as if he had guessed how she felt about Lord Wareham. She wished she could tell him about her previous encounter with the man—he'd tease her about it and then she wouldn't mind anymore—but his already poor opinion of Ralph would be confirmed.

"Would it be very shocking," she whispered to him, "if I went to sit in the morning room?"

"Running away?" he rallied her gently, with an odd note of satisfaction. "I know you to be no coward."

"I am not, but Ragamuffin can be with me there. He does not like to be banished to the stables when I am in the drawing room."

"Gammon, he likes to visit the horses, though I'd swear he misses your Sparrow since your groom took him home. Besides, you are too late to escape unseen."

Lady Lilian had told the butler to show Lord Wareham in and his steps were heard in the hall. As he appeared in the doorway, Emily who had been showing her mother her embroidery, hurriedly moved to a seat next to Mariette.

"Is he not handsome?" she breathed. "But he scarcely knows I exist."

"Good gad, Emmie," Mariette exclaimed, horrified, "he is old enough to be your father."

"I don't want him for a husband, only for a flirt. Lizzie Phillips danced with him at an assembly in Plymouth at Christmas and she says he is a splendid flirt."

"Ugh!" Mariette wondered whether it would have been better or worse if Lord Wareham had tried to flirt with her instead of turning up his nose. Worse, she decided.

"To tell the truth," Emily whispered, "I don't like him above half, and I am not sure how to flirt. Uncle Malcolm, must one like a man to flirt with him?"

"I'd say liking is not a requirement, though it makes for a vastly more enjoyable experience. At least you should not dislike him! In any case you are by far too young to think of flirting."

Emily pouted. Mariette pondered Lord Malcolm's words and regretfully decided he must be a practised flirt to speak with such expertise. He *had* been flirting with her. She must take care not to read more into his words than he intended.

What a pity she did not know how to flirt back!

She looked at him, to find him watching Lord Wareham and Lady Lilian. Bowing, the baron raised her hand to his lips and kissed her fingers. If that was flirtation, Lady Lilian did not appear to enjoy it. She looked vexed and quickly extricated her hand from his.

"Morning, Wareham," Lord Malcolm drawled in a loud voice, forcing him to turn away from Lady Lilian.

"Morning, Eden."

"B'lieve you're acquainted with Miss Bertrand?"

"Miss . . . ?" He gazed at her as if he had never seen her before. "Oh, Barwith's niece. Have we met, ma'am?"

"Once. How do you do, sir." Mariette was not forced to think up something polite to say since he was already turning back to his hostess, scarcely acknowledging Emily's curtsy. She found she did not care a groat for his disregard, now that she had supportive friends about her.

"Is he not horrid?" Emily said in a low but indignant voice. "He must know you have been ill yet he did not even enquire how you go on!"

Lady Lilian reluctantly invited the baron to be seated, indicating a chair at a little distance. He pulled it up close to her before sitting down.

"You a huntin' man, Wareham?" Lord Malcolm enquired, still in the lazy drawl so unlike his usual mode of speech. Mariette looked at him in surprise. He wore a rather vacant, fatuous expression, eyelids drooping to hide his eyes, his posture languid.

"I go out occasionally with the local hunt," Lord Wareham said, a hint of irritability in his tone.

"Was talkin' to Bolger yesterday."

And that was a downright taradiddle! Mariette distinctly

recalled his utter lack of interest in Sir Nesbit's favourite topic. She realized he had intervened to save his sister from an unwelcome tête-à-tête.

"Yes," said Lord Wareham tersely, "Bolger's our Master of Fox Hounds."

"Run a good pack?"

"Tolerable. I am no expert."

"Nor I, but I thought I might turn up at a meet or two while I'm here."

"You hunt?" sneered the baron, making no attempt to hide his disbelief.

"Lord no! Like Brummell, I don't go beyond the first field."

"I've heard the *Beau*'s afraid of dirtying his boot-tops."

"Very proper." Lord Malcolm gazed down with every appearance of satisfaction at the spotless white turnovers of his top-boots. "Shockin' bad *ton,* dirty boots."

"Not in the country, I assure you."

"Shockin' place, the country."

"Quite shocking. Do you stay long?"

"Haven't quite made up my mind," Lord Malcolm confided. "A fellow has a duty to keep his sister company, don't you know."

Mariette glanced at Lady Lilian, who seemed to be struggling with dismay, amusement, and gratitude. Her face quickly smoothed as Lord Wareham turned to her.

"I cannot regard keeping Lady Lilian company as a matter of duty," he said suavely. "Call it rather a great pleasure and a delight I constantly aspire to."

Miss Thorne's entrance at that moment was for once welcome. Lady Lilian rose and went to meet her, asking, "Did you find your new wool, Cousin Tabitha?"

"Yes, thank you, Lilian. I had put it on a shelf at the top of my clothes press and Pennick had carelessly pushed it to the back. Emily, if you are not otherwise occupied you may come and help me wind the skeins."

Emily's groan was inaudible except to Mariette. She obediently went to join Miss Thorne in her usual place near the fire. Lady Lilian sat down again, on a chair considerably further from Lord Wareham than her previous seat.

"When does the hunt next meet?" Lord Malcolm enquired. "Daresay Bolger told me but I've forgot."

"Tomorrow, I believe," said the baron impatiently. He stood up, moved to the fireplace, and held out his hands to the flames as he went on, "But I suspect you will be disappointed—or perhaps relieved?—by a cancellation. I observed as I rode over that the clouds definitely threaten snow, and a fair amount if I'm any judge."

Leaving the fire, he headed towards the chair beside Lady Lilian. She jumped up with somewhat less than her usual grace and said quickly, "Then we must not detain you, Lord Wareham. It would be beyond anything if you were caught in a snowstorm on your way home."

"Unthinkable!" said Lord Malcolm, a hint of smugness in his drawl. He had risen when his sister stood up and now advanced, sauntering yet with a purposeful air, on Lord Wareham. He took the baron's arm. "I'll see you out, my dear fellow. No, no," he insisted when the baron opened his mouth to protest, "we quite understand. It was civil in you to come all this way in such inclement weather to enquire after Miss Bertrand's health but you must not stay at risk of foundering your horse in a snowdrift."

Still chattering inanely, he drew the hapless baron out of the room.

Mariette met Lady Lilian's eyes and both at once clapped their hands to their mouths to stifle giggles.

"Uncle Malcolm is a complete hand," announced Emily.

"A clever . . ." Lady Lilian started to correct her daughter, then smiled. "You are right, Emmie, he is a complete hand." She went to the door and sneaked a peek into the hall. Returning, she sank into her chair. "Perhaps I flatter myself, but I do believe the wretched man *hoped* to be confined at Corycombe by bad weather."

"You don't flatter yourself. He said he aspires to your company," Mariette pointed out. "He admires you, ma'am."

"I wish he did not! Enough of 'ma'am,' Mariette. I could easily be your elder sister. Pray call me Lilian."

"Humph!" said Miss Thorne, starting to wind another ball of her new wool—mud brown as a change from mustard. "I hope you know what you are about."

Lilian was not listening. Lord Malcolm came in and she demanded, "Malcolm, is it really going to snow?"

"My dear, I'm no weather-glass. I didn't even go outside. I handed your importunate suitor over to Blount." So saying he strolled towards a window.

"My suitor! Surely not!"

"Your beau, then, though I don't think it a word he cares for! Yes, the sky does look very like snow."

"Suppose Captain Aldrich is caught in a snowstorm? You had better send a message postponing his visit."

"I daresay he won't start out if it is already snowing heavily. If it begins when he is on his way, I hardly think enough will fall in an hour to discommode him seriously."

"Perhaps not," she said with unwonted uncertainty. "But if it starts to snow when he is here? I cannot let him go out into a snowstorm at night! I shall tell Mrs. Wittering to make up a bed."

"An excellent notion."

As she hurried out, Malcolm returned to his seat beside Mariette. Her reaction to Wareham's arrival had reassured him that the baron was not his rival, but he wished he knew what the man had done to make her loathe him.

"So you survived Wareham's presence," he said.

"Yes, but he did not survive your brilliant manoeuvre!" She laughed—a gleam of white teeth between rosy lips— and her dark eyes sparkled. "Very neat."

"He dug the trap himself," Malcolm disclaimed modestly, "and Lilian saw it before I did. He was too eager to deprive me of my hunt meet."

"Do you truly wish to attend a meet?"

"Not in the least."

"I thought not. When Sir Nesbit talked about the hunt you did not seem precisely enthralled." She looked puzzled.

"But what was the nonsense about not riding beyond the first field? You told me you enjoyed galloping on the moor."

"I do. I was just provoking Wareham."

"Because he judged you by your waistcoat? Is that why you spoke that way while he was here, as if it were an effort hardly worth making? No, you were the same with everyone who has called."

He was disconcerted. Accustomed to playing the idle fribble to all but his closest friends, he adopted the pose automatically in company. It was not difficult. He had been an idle fribble—until disgust at his way of life led him to investigate the possibility of a career in the Navy, an institution devoid of brotherly precedent.

His foray to the Admiralty had led not to a life at sea but to a meeting with a certain gentleman. This gentleman suggested no one would suspect him of hunting out England's enemies at home since no one imagined he had anything on his mind but the design of exotic waistcoats. So Malcolm joined the hunt while continuing to hide behind his waistcoats and his mask of inanity.

He had not considered how odd it must appear to Mariette. The circumstances of their meeting had not allowed a pretence of indolence. Knowing her to be perceptive, he ought to have reckoned she would notice and be intrigued by the change in his manner.

Not that it mattered. He was convinced she was not a French spy. However, her cousin was probably in it up to his neck and she had proved she would go to great lengths to protect the wastrel. She must not guess Malcolm had any purpose in Devon but to visit his sister, even as he waited impatiently for Des's arrival and report on their elusive spy.

"Many people behave differently in company and with their intimate acquaintances," he said. "You do yourself."

"I!"

"Ask any one of our callers these last few days and they will say you are reticent, even bashful. That is not at all how I should describe you."

"Oh! How . . . ? No, I am sure I had best not ask."

He would have told her anyway but Miss Thorne interrupted. "Miss Bertrand," she said sharply, "since you are able to sit up now, I am sure you are as capable as Emily of holding my wool for me. She ought to be practising her music."

"Yes, ma'am." Resignedly she started to get up.

Malcolm put his hand on her arm. "You stay here, where all has been arranged for your comfort. Miss Thorne, pray take my place."

Grumbling, Miss Thorne gathered her wool. Emily, passing on her way to the pianoforte, leaned down and whispered to Mariette, "Sorry! When I told her I must practise I did not suppose she would call on you instead."

"I don't mind," said Mariette. "I like to hear you play."

Emily looked gratified, and Malcolm felt a sudden extra rush of love for Mariette. How the devil had she managed to bring herself up to be so utterly enchanting?

The last ball of wool was nearly finished when Lady Lilian returned to the drawing room.

"Cousin Tabitha!" she said in dismay, "Mariette should not be holding your wool for you. She is a guest, and convalescent besides."

"Humph!" said Miss Thorne, winding the last strand. "The least she can do is help where she is able."

"I don't mind, Lilian, truly," Mariette assured her, though her arms were tired and aching from holding up the skeins. "I can scarcely claim to be convalescent still." It was the perfect opening to announce that she was well enough to go home, but she hesitated. Miss Thorne would be so pleased to be rid of her! She had rather tell Lilian alone.

"Where is Malcolm?" Lilian asked, looking around the room.

"He went to take Ragamuffin for a run in case it snows later."

"As though a groom could not take the dog out!" Miss

Thorne snorted, stuffing the balls of wool into her knitting
bag.

"I expect Malcolm will be glad of the fresh air."

"Humph! Catch cold, more likely." With a sniff, Miss
Thorne marched to her preferred place by the fire.

Lilian watched her go, a tiny frown creasing her brow.

"I don't believe Lord Malcolm is likely to catch cold,"
Mariette said hesitantly, "not just from taking Ragamuffin
out for a little while."

"I wonder what . . . ? Not that she has ever been precisely
conciliatory. . . . I beg your pardon, I was woolgathering!
Malcolm catch cold? No, not at all likely. He is excessively
healthy for all his hothouse airs. But, oh dear! I do hope
Captain Aldrich will not be caught in a snowstorm and fall
ill."

"Is the captain not in good health? Somehow one thinks
of naval men as being fit for anything."

Lilian gave an embarrassed laugh. "I daresay he is, and I
am making a mountain out of a molehill. He has lost his
arm, you see, and no longer goes to sea, but of course that
does not mean he is not otherwise robust. Indeed, he seemed
quite hale and hearty."

"Mama," said Emily, coming to the end of the piece she
was playing, "may I stop practising now?"

"Go on a little longer, my love. The Clementi is still not
quite right. Perfect it and you may play it this evening for
our hero of Trafalgar. I wonder whether Captain Aldrich
cares for music?" she said to herself in a musing tone. "I do
hope so."

Mariette was eager to know more about the Navy captain
who awakened such solicitude in her hostess. "Who is he?"
she enquired. "I thought I knew the names of all the neighbours for several miles around."

"Captain Aldrich is a schoolfriend of Malcolm's, a close
friend, I collect, although some years older. As he lives in
Plymouth, or rather Devonport, Malcolm looked him up
when he came to Corycombe. They have some sort of business together, though what I cannot imagine."

"Business? Perhaps Captain Aldrich has good ideas for spectacular new waistcoats."

"Oh no, the captain is a serious man. He dresses quite plainly—perfectly gentlemanly," Lilian hastened to add, "but with nothing of the dandy, like Malcolm. No doubt their 'business' is no more than an excuse to linger over the port and reminisce about old times."

"Linger over the port?" Mariette was confused. "But the captain is coming here, is he not, not Lord Malcolm going to Devonport?"

"A colloquial phrase, my dear, which illustrates the disadvantages of not speaking the plainest English! In Society, it is the custom after dinner for the ladies to leave the gentlemen to take a glass of port or brandy."

"Oh, Uncle George always drinks a glass of brandy after dinner, but he likes me to keep him company."

Lilian looked aghast. "Surely you do not drink spirits!" She sounded aghast, too.

"You mean brandy? No, cannot like the taste! I generally have a glass of negus—sherry wine and hot water, that is. Is negus a . . . a *colloquial* word?"

"No, it is perfectly unexceptionable."

"And . . . and drinking it?"

"Also unexceptionable. Mariette, I did not mean to find fault."

Mariette waved aside her apology. "If you will not tell me, how shall I learn? For a lady to drink brandy is not acceptable?" she asked earnestly.

"Unless she is a very elderly, infirm lady, and it is for her health. My dear, do you wish to learn how to go on in Society? I should be very happy to teach you."

"You will? Oh, splendid!" Mariette clapped her hands. The movement made her arms ache slightly, from holding Miss Thorne's wool. She remembered how she had declared that she was no longer convalescent. "But I am well enough to go home," she said sadly. "I was thinking of leaving tomorrow. I cannot trespass on your kindness any longer."

"That is nothing, but I daresay your uncle is in want of

your company and we ought not to keep you from him."
Lilian pursed her lips in thought. "Perhaps you could come
over to Corycombe for lessons, whenever it is convenient?"

"May I?" She was actually invited to call! "I would practise at home," she promised.

"Practise what?" Emily abandoned her music to join
them. "Are you going to learn to play the pianoforte, Mariette?"

"No, your mama is going to teach me elegant manners."

"Mariette feels she should return home tomorrow . . ."

"So soon? Must you go, Mariette?"

"But she will come here, frequently I hope, so that I may
advise her."

"Oh, famous! And I cannot wait to see Bell-Tor Manor."

"We shall have to see about that," said Lilian, indulgent
but firm. "Now, let me hear you play your sonatina."

So they would not be calling at the manor. Mariette realized the acceptance she had won was only partial, doubtless
dependent on her progress in her studies of etiquette.

Which led to the thorny question of how she was to attend those studies. To ride across the moor to Corycombe,
astride in breeches, would be to fail before she started. By
road the distance was a dozen miles, two hours or more each
way behind the aged Bonnie in the yet more ancient, bone-
shaking trap.

The trap it must be. No difficulty was great enough to
make her give up the chance to prove to Lord Malcolm that
she was capable of behaving like a lady, neither ramshackle
nor bashful.

The trouble was, he did not live at Corycombe. How
much longer did he intend to stay?

Chapter 9

Just as Emily finished the Clementi sonatina to her mama's satisfaction, Lord Malcolm returned to the drawing room. He was wearing buckskin breeches and a riding coat, which Mariette thought became him even better than his elegant morning dress. His face had a healthy glow from the fresh, cold air. Nothing could have looked less like the languid fop he had seemed earlier.

"I killed two birds with one stone," he told her, "exercising both Incognita and Ragamuffin. That dog has excellent manners when accompanying a horse."

"Yes, he never gets underfoot—under hoof, I should say, as our cook at the manor frequently complains of his being underfoot in the kitchen."

"Any dog of the slightest intelligence hopes to trip up someone in the kitchen who is carrying something worth eating. Excuse my riding clothes, Lilian," he went on as his sister and Emily joined them. "I told Des you would not mind if he dines in his again, as otherwise he'd have to go to the expense of hiring a carriage."

"Of course, he will be more comfortable if you are not in evening dress. It is not snowing, is it?" She glanced anxiously towards the window.

"No. In fact, the clouds are thinning. I even caught a glimpse of blue."

"Drat!" cried Emily.

"Emily dear!"

"I mean, what a pity!"

"I thought you liked the captain," said her mother, obviously chagrined.

"I did, Mama. I do, and I hope he arrives safely, only I hoped the weather might be too horrid for Mariette to leave tomorrow."

"Tomorrow?" Lord Malcolm frowned. "You are leaving tomorrow, Miss Bertrand?" He looked accusingly at Lilian.

"I cannot ask Mariette to absent herself from her home any longer, Malcolm, but we have arranged that she will visit us often."

She smiled at Mariette, who gave her a grateful look. How tactfully she had phrased it, so as not to expose Mariette's need of instruction to Lord Malcolm. Of course, he knew as much as Lilian, or more, about her inadequacies, and he'd soon discover the purpose of her visits . . . if he stayed on at Corycombe.

He was gazing at her with an air of discontent. Would he be sorry to see her go? Perhaps it was just as well she was leaving. She was growing altogether too fond of Lord Malcolm's company.

Was that why she had forgotten to tell Jim this morning that she was coming home tomorrow?

"It is not too late to send a message to Bell-Tor Manor, is it?" she said guiltily. "Our groom will have to drive the trap tomorrow to fetch me."

"Nonsense, you shall . . . ," Lilian started.

"Fustian, I shall . . . ," said Lord Malcolm at the same moment. He bowed to his sister. "After you."

"I was going to say, you shall have my barouche to take you home, Mariette."

"I was going to offer to drive you in the curricle, but perhaps you will be more comfortable in the barouche," her brother said regretfully, then brightened. "Let us see when the time comes. However, I shall most certainly escort you to make sure you do not meet with an accident . . . or a highwayman."

As she thanked Lilian, Mariette met his laughing eyes and

glared at him, willing herself not to blush. However attractive, he was a shocking tease!

Lilian rang for tea. Afterwards, Mariette retired to her chamber to rest before her first dinner below stairs. She was a little nervous about the great occasion, but it did not seem to have dawned on Lilian that her table manners might be at fault. Lilian was in a flutter, apparently over the prospect of seeing Captain Aldrich, so Mariette did not like to trouble her with a request for guidance.

She managed well enough at luncheon. If she watched carefully and copied what she saw, she could not go too far wrong, she told herself. At least she knew enough not to stay to drink port with the gentlemen!

She was eager to meet the captain, to see what sort of man caused such fidgets in Lilian who remained cool and calm even when pursued by the obnoxious Lord Wareham.

Her first sight of him was a disappointment. When she went down to the drawing room, only Lord Malcolm and his friend were there. They stood by the fire, talking. The captain was about the same height as Lord Malcolm, broader in the shoulders, too thin for what should be a sturdy frame. As the gentlemen turned on hearing her entrance, she saw the empty sleeve of his threadbare riding coat pinned across his chest.

Quickly she shifted her gaze to his face. He appeared much older than Lord Malcolm, aged by pain, she guessed, as well as by a seaman's exposure to the elements. Whatever attracted Lilian was by no means immediately apparent.

"Miss Bertrand, allow me to present Captain Aldrich."

"How do you do, Captain." She knew that much was right.

Bowing, he looked at her with obvious curiosity and a hint of wariness. Shabby as he was, he must wonder why his fellow-guest was wearing a dowdy old woollen gown which had plainly seen better days. Mariette wished she had an evening dress, preferably spectacular silks and laces to dazzle Lord Malcolm, or at least a pretty muslin so his friend would not take her for a scarecrow.

Not that she cared what the captain thought of her, except insofar as his opinion might influence Lord Malcolm.

For the moment, Lord Malcolm was as solicitous as ever. "You should have sent for me when you were ready to come down," he said reproachfully. "You know I like to be there when you descend the stairs, lest you should fall. Come and sit."

"I manage the stairs perfectly well," she protested, but she took his arm and let him lead her to her waiting cushion. "Will you not be seated, gentlemen?" she said, having heard Lilian speak thus to her visitors.

Lord Malcolm gave her an approving smile as they sat down.

"You have been ill, I understand, Miss Bertrand," said Captain Aldrich. "I trust you are rapidly recovering?"

"Yes, sir, I thank you." The country people always thanked one for asking after their health. Correct or not, it was polite. Should she say something about his arm in return? No, she decided, he probably did not like to have attention drawn to it. "I am going home tomorrow," she said instead.

"You live nearby?"

"Just a mile or two over Wicken's Down, though it is quite a distance by road." That subject exhausted, she sought desperately for another and recalled *maman*'s comments on the English habit of endless polite conversation about the weather. "Is it snowing?" she asked.

"No, ma'am, the sky is clear at present and the air is very cold. However, the wind is from the southwest and a bank of clouds is visible in that direction which will probably blow in before daybreak, so we may have snow later."

Lord Malcolm laughed. He was his usual self with the captain, not the languid dandy. "Asking a sailor about the weather is like asking a tailor about the set of a sleeve," he said. "You get a good deal more information than you require."

Captain Aldrich's grin made him look ten years younger. "I'd like to send you to sea in charge of an elderly frigate and see how fast you learn to read the signs," he said. "When one's life as well as one's livelihood depends on the weather, Miss Bertrand, one becomes more weather-wise than the most farsighted farmer."

Mariette would have liked to pursue the topic. She had read about voyages of exploration from Henry the Navigator to Captain Cook, and naval battles from Actium to Trafalgar. Storms had helped Sir Francis Drake defeat the Spanish Armada off Plymouth, she knew. It would be interesting to discuss the weather's effect on other occasions.

However, Lilian had come in and heard the captain's comment. "You are ashore now, Captain Aldrich," she said gaily, "and may expect to find shelter from any storm. I have had a chamber prepared for you so you need not ride back to Devonport tonight."

He sprang to his feet and clasped the hand she offered him. "My lady, you are very kind," he said gruffly. He bowed but did not release her hand.

Recalling how quickly Lilian had removed her hand from Lord Wareham's clasp, Mariette was fascinated to see that she made no effort to extricate herself. The pair gazed into each other's eyes.

"I thought I must have dreamed you," the captain said in a hushed voice.

Lilian's cheeks, already pinker than usual, took on a deeper rose. She was looking particularly pretty, her fair hair done in a more frivolous style and a bright Paisley shawl over her grey silk dress. Stars shone in her blue eyes.

Envious, Mariette whispered to Lord Malcolm, "They only met once before? Is it possible to fall in love so quickly?"

"Yes," he said with conviction. "Are not the romances you read full of love at first sight?"

"You made plain to me the difference between Gothic novels and real life."

"May a man not be converted?"

For a breathless moment her heart stood still. Did he . . . could he *possibly* mean he had fallen in love with her?

Common sense came to the rescue before she made a cake of herself. As usual, he was teasing. Gentlemen of the first stare did not fall for dowdy country girls of foreign birth. He was talking about his sister and his friend, their spellbound pose evidence enough for any man of the existence of love at first—or at least second—sight.

The spell was broken by Emily, who had come in with her mother and was growing impatient.

"Good evening, Captain Aldrich," she said, curtsying.

At once he turned to her with a smile. "Good evening, Miss Farrar. Malcolm tells me I am in for a treat."

"A treat?" she asked uncertainly.

"He said you are going to play on the pianoforte this evening. I hope he's right, for I dearly love music and I rarely have a chance to hear anything but a bo'sun's whistle!"

"What is that?"

While he explained, Lilian recovered her countenance. She was ready when Emily said, "If you love music, sir, you must hear Mama play instead. She is much better than I am."

"I shall be happy to play for the captain any other time," Lilian said composedly, "but this evening it is your turn, Emmie."

They talked about music, Lord Malcolm joining in. Mariette knew nothing so she listened to the beautiful names of instruments, wondering what they sounded like: harpsichord, clavichord, violin and viola, clarinet, oboe, and bassoon. Then there were the composers: Scarlatti and Spohr, Mozart and Monteverdi, Handel, Haydn, and Hummel, Couperin and Cimarosa.

What a lot she didn't know, Mariette thought with a silent sigh.

Miss Thorne came in, wearing her usual stark black satin with jet beads. Blount followed and announced dinner. Lilian took Captain Aldrich's arm to proceed to the dining room. Lord Malcolm offered his to Mariette.

"Should you not take in Miss Thorne?" Mariette muttered, noting that lady's glare.

"No, thank heaven. If this were a formal dinner, as a guest you would precede her. As we are informal tonight, politeness requires me to take in the nearest lady, fortunately you! Besides, I know on which chair Blount has placed the extra cushion."

Mariette's glare was almost as indignant as Miss Thorne's. If he loved her he'd have the delicacy to show her to her chair without reminding her of her embarrassing injury. So he didn't love her, so how lucky she had not asked him to explain his conversion to a belief in love at first sight.

In response to her glare, he merely smiled and patted her hand.

The dining room was large enough to seat eighteen or twenty, but the table was of a convenient size for their small party. Either he explained to Mariette at luncheon that a number of leaves could be added to enlarge it, a device she thought most genious. At home, she and Uncle George and Ralph ate at one end of the huge old dining table.

Lord Malcolm seated her and then politely held the chair next to her for Miss Thorne, who thanked him with a frosty nod. He took the end of the table, beside Mariette.

She began to feel more confident. Though Miss Thorne would disapprove whatever she did, the only stranger, Captain Aldrich, was not likely to pay attention to anyone but Lilian. Besides, so surely the rules could not be too complicated. Even the bewildering variety of gleaming silver knives, forks, and spoons before her could be sorted out by watching what the others used.

When Blount and Charles served the soup, she waited to see how everyone else dealt with it before she ventured to take a mouthful herself. Concentrating on the way people ate as the first course proceeded, she soon realized that all the delicious dishes were easy to eat with a fork alone. Lilian had ordered the meal to accommodate the captain's difficulties, just as she had for Mariette while she could only eat lying down.

What a splendid person Lilian was! Mariette vowed not to disappoint her.

She redoubled her attention to her manners. Nonetheless, she gradually relaxed enough to listen to the conversation, though she did not join in. Captain Aldrich was talking about places he had visited, all over the world, places she had read about.

He told of an elephant hunt he had witnessed on the island of Ceylon. A herd of the gigantic animals, to be tamed not killed, were driven into a water trap by men with trumpets and drums, torches and fireworks. His description was much more vivid than one Mariette had once read, and differed in several respects. She would have liked to ask about the differences, but she was afraid of seeming to contradict him.

To her surprise and delight, Lord Malcolm asked precisely the questions which hovered on the tip of her tongue. He too had read Captain Perceval's book!

For all his admirable qualities, she had not known he liked to read anything more serious than Madame D'Arblay's novels. She wondered whether he was interested in history as well as travellers' tales.

He was asking about the sacred footprint on the island, ascribed to Adam by the Mahomedans, to Buddha by the Buddhists.

"I didn't see it," said the captain. "It is on top of a sacred mountain in the interior. But yes, it is reputed to be two feet in length, or more."

Emily held her hands about two feet apart. "Good gad," she exclaimed.

"My dear, pray mind your tongue!" said Lilian, shocked.

"But I have heard Mar—" Emily glanced at Mariette, whose face was burning, and changed her excuse. "I have heard Uncle Malcolm say it, Mama."

"I plead guilty," said Lord Malcolm at once, "and I wager Des does, too."

Captain Aldrich grinned. "Oh, undoubtedly. I'm afraid

we sailors are not noted for the purity of our speech, Lady Lilian."

"Gentlemen are permitted a great deal more laxity, Captain."

"Which is shockingly unfair," Lord Malcolm pointed out. "But as it is so, we also ought to mind our tongues, for if a lady never heard such expressions, how could she repeat them?"

"Very true, Malcolm," said his elder sister severely. "You are to blame for the whole thing and we shall now forget it."

"Humph!" said Miss Thorne, and sniffed.

Mariette did not quite dare raise her gaze from her plate, but she felt immeasurably better than she had scarce a minute earlier. In a way Lilian was right, it was Lord Malcolm's fault she had used that expression before Emily.

She remembered from her childhood that certain words were not to be pronounced by polite people. Which words, she had no way to tell, nor had she realized the rules for ladies were different from those for gentlemen. Hearing Lord Malcolm, the epitome of the Polite World, say "Good gad," she had not hesitated to say it herself. And she had been trying so hard!

The others were talking about the captain's voyages again. Lord Malcolm leaned across the corner of the table and whispered to Mariette, "Don't do this, it's very bad manners, but I must apologize for being a bad example. Forgive me?"

She smiled at him and nodded. All the same, and in spite of Emily's quick thinking, she knew she had once more proved herself no lady.

At last the meal ended and she trailed out of the dining room after Lilian and Miss Thorne. Emily took her arm.

"I'm *dreadfully* sorry," she hissed.

Mariette hugged her. "Don't be, goose. You did not mean to give me away. Indeed, you tried very hard to swallow my name."

"Well, I *have* heard Uncle Malcolm say it, too. He was

prodigious quick to admit it, was he not? I believe he likes you."

"He has grown accustomed to protecting me from disaster," Mariette said firmly, and changed the subject.

She did think Lord Malcolm liked her, at least a little. Unfortunately she wanted a great deal more. She wanted him to look at her the way the captain looked at Lilian, as if she were the most precious object in the world.

Small hope of that! As she had already told herself, a gauche, shabby, shatterbrained nobody could not hope to attract the fashionable, top-o'-the-trees son of a marquis.

At least she hoped to have his friendship. An interest in books could be a bond between them, especially if he chanced to love history as she did. However, if he was ignorant he might be embarrassed by her asking. She decided to try to find out from Lilian first.

When they reached the drawing room and Emily went to practise her sonatina one last time, Mariette apologized to Lilian for having precipitated her daughter's *faux pas.*

"My dear, I don't regard it," Lilian assured her. "If you knew everything I should not have offered to teach you. I said it should be forgotten, and it shall. You did very well at dinner."

"I was very careful. Lilian, does Lord Malcolm like history?"

"History!" She looked startled. "Whatever gave you the notion that he may?"

"He had read the same book about Ceylon as I had, and since I enjoy learning about both other lands and other times, I thought perhaps he might. History is my favourite reading."

"Oh dear, never say you are a bluestocking!"

Puzzled, Mariette stared at her. How had the conversation suddenly turned from books to clothes? "No, my stockings are black," she said. "I have white ones for the summer."

Lilian burst into laughter. Mariette had not heard her laugh so wholeheartedly before and in a way she was glad to see her so merry, though at her own expense. She could not help smiling.

"What have I said now?" she asked resignedly.

"Oh, my dear, I do beg your pardon. That was prodigious rude of me and not to be copied! A perfectly natural mistake, once again the result of using colloquial language. A bluestocking is a name given to an excessively bookish female."

"Why?"

"Truth to tell, I have not the least notion."

"I suppose only a bluestocking would want to know why. But what is wrong with being bookish?"

"Gentlemen do not care for overmuch learning in a woman," Lilian said firmly. "Now, let me explain to you how a formal dinner party differs from our dinner this evening."

Though Mariette listened attentively, at the back of her mind a little voice rebelled. Not against the rules of precedence or against speaking only to one's immediate neighbours, but against gentlemen who did not care for bookish females. She was not going to give up reading history and philosophy for anyone.

After all, the little voice argued, she had no expectation of meeting any gentlemen whose opinion she cared for. Lord Malcolm already knew the worst; one more oddity would not shock him.

All the same, she resolved not to approach him on the subject of history.

As the ladies left the dining room, Malcolm and Des resumed their seats. Blount set glasses and decanters of port and brandy on the table and withdrew.

"Brandy?"

"If you please," said Des. "I admit I've never developed a taste for port."

"I know rum is a sailor's tipple," Malcolm observed,

pouring, "but I always thought they had a liking for port. A girl in every . . . ?"

Des flushed. "Devil take it, don't bring up that old canard."

"Sensitive on the subject, hey? No, no, old chap, don't call me out, I can see it's not like that with Lilian. I wager you'll be playing host here next time I visit."

"Don't be a sapskull," the captain advised, his face redder than ever. "Your sister has only met me twice. Besides, the daughter of a marquis and a penniless, crippled sailor . . . it just won't fadge."

"A dowager viscountess," Malcolm pointed out. He lounged back, glass in hand. "She's had her lord and now she can please herself. Oh, Frederick was a nice enough fellow, but she never looked at him the way she looks at you."

"She didn't?" Des gazed into the depths of his brandy glass, then took a hearty swallow. "Do I take it you'd have no objection to my courting Lady Lilian?"

"Not the least in the world. I'm not saying it would all be smooth sailing, mind you. There's the rest of the family may blow up a storm."

Des quailed. "Lord and Lady Ashminster, Lord Radford, Lord Reginald, Lord Peter, Lord James, and doubtless any number of uncles, aunts, and cousins."

"By the dozens."

"It's a wise seaman steers clear of the shoals." He heaved a deep sigh and held out his glass to be refilled. "We had best meet in Plymouth in the future."

Malcolm shrugged his shoulders. He thought Des and Lilian would be good for each other but it was none of his affair. "To business, then," he said.

"Yes. Do I gather Miss Bertrand is going home tomorrow?"

"She insists," Malcolm said gloomily. "I can't even try to dissuade her without suggesting her blasted uncle and cousin don't give a damn whether she is here or there."

"Then you don't believe her return home will make any difference to Riddlesworth's forays to Plymouth?"

"He'll not stay home for her sake, if that is what you mean. The wastrel hasn't come to visit her once!"

"I wondered whether hers might be the mastermind behind the selling of our secrets, but from what I have seen of her she hasn't the brains."

"Miss Bertrand is exceedingly clever!" snapped Malcolm indignantly.

"In that case she dissembles exceeding cleverly. Perhaps things will change when she is in charge again."

"She is *not* in charge, I swear it. If she's involved at all it's only to protect her damned cousin by her silence." He found himself suddenly madly jealous of Mariette's loyalty to young Riddlesworth. "What changes do you expect?" he grunted, swigging down the rest of his brandy, unappreciative of its excellence. "What has been happening while I've been here cooling my heels."

"The latest sphinx letter, the one Justice Penhallow turned over directly to you—that was a complete copy Jessup brought me?"

"I copied every last word in my own fair hand before I sent it on to the Admiralty."

"So I assumed. It contained not a word of any of the false information my men have been feeding to Riddlesworth."

Malcolm set down the decanter, sat up straight, and pushed his glass away. "Not a word?"

"I should know. You left me to invent that hocus as well as the Banbury tale we wrote under your sphinx seal for Penhallow to give his tame smuggler to turn over to the Frogs."

"So everything in the letter Penhallow passed on to me was the genuine stuff?"

"It was. Stuff we'd not have the French find out for all the tea in China," Des said grimly.

"Riddlesworth must have another source he considers more reliable if he's discarding your fellows' cozenage."

"We can't be sure he's discarding it. It's my belief he's waiting for Miss Bertrand to decide whether it's reliable."

"No!" Malcolm ran his fingers through his hair. "Though

I suspect you're right that there's someone else in it with him. We'll unearth them. In the meantime, where is he getting his information? Who, besides you, knows about all those shipping movements?"

"Only one person has all the information," said Des reluctantly. "Unless we have several babblers or traitors, the only possibility is my superior, Rear-Admiral Gault."

"A turncoat admiral! Good Lord, that would set the cat among the pigeons."

The captain hurried to disclaim. "I don't think for a moment he's a deliberate traitor. He's pretty plump in the pocket, so he'd not be tempted to betray his country for money, and his son was killed at the Battle of the Nile, so he's no lover of Bonaparte, or the Frogs in general. In fact, his wife even avoids the only French dressmaker in Plymouth, though Madame Yvette is an emigré who loathes Boney."

"Who *claims* to loathe Boney."

"What? You think . . . ? It's possible, of course, and I daresay we had best keep an eye on her, but I wager we'll find Gault's been babbling in the wrong quarters. There's no denying he's a regular bagpipe, squawks away like a whole flock of gulls."

"It does sound as if he's our man."

"The trouble is, he doesn't frequent the coffee rooms and taprooms where Riddlesworth lounges and gambles. In fact, as far as I can find out, the two have never met."

"Oh hell!" said Malcolm. "I must say I don't care to spy on an admiral without more evidence—or authority from the Admiralty. I'd best write a letter at once and Jessup can set off with it tonight." He pushed back his chair. "Come on, there is writing stuff in my sister's study and no one will disturb us there."

"You don't need me," Des protested. "I've told you all I know."

Malcolm grinned. "All right, you go and join Lil—the ladies. Tell them I'll be along shortly."

His grin faded as he made his way to Lilian's private

room. How was he to persuade Des that Ma[...] traitor to her adopted land?

He was utterly sure of her. She was quite inte[...] enough to run the operation, but far too open to conceal t[...] fact. It was not just partiality, he told himself. She deserved his trust.

Whether he deserved hers was another matter, he realized with a sinking heart. Mariette was not going to be pleased when he arrested her dearly beloved cousin as a traitor.

Chapter 10

When Mariette awoke in the morning, she knew at once that it had snowed in the night. Between and around the curtains, a cold, clear, white light crept into her chamber, and the silence had a curious muffled quality. The air was chilly though a housemaid had crept in earlier to build up the fire.

How *much* had it snowed? Mariette lay snuggled beneath the bedclothes trying to summon up the resolve to emerge and go to see. If only she knew whether she wished for deep drifts or a thin, crisp covering! Of course she wanted to go home to Uncle George and Ralph, and yet . . .

She had to admit that should Fate decree several more days at Corycombe, she would not be utterly overset.

"Mariette!" Emily burst into the room, swathed in a blue velvet wrap but bare-footed. "Look!"

She dashed to the window and pulled open the curtains. Beyond the glass white flakes floated down, soft, feather-light, incessant, impenetrable. No mistress as considerate as Lilian would ask her coachman to drive out in that.

"Is there much on the ground?" Mariette asked, as the usual earthquake under her bed preceded Ragamuffin's appearance.

"Lots. Jenny says it has been snowing since before midnight, on and on and on. Good morning, Ragamuffin." She shook the paw the dog offered, scratched his head, and went on joyfully, "You cannot possibly leave today."

"And that's the truth, miss." Jenny came in bearing Emily's slippers. "I don't know when I've seen such a fall down here in the valley. The stable lad who rides into Plymton for the post couldn't get through. Here, Miss Emmie, put these on afore you get frostbite."

"I shall stick my feet under Mariette's covers." Emily bounced onto the bed. "Mariette, I have had a simply famous idea. Mama was saying only a little while before you came that it is time I learned to dance. And lo and behold, here we are stuck in the house with two gentlemen for partners, even if they are rather elderly. What could be luckier?"

"It would be fun to learn," Mariette agreed, smiling at her enthusiasm, "though I don't expect ever to have the opportunity to dance. But remember that one of our gentlemen has only one arm. He might find it embarrassing or impossible."

"Oh yes." Emily's face fell. "I should hate to embarrass Captain Aldrich. I like him, do not you? He never makes me feel as if I scarcely existed, as Lord Wareham does."

"Only think how horrid it would be if Lord Wareham had been snowbound here!" Both girls giggled as they recalled the routing of the abominable baron. "You know, Emmie, it is best if you don't ask Captain Aldrich to dance with us, but I daresay your uncle would know how to ask him without making him uncomfortable."

Emily flung her arms around Mariette and kissed her cheek. "You are a perfect lady," she declared, "whatever Cousin Tabitha may say, for you always consider other people's feelings and Mama says that is the most important thing. I shall ask Uncle Malcolm to speak to the captain."

"Lord Malcolm may not wish to teach us to dance," Mariette warned. "He is used to the London ballrooms and beautiful partners who know all the steps and perform them with grace and elegance."

"Whereas I daresay you and I may even step on his toes. Yes, Uncle Malcolm is all the crack and vastly dashing, but he is never the least bit starchy or toplofty—and *don't* repeat any of those words, nor tell Mama I said them! He has always been prodigiously kind to me."

"And to me," she said wistfully. Last night when Lord Malcolm finally came to the drawing room, he had been more charming and attentive than ever. Yet she was a widgeon ever to have imagined his conduct towards her sprang from something more than kindness.

"I shall get dressed," said Emily, "and go down at once to ask him. Shall you come down to breakfast today? Cousin Tabitha always breakfasts in bed."

"No doubt there is an etiquette of the breakfast table I ought to learn, so yes."

"Good. If *you* ask Uncle Malcolm to teach us to dance, he is bound to agree!" On this blithe note, Emily hopped out of bed and scampered from the room, without the slippers Jenny had left for her.

The abigail returned just as Mariette pushed back the covers. "Miss Emily said you'll be going down to breakfast, miss," she said. "I'll give you a hand dressing."

"Thank you, Jenny, I believe I'm well enough to manage for myself. Do you think the snow will last long?"

"There's no knowing, is there, miss? It don't often snow this much hereabouts, 'cepting up on the moor, though I've heard tell they get more in London. Could be it'll rain this afternoon and melt it all away. Could be it'll sit a few days, I reckon."

"If I have to stay a few days longer, I have a favour to ask of you."

"Ask away, miss, do."

"Your alterations made my gowns fit so much better. Would you show me how you did it?"

"Course, miss, no trouble at all. You made 'em yourself, didn't you? Ever so neatly stitched, but fitting's an art needs learning. You just send for me when you've a while to spare. Now I'd best go help Miss Emily if you don't require my help."

Pulling off her nightgown with a shiver, Mariette felt her days were filling up very nicely. She would have little time to brood over the significance of Lord Malcolm's every word and deed.

Emily came to fetch her and together they went down to the breakfast parlour. Even with snow still drifting down outside the window, the sunshine-yellow wall hangings, marigold-patterned curtains, and a blazing fire made the room cheerful and cosy. To add to the sense of comfort, the smells of bacon, coffee, and fresh-baked bread wafted through the air.

Lord Malcolm was already there, working on a thick slice of ham with fried potatoes. Smiling, he stood up, as the girls entered, and wished them good morning.

"Pray be seated, Uncle," said Emily graciously, "or your breakfast will grow cold. We shall serve ourselves." She led Mariette to a laden sideboard.

The choice was bewildering. Half a dozen dishes with silver covers steamed over little blue-flamed spirit lamps, as did pots of chocolate and coffee. A nest of napkins in a basket unfolded to reveal rolls still warm from the oven. A bowl of bottled plums swimming in purple juice flanked another heaped high with apples, a few bright oranges glowing among them.

Oranges! Mariette had not eaten an orange since her childhood.

As she piled her plate with eggs, bacon, sausages, rolls, and one of the precious oranges, Blount came in to ask if she would like tea. She was about to say, not if it meant extra trouble, but she decided even the most considerate of ladies would expect her large staff to provide freshly made tea for breakfast.

"Yes, please, Blount," she said, and was glad to see the elderly butler did not look at all put out.

She turned to the table. Lord Malcolm rose again and pulled out the chair next to him, so she sat there, opposite Emily.

"Ask him," Emily said.

"You ask him. He is your uncle."

"But he is more likely to say yes if you ask him."

Lord Malcolm and Mariette glanced at each other, both a trifle pink-cheeked. *"What* am I more likely to say yes to, Emmie?" he asked suspiciously.

"Nothing dreadful! We wondered whether you would mind helping us learn to dance."

"Dancing lessons!" He groaned and grimaced, his eyes bright with laughter. Mariette had never known eyes could laugh until she met Lord Malcolm. "Think of my poor, tender toes."

"Wear riding boots. We shan't mind, shall we, Mariette?"

"Unless he steps on *our* toes."

"Madam, you insult my reputation as a Pink of the Ton. I am much sought after as a dancing partner, I'd have you know."

Emily sighed. "Mariette said you are probably too accustomed to dance with the most proficient and beautiful ladies to wish to stand up with us."

"I'm teasing, goose. Besides, I could not ask for more beautiful partners. Of course I shall help, and I wager Des will, too."

Mariette explained their qualms about inviting the captain to dance. Lord Malcolm covered her hand with his and said softly, "How like you to be concerned for his feelings. I shall put it to him privately. Would you like me also to explain to him about Lilian teaching you? She has told me of your wish to learn how to go on in Society."

"Will you? Then I shall not have to worry about making mistakes in front of him. He must have been shocked last night, when . . ."

He grinned as her voice trailed off. "Good gad, no! Sailors are not so easily shocked."

"Practically shock-proof," agreed Captain Aldrich, coming into the room. "Good morning, ladies. Morning, Malcolm. Thanks for the loan of the togs." He wore morning dress, the blue coat strained across his shoulders though rather loose below, with his own modest snuff-coloured waistcoat.

Malcolm eyed him critically. "Lackluster. Are you sure

you won't borrow a waistcoat?" This morning he had on his burgundy coat and cherry-striped waistcoat.

"Not me! Now that would be a shock, seeing myself in the looking-glass in one of your garish creations."

Emily was disconcerted by their badinage, but it emboldened Mariette to do her own explaining.

"We are outclassed, Captain," she observed with a smile. "You will never match Lord Malcolm's sartorial splendour, and I shall never match Lilian's or Emily's polite polish. I was not brought up to it, you see, but I mean to try. Lilian has offered to assist me."

"Good for her, Miss Bertrand, and good for you. I confess, though, I've no desire to match Malcolm's frippery foppery."

Mariette shook her head. "Let us agree to disagree then, sir, for I am a great admirer of his waistcoats."

"If that is all you admire in me, Miss Bertrand," said Lord Malcolm mournfully, "then I am undone. Des, you will be undone by hunger if you don't go and serve yourself." He waved at the sideboard.

"Good gracious!" cried Emily, jumping up, "you must not copy me, Mariette, for I am not doing my duty as hostess. Come and see what you would like, sir."

" 'Good gracious,' " Mariette mused. "Yes, I have heard Lilian say that. What other exclamations are unexceptionable?"

"Good heavens," Emily suggested, lifting lids for the captain.

"Or under extreme provocation," Lord Malcolm proposed, "you might even venture upon 'gracious heavens!' "

Lilian came in and smiled to see them all laughing.

"Good morning, all," she said. "It looks as if you will be staying with us a while longer, Mariette, and you, Captain."

"There's nowhere I had rather be," vowed Captain Aldrich as Lilian moved across to the sideboard.

"Nowhere?" She looked up at him through her lashes, a trace of a smile lingering on her lips.

"Say rather, anywhere suits me. It's not the 'where' that matters, it's the company."

"We are a very small company. I should have foreseen the snow and gathered a house-party to entertain you."

"Then you would be occupied in entertaining the crowd, with no time to spare for any particular guest."

"One can always make time for those with whom one particularly wishes to spend time."

Mariette exchanged a significant glance with Emily, who had returned to her muffin with strawberry jam when her mother joined Captain Aldrich at the sideboard. *Now* that *is flirting!* their glances agreed. Mariette resolved to watch Lilian more closely than ever. She doubted lessons in coquetry would be included deliberately in her syllabus and she wanted to learn.

She missed the captain's response as Lord Malcolm at that moment said to her, "Let me peel your orange for you, Miss Bertrand. I consider myself something of an expert."

"Please do," she said. She had been wondering how to tackle the messy fruit. After taking it she had remembered the mess but not the technique. "I have not had an orange since I came to Devon," she confided. "I did not know one could buy them here."

"I'm sure they must be available in Plymouth, but these come from Lilian's orangery. I'll take you to see it one of these days." Stripping off the last piece of peel, he divided the orange into segments and popped one into his mouth before putting the rest on her plate. "My reward," he said as he wiped his fingers on his napkin.

"Do have another slice."

"I believe I shall have a whole one to myself."

"Then let me peel it for you. I watched how you did it."

"I suppose you will insist on taking a slice as a reward?"

"Of course," she said, laughing.

He went to the sideboard, where Lilian and Captain Aldrich were still talking, food forgotten. His arrival returned their minds to breakfast, and they followed him back to the table with their plates.

"What shall I do with the pips?" Mariette hissed at him.

"You could see how far you can spit them," he suggested consideringly, "or . . ."

"Malcolm! I mean, Lord Malcolm!"

He grinned. "Make a fist, like this, and discreetly deposit them in the hollow on top—you see? Then transfer them to your plate. In more formal situations oranges are seeded in the kitchen before they are brought to table."

Thankfully Mariette disposed of the pips. She took his orange and prepared it as she had seen him do, only she cut a trifle too deeply and made considerably more mess. "There!" she said with satisfaction, eating her piece and giving him the rest.

"Not bad. You need practise. I prescribe an orange a day as long as the supply holds out. Lilian, have you many oranges this year?"

"Yes, an excellent crop." She had one on her plate, along with a modest half a buttered muffin, and she started to peel it as she spoke. "I like to eat an orange for breakfast every day, Captain, but a whole one is rather more than I really want. Will you share this with me?"

"I shall be more than happy to share anything you choose to share with me, Lady Lilian."

"Anything, sir?" Lilian glanced up at him, her lips pursed in thought, her eyes sparkling. "Let me see. There are meals to be planned and I simply must deal with my accounts this morning. Then Mrs. Wittering mentioned checking all the tablecloths to see which may be mended and which should be thrown out."

The captain rose nobly to the occasion. "Madam, I am yours to command."

"Gallantly spoken, Captain Aldrich. I shall keep you busy, I vow."

Mariette realized she had missed an opportunity to flirt with Lord Malcolm over their shared orange. Who would have guessed so simple a thing could lead to such a delightful exchange? Perhaps, with the right person at the right moment, any opening might serve.

She looked sideways at Lord Malcolm, who was regarding his sister and his friend with amusement. No, she thought, she'd not try to flirt with him until she had a better idea how to go about it. Failure would be too utterly dispiriting.

Both Captain Aldrich and Lilian agreed to the dancing lessons. The carpet in the drawing room was rolled back and Mariette and Emily started to learn the basic country dance steps.

Mariette was stiff and tired quickly, so the first lesson was short, but she enjoyed it. Though at first it was a trifle disconcerting to reach for the captain's arm to turn or promenade and find it not there, both she and Emily quickly adjusted. As she said to Emily later, "When you go to balls you are bound to meet with partners who don't know the steps properly. This will give you confidence to carry on as if everything is quite all right."

Her own confidence grew by leaps and bounds as the day passed. Following Lilian's example as much as her advice, she made fewer and fewer mistakes, "and never the same one twice," as Lilian pointed out approvingly. Whenever she found herself at a loss, Lilian or Emily or Lord Malcolm was there to help.

Miss Thorne continued to turn up her nose. This failed to daunt Mariette, since the shrewish companion found fault with everyone, even Lilian. In fact, she seemed still more disgruntled by Captain Aldrich's presence at Corycombe than by Mariette's. Mariette overheard her remonstrating with Lilian about her undue familiarity with a mere sea captain.

Lilian continued to smile a great deal and to dress up her grey gowns with colourful shawls and ribbons.

Snow fell on and off all day. In the night the clouds cleared and in the morning the pristine white hills and valley sparkled brilliantly under a frosty sun. Servants swept the terrace to the south of the house to permit the ladies and gentlemen to take the air.

Lord Malcolm was very dubious about allowing Mariette to go out in the icy cold after her illness.

"But I did *not* take an inflammation of the lungs after lying on the moor," she pointed out, "so a stroll on the terrace is not at all likely to harm me."

Nonetheless, he insisted on bundling her up in a hooded duffel cloak borrowed from one of the maids and a vast woolly muffler from the coachman. Mariette was quite glad when she recalled that the only outdoor clothes she had here were Ralph's outgrown greatcoat and the antique chapeau-bras she had worn as a highwayman.

Emily found the heaps of swept snow at either end of the terrace irresistible. In no time she had her uncle helping her to build a snowman. Copying Lilian, Mariette wistfully refrained from joining in—after all, Emily was still in the schoolroom.

However, once a hat had been provided for the snowman's head and Captain Aldrich had thrown the first snowball in an attempt to knock it off, Lilian herself threw the second. After that, Mariette had no qualms about taking the third shot. The snowman was subject to a veritable bombardment which the captain declared worthy of a forty-gun frigate.

In the end it was one of Mariette's snowballs which knocked off the hat. "Only because you were not really trying," she accused Lord Malcolm as they all returned pink-cheeked and merry to the house. "Your shots could not possibly have gone so wild if you had aimed properly."

"My dear," said Lilian, "I fear you will frequently discover in gentlemen an odious propensity to allow ladies to win."

"*I* think it is splendid," Emily said stoutly.

"No, Emmie, your mama is right, it is odious," Mariette averred. "It indicates their belief that we cannot win on our own merits. Besides, if it is all a cheat, where is the pleasure of victory?"

"Well, in this case," said Lord Malcolm, "yours was a good throw and my failure did not necessarily lead to your success. As a matter of fact, I didn't want to spend all my time putting the dashed hat back on his head."

"Such modesty!" exclaimed the captain.

"Oh, I'm a modest fellow." Lord Malcolm grinned. "But I shall remember your words, Miss Bertrand. Beware when I challenge you to a game. I shall give no quarter."

Mariette laughed. "Then I had best issue the challenge. Since we are not discussing a duel, that will give me the choice of weapons. Do you play backgammon?"

"Yes, but you had best rest awhile before we play, and recruit your strength, for I mean to give you a strenuous time of it."

The bombardment of the snowman had wearied Mariette a little. She decided to lie down with a book for half an hour. Having finished *Cecilia,* she asked Blount the way to the library.

In this, at least, Corycombe was no match for Bell-Tor Manor. Before taking up sculpture, Uncle George had been something of a bibliophile with a particular interest in history. His books and those of his predecessors filled ceiling-high shelves on four walls of a large room, overflowing into dusty stacks on chairs and tables.

In Mariette's eyes, the library at Corycombe scarce merited even the name of book-room. The four matching cabinets were elegant pieces of furniture but each had no more than five or six glass-fronted bookshelves above closed cupboards. Among a preponderance of poetry and novels, there was something for every taste, something to occupy the idle moments of occasional guests, both ladies and gentlemen.

And judging by what Lilian had told Mariette about bluestockings, the volume she chose was undoubtedly intended for the gentlemen.

An hour later, Malcolm ran Mariette to earth. She was curled up on one of the Chippendale settees Lilian considered suitable furniture for a library—at least they matched the bookcases. Her nose was buried in a book, but as he entered she glanced up, she hurriedly closed the volume, and pushed it down behind a cushion. Then she uncurled and fished with her stockinged feet for her slippers.

"Put your feet up again," Malcolm ordered. "You are supposed to be resting, not demonstrating a ladylike posture."

"I meant to go up and lie on my bed," she explained, "but . . ."

"But?" he asked when she stopped. "You found a book so fascinating you couldn't put it down? What are you reading?"

"Oh, nothing," she said uneasily.

"I already know your predilection for Gothic novels, remember."

"I shall never read another one!"

Amused by her vehemence, he wondered what the deuce she had found in Lilian's minimal collection to which anyone could possibly take exception. "Come on," he coaxed. "Let me see it."

Reluctantly she fished it out from behind the cushion and handed it to him.

"Voltaire's *Essay on History*" he read. "Good gad—I beg your pardon—good gracious!"

Mariette looked more defiant than abashed. "Lilian told me ladies are not supposed to care for serious subjects, but I have been wanting to read it this age. The edition at home is in French. I didn't know it had been translated into English."

"You don't read French?"

"Only the easiest bits. *Maman* stopped teaching me French when she married my step-papa, and I have forgotten a great deal."

"I expect you could manage with a dictionary."

"We have Dr. Johnson's dictionary," she said uncertainly.

"No, a French-English dictionary, which lists French words and gives their translations. Perhaps lexicon is a better word."

"I didn't know there was such a thing! I wonder if the book shop in Plymouth might have one."

"Probably."

"Do you think it would be very expensive? It would be worth spending my allowance on, though."

"A few shillings." When he married her, she should have every book her heart might desire, even if he had to do without his spectacular waistcoats. He must not be precipitate though, and risk frightening her off. "I'm sure Lilian would lend you this Voltaire."

"There are other French books at home. Besides, I don't want her to know I am reading it. You won't tell her, will you?"

"Truth to tell, I'm amazed to find this in her house, and I'd be astonished to learn she had read it. Some guest must have left it by mistake."

"And you were shocked to find me reading it."

"Not shocked, surprised. You must admit you have never given me the least hint that you are a bluestocking."

"Is it so dreadful to be a bluestocking?" Her dark eyes were wistful, appealing. At that moment she could have asked whether it was dreadful to be a cannibal and he'd have heartily denied it.

"Not at all, or only to men afraid to discover that women are as intelligent as themselves."

"Which must be most men, or Lilian would not have warned me."

"I daresay," he agreed ruefully.

"And you?"

Did she just want his opinion, or did she really care what he thought? If he advised her to give up reading history, would she do so, or would he have lost her forever? Did he *want* her to abandon her studies, to join the ranks of young ladies with nothing on their minds but fashion, gossip, their own sensibilities, and the hunt for a husband?

Heaven forbid!

"There are not so many men with whom one can hold an intelligent conversation," he said, "that one can afford to exclude women. What do you think of Voltaire's history so far?"

"Have you read it?" She beamed as he nodded. "Oh, splendid! I have a hundred questions and it may be days before I can ask Uncle George."

"You must not expect my learning to equal your uncle's," he protested, "but let's see what I can do."

He found her mixture of historical erudition and worldly naïveté utterly enchanting. Somehow they ended up in a vigorous argument about Elizabeth Tudor and Mary Queen of Scots, Mariette supporting the practical and accomplished Elizabeth, Malcolm the romantic, tragic Mary.

Time passed unnoticed until they were summoned to luncheon.

"We shall have to agree to disagree," said Mariette, retrieving her slippers.

"What, has my powerful male reasoning not convinced you?"

"Not a bit. You won't tell Lilian, will you?"

"My lips are sealed. I'll even smuggle the book up to your chamber for you."

Laughing, she took his arm. "I am so glad it was you who won Ralph's ring."

So was he, or he'd never have met her. And yet, once she learned what use he was making of the sphinx signet. . . . He had to make her love him before she found out, but he could not in all honour ask her to be his wife until she knew the worst.

The weather remained clear and cold, with no sign of a thaw. As the days passed, Mariette recovered her strength—and her energy.

Lilian taught her to bridle her energy, to walk at a decorous pace, to glide up and down stairs instead of running, to gesture with languid grace. Mariette mastered every movement, but she was left with a restless need for vigorous exercise which the dancing lessons only partially appeased.

The servants cleared the worst of the snow from several paths around the house, so she and Lord Malcolm took Ragamuffin out for a run two or three times a day. Sometimes Emily or the captain accompanied them, in which case Mariette strolled with ladylike sloth, leaning on Lord Malcolm's arm. When they were alone, she matched her stride with his. *He* did not mind.

One afternoon when they returned to the house, Lilian drew Mariette aside.

"I happened to look out of the window," she said, "and saw you traipsing along at a great pace. Since we are so isolated at present it scarcely matters here, to be sure, except that it may become a habit."

"I fear walking fast is already a habit with me, but I am trying to break it, truly."

Lilian smiled. "I am sure you are, my dear. And you will not forget, when you go home, that riding astride in breeches is not at all the thing?"

"You shall never see me riding astride again," Mariette promised. She simply must get hold of a sidesaddle somehow, so that she could ride to Corycombe. As for her gallops on the moor, Lilian never went up there. Nor did anyone else but shepherds and occasional poachers, neither in the least likely to give her away.

"You are a most satisfactory pupil," said Lilian. "I doubt there is a great deal more I can teach you. I hope you will come often to Corycombe when the snow melts, nevertheless."

"If I may. I shall need reminders and practise."

The trouble was that all the lessons were directed towards proper conduct in company—of which there was none at Bell-Tor Manor—and catching a husband. Even if she ever met other gentlemen, she could not imagine wanting any husband but Lord Malcolm.

As for Ralph, she thought guiltily, her long-held notion of marrying him now appalled her.

Chapter 11

"Blount tells me the path to the orangery is cleared,"
Lord Malcolm informed Mariette as Ragamuffin bounded
ahead of them down the terrace steps.

"Yes, we ate the last oranges for breakfast today. I doubt
they need have dug out the path, though." She glanced up at
the grey sky.

During the morning a west wind had risen, a warm, soft,
moist wind, a harbinger of spring. Now the clouds hung
heavy overhead. Already melting snow dripped from the
eaves and the flagstoned terrace had puddles here and there.
Lord Malcolm took her elbow to steer her around a large
one.

"It will take a day or two for so much snow to disappear," he said.

"Not if it rains."

"You must be eager to go home."

She could not tell him she wouldn't mind being snowbound forever as long as he was there. "I am a little anxious
about Ralph and Uncle George," she said, and found it was
true. "Uncle George is quite capable of forgetting to eat if I
am not there to remind him. As for Ralph, being stuck at the
manor for nigh on a week must have bored him to desperation."

Their feet crunching on the gravel, they turned the corner
of an ilex hedge, down a walk Mariette had not traversed
before. Ragamuffin brushed against the hedge and was

showered with mushy snow. He shook himself vigorously, transferring the slush to Mariette's borrowed cloak. She brushed it off, noting how fast it turned to water.

Another turn or two and they came to a formal garden, laid out in an intricate pattern of squares. Snow-capped Classical statuary stood about, looking so chilled—what with white marble and exiguous draperies—and so lifelike that Mariette almost expected the gods, goddesses, and heroes to shiver.

Poor Uncle George, struggling with his pig-badger!

On the far side of the garden, facing south with its back to a steep-sloped spur of Wicken's Down, stood the orangery. From up on the moor Mariette had seen the vast expanses of glass glittering in the sun and wondered what it was. Close to, it was still more impressive. Some seventy feet long and two stories in height, the façade was all windows from ground level up, separated and supported by unadorned Doric pilasters. The roof, too, was of glass, upheld by a tracery of ironwork.

"My brother-in-law's grandfather built it," Lord Malcolm said, "at the same time as the house. Corycombe was the furthest south of his estates. Now, of course, the produce is all Lilian's though I believe she occasionally sends a gift of oranges to the present viscount."

Because of reflections, little of the interior was visible from the outside. "May we go in?" Mariette asked.

"Yes, I have brought the key. It's kept locked so that the door is not left ajar by accident. The place is heated, as you will feel." He took a key from his pocket and opened the French door.

Mariette went first, Ragamuffin at her heels. His claws clicked on the stone floor. Dry heat; she pushed back her hood. A sweet, exotic fragrance.

Despite all the windows, after the glare of the snow outside Mariette's sight took a moment to adjust. Then she saw the trees, ranked along the back wall in huge terracotta pots. Against the glossy dark-green leaves, the orange globes of the fruit seemed to glow, while clusters of snow-white blossom sent forth their aromatic, sensuous perfume.

"Oh, beautiful! I did not know they bloom at the same time the fruit ripens." She looked up at Lord Malcolm to share her delight.

"This is the best time," he said in an odd voice. And then he kissed her.

His lips brushed hers, feather-light. His arms went around her, pulling her close. He had unbuttoned his great-coat and his body was hard against hers, his mouth now firm, insistent, demanding. Mariette put her arms round his neck and clung to him as a wave of shuddering warmth flooded from her lips to her toes and back to the centre of her being. The world was lost; the only reality was his touch, his . . .

"Woof!"

They sprang apart. Mariette's face burned as if Lilian, not Ragamuffin, had interrupted the embrace.

"Woof?" He had found an orange and brought it to lay at Lord Malcolm's feet, in the clear belief that the dearest desire of his lordship's heart was to play catch.

Lord Malcolm obliged, his cheeks as fiery as Mariette's felt. She crossed to the nearest tree and buried her face in its blooms. So that was a kiss, she thought dizzily. No wonder the heroines of romances lost their heads as well as their hearts!

What did it mean? In books, villains as well as heroes kissed, and even gentlemen did not always reserve their kisses for their beloveds. Lord Malcolm was no villain. He was too much the gentleman to wish to take advantage of her, as his discomfiture proved. But had his embrace been a casual gesture such as gentlemen were prone to, or had it shattered his world as it had shattered hers?

Her outward composure regained, she turned to observe him as he threw the orange for the indefatigable dog. Though his colour was still heightened, that might easily be from heat and exercise. The heat and the blossom's perfume were becoming overpowering.

He glanced at Mariette and smiled, but she was too far away to be sure of his expression.

Ragamuffin returned once more with the orange. "Enough," cried Lord Malcolm, laughing. "Slobber is one thing, but now you have punctured it and it's sticky with juice as well."

He went to the door, opened it, and hurled the revolting object into a snowdrift. Ragamuffin eagerly plunged after it.

Lord Malcolm scrubbed his hand with a handkerchief, put his gloves back on, and buttoned his coat. Apparently studiously intent on each action, he did not look at Mariette until he had finished.

"Shall we go?"

She nodded, unsure of her voice. Raising her hood, she moved at her most ladylike glide past him and out into the cold. The stiff breeze no longer felt balmy. She shivered.

Turning from locking the door, he offered his arm and she took it, just as if nothing had happened between them.

"I must beg your pardon," he said softly as gravel crunched once more beneath their feet. "That was unconscionable, unforgivable of me."

"Not unforgivable." Mariette had to clear her throat. "I fear the fault was not entirely yours." After all, she had not pushed him away, had not struggled, let alone slapped his face. In fact, she admitted, once he was well embarked upon kissing her she had positively encouraged him.

"I assure you, gentlemen are permitted to assume the entire blame." Stopping, he looked down at her with a smile. But his eyes were full of warmth with no hint of teasing laughter. "You won't tell Lilian?"

"No." For a moment she thought—hoped?—he was going to kiss her again, but he resumed walking. Mariette sighed. "It seems her insistence on a chaperon is vindicated."

"Yes." Now he was laughing. "Ragamuffin performed that rôle most excellently, do you not agree?"

And she had to laugh, too, and once more they were on the easiest of terms.

As Ragamuffin emerged backwards from the drift, looking like a snow-dog, heavy raindrops began to fall. After a good shake, he pranced forward, very proud of himself, and laid the squishy orange at Lord Malcolm's feet.

"Not a chance, old boy! After the orangery it's cold out here, and wet, and we are going back to the house. Though, come to think of it, the stables are undoubtedly the place for you at present. If you'll excuse me, Mar—Miss Bertrand, I shall desert you and take him to be dried."

Mariette was quite glad not to face the others with him at her side, and also glad of a little time to think before she faced them. At the next corner they separated and under an increasing downpour she hurried towards the house.

To return to their old, friendly footing was better than to wallow in embarrassment until she returned home. Yet how she wished he had declared his love, offered his heart, begged her to marry him. It had been a casual kiss after all, the result of mild affection meeting the luxuriant scent of orange blossom. She was indeed at fault for responding with such fervour. He was a true gentleman to take the blame upon himself.

She stopped stock-still on the terrace steps as a thought struck her. He was a true gentleman, and a gentleman did not offer for a lady without her father's or guardian's permission. Was he waiting to speak to Uncle George?

It was almost too much to hope for—but not quite.

"Is this land your uncle's?" Lord Malcolm enquired as the bays trotted sloshily along the muddy lane.

"Yes, the Bell-Tor Manor estate begins where we drove out of the woods back there."

From the high seat of the curricle, Mariette could see over the bare hedges, neatly pruned down for the winter. On either side spread dun meadows grazed by red Devonshire cattle, interspersed with ploughland already hazed with green winter wheat. The rain had stopped in the night; the sun shone, and the snow was gone except for streaks on the north side of hedgerow and copse. Spring was definitely in the air in this favoured southwestern corner of the realm, though gales and storms might yet be on the way.

Ragamuffin, sitting on Mariette's feet, snuffed the air with an expression of bliss.

"The farms look to be in good heart," said Lord Malcolm, sounding surprised.

"Mr. Taffert is an excellent bailiff, as I told you, and Uncle George does not begrudge the expenditure necessary to keep things running smoothly."

"Very wise."

"Ralph grumbles that it is all run on shockingly old-fashioned lines."

"Your cousin is interested in farming?" Now Lord Malcolm sounded astonished.

"Well, no," she confessed reluctantly. "He talks grandly of modernization, but I fear it is no more than a word to him. However, if he were to try, I doubt Uncle George would oppose him."

"Mr. Barwith must be the most easy-going of men."

"Oh, he is. He's a dear."

"It's a pity your cousin don't make the effort, for the new methods of agriculture, new breeds of animals and varieties of crops often produce impressive results."

Mariette turned her head to stare at him. "You know about agriculture?" she asked.

"Very little. I've had no cause to study but I grew up on a great estate. My father owns a vast number of acres, and he and my eldest brother are both progressive landlords. It's interesting and one cannot help learning a bit."

"I know what you mean. From simply talking to the tenants and Mr. Taffert I have learned a little. Like living in a house with a library full of history, it is inevitable—except that Ralph has succeeded admirably in avoiding any interest in either history or farming. Oh, I do hope he has not fallen into the suds while I was away!"

"You are not responsible for rescuing him from his difficulties."

"Perhaps not." Yet she still felt guilty for abandoning the notion of marrying him and devoting her life to taking care of him. "I suppose it has become a habit. When he was little it was things like tracking mud into the house and stealing jam tarts. I used to intercede with Cook or Mrs. Finney on his behalf. Then with Jim Groom, when Ralph left the paddock gate open and all the horses wandered off up to the moor. And the dairymaid, the time he used milk churns as giant skittles and knocked over a full one."

"Giant skittles!" Lord Malcolm exclaimed. Lilian's groom Benson, sitting up behind, gave a snort of laughter.

"He thought they were all empty. It was a mistake. He was never naughty on purpose," she said earnestly.

"I daresay."

She tried to make him understand. "Ralph was only nine when he came to live with us. His parents had just died and he was dreadfully unhappy. I had already been there for some time so it was natural to do what I could to—Oh, slow down a minute! Ragamuffin wants to get out."

He reined in the bays and Ragamuffin took a flying leap. Mud spattered in all directions.

"Oh bother! I shall have to bathe him."

"Surely your groom . . ."

"Jim is an old man and sadly rheumaticky."

"Begging your pardon, m'lord, but if you was to stay a half an hour to rest the hosses, I c'd wash the dog for miss afore we leave."

Mariette smiled at him over her shoulder. "Thank you, Benson, I shall accept your kind offer. It is *not* one of my favourite tasks!"

The groom flushed. "My pleasure, miss," he muttered.

Ragamuffin, having thoroughly investigated the enticing smell, returned to the curricle, quite prepared to launch himself into the moving vehicle.

"Oh no, you don't," said Mariette severely. "You are filthy. You'll have to run the rest of the way."

They drove on up the valley, through a village which was no more than a few rows of whitewashed cottages, a tavern, a forge, and the tiny church of St. Elwyn. No resident vicar—a curate came over from Plympton once a fortnight. Mrs. Finney had taken Mariette and Ralph to services for the first year or two, until they started to disappear on Sunday mornings and she gave up. Mariette had attended once when she was older. The curate's hurried sermon and evident anxiety to be gone disgusted her, and now she only went to tenants' christenings and weddings.

She had no intention of explaining this to Lord Malcolm. From their discussion of Voltaire she suspected he was no faithful churchgoer, but she knew Lilian attended St. Bride's every Sunday. As the curricle approached St. Elwyn's, she waved to the blacksmith on the other side of the street and told Lord Malcolm how he had shod the ponies free when she and Ralph were children.

"Welcome home, Miss Mariette!" he bellowed, a huge grin splitting his grizzled beard.

Heads popped out of doors and windows. Women and children and old men waved, the bolder calling out, "Welcome home, miss!" "Glad you'm better, miss!"

Mariette waved and smiled, blinking back tears. "How lucky I am to have so many friends," she said to Lord Malcolm.

"You have made your own luck, I should say," he responded.

While she was puzzling over this, they left the hamlet behind. As the valley narrowed, the lane ran through woods, close to Bell Brook, now a swirling torrent in flood. They drove over several stone bridges across the stream's windings, and Mariette pointed out the one from which she had caught her first fish.

Lord Malcolm laughed. "D'you know, I don't believe I have ever met anyone who ever forgot the precise spot where they caught their first fish. I certainly have not. How about you, Benson?"

"Like it were yesterday, m'lord."

Now the manor was visible through the bare trees, huddled under the steep slopes of Bell Tor and Grevin Moor.

No sign of life but the smoke rising lazily from the chimneys into the clear air. Mariette clasped her hands tightly, suddenly nervous.

What if Lord Malcolm and Uncle George took each other in dislike? What if Ralph, instead of thanking his lordship for the return of the ring, took it into his head to accuse him of being a Captain Sharp? What if Lord Malcolm turned up his nose at a household with neither butler nor footman, none of the elegancies to which he was accustomed?

She stole a sideways glance at him. No, he would not turn up his nose. He was too courteous and too kind, never starchy, never toplofty.

In fact, he was nigh on as perfect as a man could be.

The curricle drew up before the front door. Benson jumped down to take the reins and Lord Malcolm handed Mariette down. Ragamuffin arrived, panting.

Mariette fended him off. "Go with Benson," she ordered, pointing. Fortunately, after giving her an injured look, the animal obeyed. He knew the groom from the Corycombe stables.

The moment had come. Taking a deep breath, Mariette turned the massive wrought-iron door handle, pushed open the door, and stepped across the threshold. Dust motes floated in the sunbeams fighting their way through the grimy clerestory windows. From the depths of the hall came the clink of hammer and chisel.

Lord Malcolm followed her. "Good gad!" he said in a low voice. "I mean, good heavens!"

"I believe 'gracious heavens' might be permitted," Mariette said wryly.

"Good . . . gracious . . . heavens!" He turned his head slowly, his gaze embracing the hall full of statues, then walked slowly around the nearest, examining it more closely. "A pony?" he asked doubtfully.

"How clever of you. It started out as a Dartmoor pony but its legs and muzzle turned out too thin so Uncle George changed it into a deer. Hence the tail, or lack thereof."

"I did not mean to insult Mr. Barwith's abilities."

"Poor Uncle George is only too aware of his own lack of skill, I fear. It does not help that his eyesight is rather poor, which is why he had to give up the study of history. Give him your honest opinion, as I do, and he will not like you the less for it."

"But you are family and I am an outsider," Lord Malcolm protested. "I shall exercise the utmost tact."

She smiled at him. "Very well, but no flummery, for you will not deceive him. Uncle George!" she called, leading the way towards the centre of the hall. "I'm home. Let us meet by the lion."

"Mariette? My dear child!" Hammer in hand, Uncle George came round the end of the granite crag, small and shabby, his wig crooked, reddish from sandstone dust, and thinner than ever. He *hadn't* been eating properly. "My dear child, I have missed you."

Mariette hugged him and kissed his cheek. "And I you, Uncle. Let. . . ."

"I have been working on the lion, Mariette, but it goes very slowly. Come and see."

"In a moment, Uncle. Let me make you known to Lord Malcolm Eden."

Uncle George peered vaguely at the visitor. "Eden? Your pardon, sir, I didn't observe you. How d'ye do, sir, how d'ye do. A friend of my niece, are you?"

Lord Malcolm bowed. "I hope I may call myself Miss Bertrand's friend, sir. I am delighted to make your acquaintance."

"Lord Malcolm came to my rescue on the moor, Uncle."

"Much obliged, sir, I'm sure. Mariette, my dear, now I come to think on it, did not Mrs. Finney tell me you were injured?"

"I was, Uncle, but I am quite recovered, thanks to the kind offices of Lord Malcolm and his sister."

"Excellent," said the old man happily. "Simply splendid. Now do come and see what I have done while you were away."

Mariette glanced apologetically at Lord Malcolm but he seemed quite content to follow them around the granite. Uncle George pointed out the spot below one ear where he had been working.

"Oh dear, I cannot tell the difference."

He nodded, resigned. "It goes slowly, very slowly indeed. Now you are home, I believe I shall return to work on the pig."

"I am vastly impressed by your industriousness, sir," said Lord Malcolm.

Uncle George gave him one of his suddenly shrewd looks. "Most obliging of you. I haven't quite got the knack of it yet, but I mean to keep trying. You'll take a glass of Madeira wine, my boy? Mariette, is there any Madeira?"

"I don't know. I'll have to go and ask Mrs. Finney while you take Lord Malcolm to the drawing room."

No Madeira, but Mrs. Finney had prepared a tray with brandy, sherry, and the tea things, and Cook had the kettle on the boil.

"Jim Groom reckoned his lordship might bring you home," Mrs. Finney explained.

"We was that happy, dearie," said Cook, "when he come back from Corycombe this morning wi' the message you was coming home."

She had baked a celebratory apple cake and the kitchen smelled of cinnamon and cloves. Sniffing the delicious odour, Mariette realized she had never entered the kitchen at Corycombe. What real ladies missed by not frequenting their kitchens!

Kissing both the plump, grey-haired women, she asked Mrs. Finney to take the tray to the drawing room, and sped upstairs to take off her borrowed cloak and tidy her hair. When she came down, she found the gentlemen chatting amicably about the estate. She gave Lord Malcolm the cloak to be returned to the helpful housemaid.

"I should like to give her a shilling," she said, opening her purse which she had brought down, "and another to Benson for washing Ragamuffin. Would that be proper?"

"Quite proper," Uncle George confirmed. "You left vails for Lord Ferrar's servants, I trust?"

"Lady Lilian's, Uncle. Lord Ferrar died some years ago. What are vails?"

"A tip, my dear. What the French call a *douceur,* to sweeten service, or a *pourboire,* though one must hope not necessarily to be laid out in drink."

"Oh, I was forgetting," Mariette cried. "Lord Malcolm, will you drink brandy or sherry?"

"Tea will do me very nicely, Miss Bertrand, and may I hope to be offered a slice of that most appetizing cake?"

"Of course, sir. Cook's apple cake is my favourite."

As she served him, carefully following Lilian's directions, Mariette noted the unmatching glasses and china. Thence her gaze took in the whole drawing room, so familiar she had never really observed it before. The upholstery and curtains were faded, the woodwork dingy, dusted but not polished with any vigour. The contrast with Corycombe was extreme, though Lord Malcolm was far too polite to give any sign of noticing.

Before he came again, she vowed, she would see everything done that could be done without spending money to brighten the manor's public rooms.

Uncle George also chose tea. Pouring for him and herself and passing slices of cake, Mariette returned to the subject of vails. Lord Malcolm suggested that a crown would suffice. He undertook to divide it appropriately between the claimants at Corycombe.

"And will you please give Jenny Pennick this," Mariette said, handing him a little brooch of ivory carved into a rose. It cost her a pang to part with it—her step-papa had given it to her for the birthday before he died. "It is nothing much, but I cannot think of anything else suitable. She was particularly helpful when she might have reasonably resented being presented with an extra lady to care for."

"I'm sure Jenny will be delighted." He wrapped it up safe in his handkerchief and tucked it into the inside pocket of his coat.

Today he was wearing a waistcoat in sober dark blue and brown checks. Mariette wished she dared think he was trying to impress Uncle George with his sedate suitability as a husband. But she had left them alone for a good fifteen minutes and all they had talked about was the estate. It would seem he had no interest in marryng her at all.

Chapter 12

At that moment Ralph burst into the room. "The Fish said Eden is here!"

"Don't call Mrs. Finney the Fish," Mariette said automatically. "You know she dislikes it."

Ralph paid her not the least heed. Spotting Lord Malcolm, he bowed and blurted out, "It was jolly handsome of you to send my ring back, my lord. I can pay what I owe you now. I got stuck in Plymouth with the snow and I've had a run of luck." He pulled a roll of banknotes from the pocket of his riding coat.

"I sent it because your cousin was ill and fretting about it," said Lord Malcolm coldly. "I have brought her home and I am happy to inform you that she is quite recovered."

Though he had the grace to look a trifle conscious, Ralph said airily, "Oh, Mariette's healthy as a horse. I didn't worry about her. All the same, coz, it's good to have you back. You look capital. What have you done to your hair?"

"Lady Lilian's abigail cut it for me," she said, putting up a self-conscious hand to touch the locks on her forehead. "She just shortened a bit at the front and sides and showed me how to curl it."

"Makes you look quite pretty." Losing interest in Mariette's health and appearance, he turned back to Lord Malcolm. "If I recall correctly, my lord, I pledged my signet for fifty pounds."

Mariette gasped. She had not realized he was playing so

deep—he had pledged the ring to Lord Wareham for ten guineas. Remembering her blithe offer to redeem it from Lord Malcolm, she could only be glad he had not accepted.

"Fifty guineas was the sum, I believe," his lordship drawled.

"Oh yes, guineas," said Ralph, discomfited. "I've only the flimsies on me. Mariette, lend me two pounds ten."

"Certainly not," Lord Malcolm snapped. "I don't take blunt from females. You may continue to owe me the shillings."

As Ralph sulkily counted out the notes, Mariette was relieved to see that Uncle George had at some point drifted out of the room. He had eaten the whole of his small slice of cake. She would soon put the lost weight back on him.

"Will you take tea and some cake, Ralph?" she asked.

Glancing from the bottles on the table to Lord Malcolm's teacup, he accepted, and even brought his lordship's cup to be refilled. As he took his plate of cake, he looked round again in sudden dismay. "Where's Ragamuffin? Oh, Mariette, he wasn't shot, was he?"

She reassured him, saving for later the tale of how the dog's presence had been responsible for *her* being shot. She did not want Ralph and Lord Malcolm discussing her career as a highwayman, whether they agreed on the subject or, more likely, violently disagreed.

"Ragamuffin doesn't understand about guns," Ralph explained to Lord Malcolm. "I bought him for Mariette when he was a pup, in Plymouth from a sailor, so I never tried to train him though I believe he's some sort of setter. That reminds me, Mariette, I thought I'd better get your next birthday gift while the dibs are in tune. Do you want it now or will you wait till your birthday?"

"That's not for six months!" By then her present might well have been sold to fill his emptied pockets. "I should like it now."

"I'll go and get it." He dashed out, his slice of cake in his hand.

"You see," she said to Lord Malcolm, "he is not the utterly selfish scapegrace you supposed."

"I'm glad he spares you an occasional thought," he said dryly, then at once looked as if he regretted his words. "No, I don't mean that. He is obviously fond of you."

"He is young and heedless. I expect you were once."

"Thank you, ma'am, I do not yet consider myself in my dotage!"

"No?" she teased. "No, but you are a man and Ralph is still a boy. Were you never careless and frivolous?"

He winced. "You cannot expect me to damn myself from my own mouth! I will admit my family has been known to describe me as a fribble and even a sad rattle."

"There you are. And all that is left of it is a taste for fancy waistcoats. Ralph will grow out of his careless ways."

"I daresay."

His tone was unconvinced but she had no time to persuade him for Ralph returned. He handed her a small package wrapped in layer upon layer of tissue paper.

"I hope you will like it," he said anxiously as she unwrapped, smoothed, and folded each sheet for future use.

In the middle was a gold chain with a pendant in the form of a Tudor rose, enamelled in red and white. "Oh, Ralph, it's perfect," she cried, and burst into tears.

"Devil take it, Mariette, there's no need to cry. I didn't mean to distress her," he justified himself to Lord Malcolm.

"I don't imagine you have," his lordship said uneasily. "Females are given to odd crotchets. There wouldn't be a vinaigrette about, would there?"

"I don't need smelling salts." Mariette sniffed and wiped her eyes. "I'm sorry to make such a cake of myself. And I am *not* given to odd crotchets." Though she could not explain her unexpected outburst to herself let alone to them.

"She has been ill," the gentlemen reminded each other with relief. "She's tired."

"I had best be on my way," said Lord Malcolm, standing

up. "No, don't move, Miss Bertrand. Put your feet up. Sir Ralph will show me out."

However, Mariette felt perfectly well and insisted on accompanying him to the front door while Ralph went to tell Benson Lord Malcolm was ready to leave.

In the hall they found Uncle George frowning over his pig, which somehow now looked more like a badger than it had when that had been his aim. He shook Lord Malcolm's hand heartily, peering at his face, and said, "How d'ye do, sir? My girl seems to have made a lot of new friends while she was away. Delighted to make your acquaintance."

Mariette gently explained that he had already met Lord Malcolm, who was come to wish him goodbye. Before she finished, his attention had returned to his pig—badger?—so they gave up and moved on. A cry followed them: "Goodbye, goodbye, do call again."

"Perhaps when I have called often enough Mr. Barwith will begin to recognize me," said Lord Malcolm, smiling. "What a pity his poor sight cannot be corrected by spectacles."

Mariette clutched his arm. "Spectacles? Good heavens, I never thought!"

"You mean he has not tried them?"

"Not since I have lived here, and his eyes have grown worse all the time."

Lord Malcolm shook his head. "Having met the gentleman, I should not be surprised if the notion never crossed his mind."

"Where can I buy them?" Mariette asked eagerly as they reached the front step.

"There is bound to be a spectacle-maker in a city the size of Plymouth. Each pair must be made for the specific individual, I believe."

"Oh, I shall get Uncle George to Plymouth if it's the last thing I do. How can I ever thank you? I am so much obliged to . . ."

"No more thanks," he said firmly. "You expressed your sense of obligation in every conceivable way before we left

Corycombe. You will take care of yourself now Lilian and Emily are not at hand to fuss over you, will you not? Ah, here's Benson with the curricle, and Ragamuffin to bid me farewell."

A moment later Mariette was waving to him as he drove off. The damp dog bouncing ahead, she hurried into the house to discuss spring cleaning with Mrs. Finney.

"When I have called often enough . . . ," he had said. He might even come tomorrow. It sounded as if he *wanted* Uncle George to learn to recognize him—before he asked for her hand? The possibility no longer seemed such a castle in Spain.

Threading her way between the statues, Mariette danced.

As Malcolm turned the bays into the stable yard, Jessup came out to take their heads. He looked tired and travel-worn.

Malcolm sprang down from the curricle. Despite a drive of four-and-twenty miles through fetlock-deep mud liberally provided with potholes, he was full of energy. He liked Mariette's absentminded uncle, and rather thought the old man had taken a liking to him, even if he had not recognized him ten minutes later.

Ralph Riddlesworth was more fool than villain, he suspected. He'd do what he could to save the sapskull's skin. Now here was Jessup come back with instructions from the Admiralty. With any luck he'd get the spy business cleared up in a few days.

Then he'd be free to propose to Mariette.

"Just got back half an hour ago, m'lord," Jessup said in answer to his query. "Bloody hell, what a journey! Snow, ice, fog, the lot. I brung you a letter, gave it to Mr. Padgett."

Malcolm tipped him and told him to leave the horses to the Corycombe grooms and get some rest. "I'll be sending you down to Devonport in the morning, I expect."

"I c'n go this evening if your lordship wants," said the groom valiantly, swaying with fatigue.

"No, the morning will do. You're asleep on your feet, man."

Malcolm went into the house, took the stairs two at a time, and rang for his valet. The man knew better than to leave Admiralty papers lying about in his chamber.

Padgett had the letter stowed away in his inside breast pocket. As he extracted it, he asked, "Miss Bertrand arrived safe at home, my lord?"

"Yes, the journey did not appear to discommode her. Here." He handed over a pound note in exchange for the letter. "She asked me to distribute this among the servants. You'll know better than I, or you can find out, how a lady's largesse ought to be distributed. Oh, and there is this token for Miss Pennick. You may tell her Miss Bertrand did not part from it without regret."

"Certainly, my lord. An amiable lady, Miss Bertrand."

Malcolm smiled. "A most amiable lady, Padgett."

He turned to the letter. The blob of sealing wax was discreetly stamped with an intricate design difficult to reproduce rather than the Admiralty's easily recognized mark. He slit it and unfolded the paper. There at the bottom was the official seal, and the signature of a certain gentleman.

The body of the letter was short. It said, "Return to Town immediately for consultations."

"Confound it!" said Malcolm. "Hell and damnation! Oh bloody hell!"

"Indeed, my lord?" said Padgett.

"Indeed! I'm called back to London, urgently. You had best start packing."

"Everything, my lord?"

Malcolm stopped reacting and started thinking. He'd be coming back to Corycombe soon whether he remained in charge of the sphinx seal mission or not. The sooner he departed and the faster he travelled, the sooner he could return.

"I'll leave at once, on Incognita, so pack just enough linen for the journey. In the morning, when Jessup has recovered, he can take a message to Captain Aldrich, then you and he can come on in the curricle."

"Very good, my lord."

"I must go and tell my sister." Malcolm groaned. He could not explain why he was dashing off. What on earth was Lilian going to think?

And Mariette?

Lilian was in her private room, thank heaven, so he did not have to stumble through his story in the presence of Emily and Miss Thorne. "I have to go up to Town," he said lamely. "Urgent business."

Taking off her spectacles, she raised her eyebrows. "Urgent business? Oh, I suppose some dunning tailor is threatening to set the bailiffs on you and you have to rush off to rescue your worldly possessions."

"Not at all," he said, but he was not sorry to leave her with the impression that his business might be something of the sort. He explained that he was leaving at once, his servants following on the morrow. "I shall give you a note for Mariette," he added.

"Has her uncle given his permission for a correspondence?"

"No. Dash it, I had no notion I should need to write to her, and anyway the old man scarcely knows who I am."

"Then it would be most improper in me to countenance clandestine letters, still more so to be your messenger."

"At least you will tell her I shall be gone for a few days?" Malcolm pleaded. "I have every intention of returning to Corycombe in short order, if you will have me."

"You know you are always welcome, my dear. However, I am afraid it would be most unwise to allow Mariette to expect your rapid return. When you are in Town, among a hundred beautiful and sophisticated ladies, you may find yourself looking back on your rustic love with dismay and disbelief."

"Balderdash! She is the only one for me."

"Nonetheless, I will not do more than make your excuses

to her. I am grown fond of Mariette, Malcolm, and I don't want to see her hurt."

Malcolm was silent. He had no hope of avoiding hurting his beloved when he unmasked her traitorous cousin. If she could not forgive him for an unexplained departure, she would never forgive him for that.

Half an hour later, he cantered down the lane along Cory Brook. The drumming of Incognita's hooves beat a repetitive refrain in his head:

"I *could* not *love* thee, *dear,* so *much*

"Loved *I* not *hon*our *more.''*

Was it true?

"Who was your fine beau, my dear?" asked Uncle George, chipping away at the sandstone. "Charming fellow."

Smiling, Mariette demurred. "I'm glad you liked him, but he is not my beau. Lord Malcolm Eden is Lady Lilian's brother. He was staying at Corycombe while I was there and he was kind enough to bring me home in his carriage. Uncle George, have you ever tried wearing spectacles?"

"Spectacles?" The chipping stopped and he turned to stare at her. "Why, bless my soul, no! What a simply splendid notion. I cannot imagine why I didn't think of it years since."

"It was Lord Malcolm's suggestion. He says there must be a spectacle-maker in Plymouth. Will you go and consult him? You don't suppose they would be too expensive, do you?"

"No, no, surely not. Spectacles! Good heavens!"

"Because Mrs. Finney would like to hire two or three village women to help with the spring cleaning?"

"Is spring here already?" he said in surprise, glancing up at the sunny windows.

"Nearly."

"Then we must certainly have spring cleaners."

"The thing is, Uncle George, Lady Lilian has been teaching me to conduct myself as a lady, and I should like to go on riding over for lessons—it's such a long way by road—but I cannot ride astride to Corycombe because then she would think I had ignored her advice, so . . ."

As she ran out of breath, her uncle shook his head in dismay. "A young lady ride astride? That will never do, Mariette!"

"Well, I always have, because Jim Groom disapproves of sidesaddles."

"My sister was badly hurt in a riding accident," said Uncle George sadly. "Not Ralph's mother, another sister, who loved to gallop on the moor. She died young."

Mariette patted his hand. "I shall ride astride when I gallop up on the high moor," she promised, "but for riding to Corycombe I should like to purchase a sidesaddle. Only, of course, your spectacles are much more important, and I don't know what a sidesaddle costs."

Uncle George waved away her doubts with his chisel. "Don't worry your pretty head about that," he said. "You must certainly have a sidesaddle. Just have them send the bill to me."

"And Jenny Pennick, Lady Lilian's abigail, says I shall need a proper riding habit, so as not to expose my legs . . . limbs. But I daresay I can add a train to one of my dresses."

"Nonsense, buy yourself a habit, my dear, and a new gown to dazzle your beau while you're about it. You're a good girl, Mariette. Spectacles! Well I never! Perhaps I shall be able to see where I'm going wrong." He turned back to contemplate his pig/badger with a hopeful air.

Mariette went out to the stables to tell Jim she was going to get a sidesaddle, and to ask his advice if she could persuade him to give it. Once convinced nothing he said would sway her, the old man unwillingly admitted there was an old sidesaddle hidden away in the hayloft.

"I didn't want you a-using of it, Miss Mariette," he said with a heavy sigh, "but being as you're set on it, I 'spect it'll furbish up nicely."

That evening Mariette searched out a piece of stout worsted material left over from making a pelisse. She cut and sewed it into a sort of train which could be pinned to the skirt of the pelisse to make a temporary riding habit. While she worked, Ralph told her about his enforced stay in Plymouth.

"And then I found a gambling hell," he said, tossing a gleaming gold sovereign in the air and catching it.

"What is that?" she asked.

"I daresay you'd call it a gambling parlour or a gaming house now you've turned ladylike. It's just a place devoted to cards and dice, rather than an inn which is really for travellers and eating and drinking and such."

"Oh, Ralph, nothing but gambling?"

"It's all right, there's no EO or roulette like they have in London, though I must say I wouldn't half mind having a go at them. Anyway, you've no reason to fuss. I told you, I've been winning. The place has brought me luck."

She had long since learned the futility of arguing with her cousin about his views on luck, but she could not repress a grimace.

"Stuck the needle in your finger?" Ralph enquired with a carefree laugh. "Oh, stop fretting, Mariette. I shan't wager my signet again, I swear it. I'll tell you what, you take it and keep it safe for me." He removed the ring from his finger and tucked it away in a corner of her work-box. "There. Satisfied?"

Mariette endeavoured to stop fretting and be satisfied.

She finished her sewing in the morning. Though she was moderately pleased with the result and Jim had polished the old sidesaddle to a glossy shine, she stayed close to the manor all day. In fact she only left the house to practise riding sidesaddle in the paddock behind the stables. Lord Malcolm might come.

When he failed to brave the gentle mizzle, she was disappointed but not surprised. It had been too much to hope for. If he cared for her at all, he was by no means ready to declare himself, and to come so soon would appear most particular.

By the second day, she was so impatient to see him she decided not to wait again but to ride over to Corycombe.

She owed Lilian a courtesy call to thank her, so there was no reason for anyone to guess Lord Malcolm was the one she most wanted to see. Should she arrive at Corycombe to find he had left for Bell-Tor Manor, she could easily think up an excuse to stay until he returned.

Jim insisted on going with her. She was glad of his company, not because of the sidesaddle, on which she already felt quite at ease, but because a lady was not supposed to ride alone. A lady was not supposed to chat with her groom as they rode, either, but there was no one by to hear—not even Ragamuffin who vanished on the trail of a rabbit soon after they set out.

It was a cool, clear day, the air calm even on the crest of Wicken's Down. The grey-green gorse thickets were already dotted with yellow bloom that would soon gild the hillsides. Every step Sparrow took reminded Mariette of the last time she rode this way.

She could not regret her highwayman adventure. Lord Malcolm might have chosen to drag her before a magistrate, in which case she'd now be sitting in a cell awaiting the Assizes, but he hadn't. If she had tamely gone to ask him to let her redeem the ring, she would in all likelihood never have seen him again. Even if he did not love her, even if he never asked her to be his wife, she could hope to see him now and then when he visited Lilian, and she had memories to sustain her.

As they reached the shoulder on the west side of the hill, Mariette drew rein and gazed down at the red-brick house: memories of his kindness, of his teasing, his readiness to discuss history with her instead of condemning her as a bluestocking. Her gaze moved on to the glittering glass of the orangery: memories of his kiss. If Ragamuffin had not barked. . . .

She sighed and rode on.

The Corycombe stable yard was crowded. Mariette and Jim stopped under the arched entrance at the sight of a car-

riage and four, a smart dogcart and pair, and a humble gig
with a single bony nag. Benson came round the gig to greet
them.

"Who is here?" Mariette asked him.

"Lord Wareham, miss." He hooked his thumb at the
dogcart. Then the carriage and gig: "Squire Bolger and family, the vicar and his missus. The Captain's here, too," he
added with considerably more approval in his tone, handing
her down from Sparrow's back.

"You'll take care of Jim, won't you, Benson?" She was
not sure whether it was correct to ask but she wanted to be
sure poor old Jim did not get lost in the crowd of smart
grooms and coachmen.

"Aye, miss, to be sure. There's a bumper of ale for Mr.
Anstey in the servant's hall."

"Thank you." Mariette was so used to thinking of him as
Jim Groom, to distinguish him from Jim Gardener, that the
name Anstey took her by surprise. She smiled at the old
man. "Keep an eye out for Ragamuffin. I expect he will turn
up sooner or later. I shall see you later, Mr. Anstey."

He shook his head at her. "Jim'll do, like always, miss."

Entering the house by the back way, she recalled too late
that she ought to have dismounted at the front door and let
Jim take Sparrow round to the stables. She'd never be a perfect lady like Lilian, automatically doing the right thing.
Did Lilian really wish her to visit? Was her invitation just
politeness? Would she be dismayed when Mariette walked
in to join her genteel callers?

She was glad she had not gone in through the front door.
Warned of the crowd, at least she could remove her temporary train before anyone saw the makeshift creation.

In the back passage, she met a housemaid and asked for
Jenny Pennick. The abigail was delighted to see her, and
warm in her gratitude for the little ivory rose brooch. Train
unpinned and hair tidied in Lilian's dressing room, Mariette
smiled as she glided down the stairs.

Blount awaited her at the bottom. Gravely bowing, he enquired after her health as he escorted her across the hall. His

impassive face softened in a pleased look when she said she had never felt better. She grew more confident of her welcome at Corycombe.

The butler opened the drawing room door. "Miss Bertrand," he announced.

"Mariette!" Emily deserted Miss Bolger and sped to hug her friend. "I have missed you so!"

"It is only two days since I left, Emmie." Over Emily's head, Mariette scanned the room for Lord Malcolm.

Though she had never seen so many people in Lilian's drawing room, there was space for plenty more. If he had been present she could not have missed him. Perhaps he had fled on the arrival of the vicar and his wife, or the Bolgers. Of none of them was he fond, still less of Lord Wareham but he'd never turn tail and leave his sister at the baron's mercy—unless he considered Captain Aldrich sufficient protection. The two gentlemen sat on either side of Lilian. Though Mariette's entrance forced them to rise, it did not hinder for more than a moment their glaring daggers at each other.

Was Lord Malcolm even now at Bell-Tor Manor? She wondered how soon it would be proper to enquire after him.

As she curtsied to the company, Lilian rose and came to greet her. "Will you stay to luncheon?" she asked in a low voice. "I hope to rid myself of all . . . most of the rest before then."

"Thank you, I should like to." She didn't even need to think up an excuse to stay!

Lilian returned to her guests, seating herself between the captain and Lady Bolger. Emily drew Mariette to a sofa at a little distance from the rest and chattered away about how Miss Thorne had taken to her bed with the sniffles. Above the girl's voice, Mariette heard Lady Bolger's.

"I daresay we shall see Lord Malcolm in Town," said the squire's wife hopefully. "We are going up at the end of the month to order my daughter's gowns to be made. Can you recommend a good modiste, Lady Lilian?"

"Wasting good money on fripperies and frivolities," snorted Sir Nesbit.

"Such is London life," put in Lord Wareham with a sneer. "Lord Malcolm did not long honour us with his presence in our rustic backwater. No doubt he was eager to return to the dissipations of the Fashionable World, and to visit his tailor."

A cold hand clutched Mariette's heart, robbing her of breath. "Is your uncle gone?" she asked in a choked whisper.

"Yes, he left as soon as he returned from taking you home," said Emily. "He rode instead of driving, so he must have been in a great hurry to return to the Fashionable World. I hope he tears himself away and comes to stay again soon, do not you?"

"Yes," she said, but she was not sure if it was true.

He had departed without warning, without a word. He could at least have told her he was going! She had feared to mistake friendship for fondness, yet now it seemed he did not even consider her a friend.

Chapter 13

Pride came to Mariette's rescue. Concealing her hurt from Emily, she suggested that they both go and talk to Miss Bolger, who sat alone now looking a trifle disconsolate.

Emily wrinkled her nose but assented. Though Miss Bolger seemed to have got over her positive alarm at the sight of Mariette, she was a tongue-tied young lady. No doubt she rarely had a chance to squeeze a word in edgewise at home, to judge by the way her mother was rattling on to Lilian and her father was holding forth to Lord Wareham and Captain Aldrich.

In her company, Emily at once became prim and bashful. Mariette struggled to keep up an innocuous exchange on the recent storm, but she was not sorry when Mr. Bolger joined the young ladies.

"I hear Riddlesworth won a mint t'other day," he said to Mariette. "At that club near Peverell, wasn't it? Dashed if I can see how he managed to become a member!"

"A member?" she asked uncertainly.

"Only members can play there, and you have to be invited to join. Wouldn't have thought Riddlesworth sported enough blunt to be admitted, the lucky dog. They play deep. M'father'd throw a fit if I went within a mile of the place," he added with a resentful scowl at Sir Nesbit's oblivious back.

Mariette would have liked to know more, but Emily and

Miss Bolger were all agog and she was sure a gambling hell was no fit subject for their young ears. "Your father is Master of Fox Hounds, is he not?" she said. "Do you enjoy hunting?"

Mr. Bolger brightened. For several minutes he held forth, very much like Sir Nesbit, on raspers, oxers, bullfinches, doubles, and in-and-outs he had cleared on his galloper. Mariette understood not one word in three and Emily's blank face suggested she was no wiser.

The Bolgers departed, followed shortly by the vicar and his wife. Lord Wareham stood up, but only to move to the fireplace where he leaned against the mantel, looking down at Lilian and Captain Aldrich.

"I suppose you don't hunt, Captain," he said with a sneer, his gaze on the empty sleeve.

"We sailors are not noted for our horsemanship," the captain responded calmly.

"I marvel that *you* are able to ride at all."

"You find you need two hands to control a horse, do you, my lord?"

Mariette grabbed Emily's hands as she raised them to applaud.

Lilian looked most uncomfortable. Captain Aldrich leaned towards her and said something in a low voice. She smiled and nodded. He stood up, bowed over her hand, then came over to Mariette and Emily.

"I am invited to lunch," he said softly, "as I gather you are, too, Miss Bertrand."

"Yes, sir."

"Wareham will never leave as long as I'm here, so I'll retreat to the morning room until he's gone. It goes against the grain to let him think he has bested me, but I will not have Lady Lilian distressed."

"We shall help her get rid of him!" Emily whispered with glee.

Grinning, he patted her cheek in a decidedly fatherly way. "Good girl! I rely upon you."

As he strode from the room, Lilian in turn rose to her feet.

"Emily," she said, "it is time for you to practise your music. I daresay Mariette will be good enough to turn the pages for you. Lord Wareham, may I beg you to excuse me? My cousin is ill abed and I must go and see that she wants for nothing."

Common courtesy allowed the baron no choice but to take his leave—he did, after all, claim to be a gentleman. The moment the door closed behind him and her mother, Emily clapped her hands.

"Famous! I should have known Mama would need no help." She started towards the door. "Let's go and release Captain Aldrich from durance vile."

"Wait, Emmie, until we can be sure Lord Wareham does not linger in the hall. In fact, you had best play upon the pianoforte for a few minutes at least."

"Oh yes, loudly. It would be simply dreadful if he guessed he has been tricked. He is horrid enough without making him angry."

"I thought you wanted to flirt with him?"

Emily shuddered. "Not anymore. Uncle Malcolm was right, flirting with someone one dislikes would be horrid."

But flirting with someone one loved must be delightful, Mariette thought, especially if he loved one, too. She was not likely ever to have a chance to find out. Sighing, she helped Emily open the pianoforte.

The second time Mariette rode over to Corycombe, she wore her new riding habit. It was a splendid garment, far finer than she would have purchased had Uncle George not gone with her to Plymouth. Emerging from the spectacle-maker's shop with a pair of steel-rimmed glasses perched on his nose, he had joined her at the draper's. The drab cloth she was examining had not met with his approval.

She did not dare guess what he had paid the dressmaker to make up the habit in half a day.

So she was decked out in burgundy velvet trimmed with black braid, and on her head a new hat, black with burgundy ribbons—"Fine as fi'pence," as Jim said, and no Lord Malcolm to see her.

As she and Jim rode up to the front door, around the corner from the stables came Lord Wareham's dogcart. Driven at a trot by a tall, skinny groom with surly, lantern-jawed face, it pulled up nose to nose with Sparrow in a flurry of gravel. Firmly suppressing the gelding's attempt to rear, Mariette called to Ragamuffin who was barking his head off at the unmannerly vehicle.

Lord Wareham ran down the steps. "Keep your dog away from my cattle," he said curtly, "if you know what's good for him."

Emboldened by her dashing habit, Mariette gave him a haughty stare without deigning to answer. He responded with his usual sneer. Jumping into the dogcart, he slashed at Ragamuffin with his whip, missing as the dog dodged, then whipped up his pair and swerved around the two riders in another flurry of gravel.

Jim Groom stared after him. "Blacker nor thunder over the moor," he said. "I'd give a groat to know what's put yon fine gentleman in a passion."

"I hate to think," said Mariette, sliding down onto the mounting block and giving him Sparrow's reins. Her train over her arm, she hurried up the steps.

The door opened as she reached it. "Come in, miss, come in," the footman invited her urgently. "Her ladyship'll be that glad to see you."

"What has happened, Charles?"

"I'm sure I don't know, miss, but I was told to make sure his lordship went off right and proper, and Mr. Blount's pouring Madeira for her ladyship, who don't never touch a drop. In the morning room, miss."

Decorous pace forgotten, Mariette sped to the morning room. The butler came out as she arrived. His shaken expression lightened at the sight of her. He stood aside and held the door for her.

Miss Thorne's censorious voice came from the room

beyond. "Really, Lilian, that was no way to treat a gentleman."

"Gentleman!" Lilian exclaimed, her tone near the edge of hysteria.

"You were splendid, Mama," said Emily as Mariette went in. On her knees beside the sofa where Lilian reclined, she looked round and scrambled to her feet. "Mariette, I am so glad you are come! Lord Wareham has been most shockingly rude to poor Mama."

"His language was a trifle intemperate," Miss Thorne allowed, "but you have sorely tried his patience, Lilian. Why, from your conduct towards them, no one would guess Lord Wareham to be a peer and Captain Aldrich to be a penniless cripple."

"Enough!" said Lilian sharply. "I believe you are not quite recovered from your indisposition, Cousin Tabitha. Perhaps you ought to lie down upon your bed for a while."

"Humph! I can see where I am not wanted." With a sniff as she passed Mariette, Miss Thorne marched out, every rigid inch vibrating with affronted dignity.

Emily sped to shut the door behind her. Mariette went to Lilian and without a word pressed her hands. Despite her firmness to Miss Thorne, they quivered pitiably.

Noticing the disregarded glass of Madeira wine on the table at the end of the sofa, Mariette picked it up. "Here, do take a drink of this, my dear," she said soothingly. "Blount seems to think it will fortify you, and I daresay he knows best."

Lilian ventured a shaky smile. "I suspect butlers always know best," she said, and sipped the wine. "You must be wondering what on earth happened."

Mariette managed to restrain her burning curiosity. "Do you want to tell me? I saw Lord Wareham drive off in a prodigious miff."

"He accused me of playing coy with him and of . . . of coquetting with Captain Aldrich to make him jealous."

"No!" Mariette burst into peals of laughter. "I am sorry," she gasped, seeing Lilian's and Emily's bewildered faces, "but how can he have so mistaken you? Now, if you had coquetted with *him* to make the captain jealous it might be understandable, but you have no need, have you?"

A delicate colour suffused Lilian's face and she smiled. "Do you think not?"

"I am sure not."

"If only he does not let false modesty deter him," Lilian said wistfully. "How I wish he had been here this morning! He is a match for Lord Wareham."

"You were splendid, Mama," Emily insisted. "She said only a coward insults helpless females, Mariette, and then she rang the bell and told him he was no longer welcome at Corycombe, and Blount came to show him out."

"He went without demur, but I confess I was quite frightened for a moment. I have never seen him in a passion before. In fact, I always thought him a very cool and collected man. I wish Malcolm had not gone away!"

"Are you sure he did not say in his letter when he will come to stay again, Mama? I shall write and tell him we need him."

"No, don't do that, Emmie dear. Your uncle has his own life to lead. I received a letter yesterday, Mariette. Malcolm desires to be remembered to you." She hesitated. "He asks me to convey his apologies for leaving without a word of farewell. He was called urgently away and I would not let him write to you, so you may hold me to blame. Perhaps I have not told you before that a private correspondence between a young man and an unrelated young woman is not at all *comme il faut.*"

Mariette's hurt was assuaged, though her heartache remained. At least he had not forgotten her but he was still far away, with no suggestion of returning soon to Corycombe.

She missed him! She wanted to tell him about Uncle George's new spectacles and his dismay at his own unrealized shabbiness; how he had gone to a tailor, only to recoil in horror on being offered trousers instead of breeches. With Lord Malcolm, unmentionables were perfectly mention-able—she did not have to try to impress him with her lady-like manners.

But she would have liked a chance to impress him with her new habit.

At that moment both Lilian and Emily noticed her finery. As compliments flew, Boult and Charles came in with a tea-tray, Mrs. Wittering and Cook having agreed that a nice cup of tea would set her ladyship up much quicker than any amount of wine.

Lilian's composure restored, the rest of Mariette's visit passed pleasantly, uninterrupted by any further callers. She had numerous questions on etiquette for Lilian, questions which had not crossed her mind while immersed in the busy-ness of her stay at Corycombe. For the most part, learning kept her distracted from the fact that every little thing her gaze alighted on reminded her of Lord Malcolm. She simply had the wrong temperament to let blighted love send her into a decline like the heroine of many a novel, she decided, half regretfully.

For the next two days, a gale accompanied by torrential rain kept her at home. Ralph was irritable. He had already lost most of his winnings and he was anxious to be in Plymouth recovering his fortunes, but the weather was bad enough to coop him up. Mariette did her best to entertain him with endless games of backgammon, draughts, and cribbage.

Nonetheless she found time to make considerable progress on the new dresses she was sewing. Uncle George had insisted on her purchasing several lengths of pretty materials, though she had held firm against the expense of a seamstress for anything but the habit.

On the third day the wind calmed and the rain ceased. In spite of heavy clouds hanging over Bell Tor, Mariette and Jim set out for Corycombe.

In the drive, they caught up with a hired chaise. Mariette was astonished and alarmed to see Captain Aldrich within, fearing some injury or illness had prevented his riding from Devonport. However, when he stepped down at the front door he looked perfectly well, though a trifle flushed when he turned to smile at Mariette.

"I daresay, Miss Bertrand, you wonder at my hiring a carriage," he said self-consciously, offering his hand to help her down.

"Yes, sir," she agreed, though she had guessed as soon as she saw him, "but I feel sure Lilian would say that is a personal question I ought not to pose."

Instead of his usual riding clothes, he wore dress uniform: white breeches, stockings, and waistcoat, blue coat with gold braid and epaulets, cocked hat, and his dress sword at his side. "I wanted to arrive in parade order," he confided as they ascended the steps.

"You look very smart, Captain."

He failed to return the compliment, but Mariette willingly forgave him. Under the circumstances he could not be expected to notice her elegant habit—she was sure he intended to try his luck with his beloved.

She would not for the world embarrass him by wishing him luck. Besides, he did not need it.

He rapped twice with the gleaming brass lion's-head doorknocker. They heard raised voices, then running footsteps. Charles flung open the door.

"Thanks be you're come, sir!" he cried. "Mr. Blount, 'tis the captain!"

"Thank heaven, thank heaven!" quavered the aged butler, hurrying forward as Captain Aldrich strode into the hall, Mariette at his heels.

"What's to do?" he demanded.

Emily reached him first and seized his arm. "Sir, sir, you will help Mama, will you not? Miss Thorne says they are not to be disturbed and Blount doesn't know what to do and Charles dare not interfere without an order and Miss Thorne says I am only a child and not fit to give orders against . . ."

"Hush, Emmie." Mariette put her arm about the weeping girl. "Hush, my dear, and let Blount explain to the captain."

"Captain Aldrich has nothing to say in the matter!" Miss

Thorne stood in the middle of the hall, arms akimbo, her sharp face pale with anger. "Blount, I forbid you to discuss her ladyship's affairs with a stranger."

The butler threw her a look of deep dislike. "It's this way, sir. Lord Wareham must have come in the back way for the first we knew of it was Charles here heard him in my lady's private room. Shouting something dreadful he was, but it's true as madam says we've instructions not to go in there 'less her ladyship rings. . . ."

His last words were spoken to the captain's back as he headed for the passage to Lilian's room.

Miss Thorne called shrilly after him, "If you will meddle, I wash my hands of the whole business."

"Good!" said Emily, speeding after him.

"Emily, come back!" Mariette's cry was ignored. Recalling Lord Wareham's attack on Ragamuffin, she was horribly conscious of his propensity for violence—and of Captain Aldrich's infirmity. "Blount," she ordered, "fetch the grooms at once. Charles, come with me."

"At once, miss!" The butler scurried off.

"I'm right wi' you, miss."

Running, Mariette and the footman reached Lilian's room as Captain Aldrich, having paused for a moment to listen, threw open the door.

"Unhand her, villain!"

Just like all the best Gothic romances. Mariette felt a giggle rise in her throat though she had never felt less like laughing. She grabbed Emily.

Trapped in Lord Wareham's arms, Lilian beat on his chest with impotent fists. The captain's eruption into the room wiped the smug smirk from the baron's face but he did not let her go.

"Get out," he snarled, "or I'll see you cashiered. With the greatest pleasure."

Lilian turned her white face towards the door and ceased to fight. "Desmond!" Her voice cracked on his name.

With a sweeping gesture, he drew his sword. "Let her go," he repeated through his teeth.

Lord Wareham's hands dropped to his sides and Lilian stepped back to lean weakly against the wall. Mariette pulled Emily aside, speechless with fright, so that Charles could go to the captain's aid if necessary.

"It's easy to draw on an unarmed man," taunted Lord Wareham.

"It's easy to persecute a defenceless woman," Captain Aldrich retorted. "I'm ready to meet you any time, anywhere. Name your seconds, my lord."

"You cannot suppose I'd fight a duel with a one-armed nobody!"

The captain laughed. "So you need two hands to wield a sword, too, do you?"

His face livid with fury, the baron started forward. Captain Aldrich stepped aside and, bowing slightly, with his sword gestured him onward to the doorway. Charles slipped through and stood opposite the captain, his back to the open door as if seeing out any departing guest. His rigid pose was properly footmanly, his eyes fixed on the middle distance, but his large fists were clenched.

Lord Wareham hesitated.

From the front hall came a thunder of heavy boots in a hurry. Mariette looked back to see Benson, the head groom, and three stableboys galloping along the passage, followed at a creaky trot by Jim and Blount.

"Goodbye, my lord," said Captain Aldrich coolly. "I trust you will remember in future that Lady Lilian is *not* a defenceless woman."

"Rest assured I shall forget nothing, Captain," Lord Wareham hissed. "You have not heard the last of this!" He strode out.

The grim-faced stablehands opened a way for him then closed in behind and tramped after. Charles took his lordship's hat and gloves from the small table by the door, and murmured to Mariette, "Don't want to give him an excuse to come back. We'll see him off atween us, miss, never fear."

As he dashed off, Lilian ran to Captain Aldrich and flung herself on his chest, weeping. His sword clattered to the floor and he clasped her close in what she appeared to find an eminently satisfactory one-armed embrace. Mariette was debating whether she ought to play chaperon or allow the pair their privacy when Jenny hurried up.

"Well, bless me!" she gasped. "They said Lord Wareham . . ."

"It is all right, Jenny," Mariette assured her. "Her ladyship does not need you for the moment. Will you tell Blount to be prepared to produce a bottle of champagne?"

"That I will, miss," said the abigail, beaming. "This very minute!"

Emily had none of Mariette's qualms. She pulled Mariette into the room and shut the door. "In case Miss Thorne comes," she whispered. "Mama does not mind the captain holding her, does she? Not like Lord Wareham?"

"Not at all."

"I'm so glad." She heaved a satisfied sigh. "I shall like to have Captain Aldrich for a step-papa."

"Hush!"

In fact, oblivious of both company and decorum, the happy couple were fully occupied in exchanging vows and kisses in equal measure. Emily watched and listened, fascinated.

Mariette, embarrassed and envious, drew her away to the window. Thence they had the felicity of seeing Lord Wareham's dogcart race past as if pursued by forty devils, though his only pursuers were Benson and the stableboys. The four stopped at the corner of the house and continued the pursuit by means of jeers and catcalls, fortunately indistinct within the house, and rude gestures, all too visible.

Emily applauded.

"Oh!" Very pink, her cap awry, Lilian broke away from the captain's embrace, leaving him with a grin liable to split his weathered face in two.

Emily ran to her and hugged her. "I'm so happy for you, Mama."

"Truly, Emmie? You will not object to having a step-papa?"

"As long as it is Captain Aldrich. Did Lord Wareham want to marry you, too?"

"Yes, but only because he is deeply in debt. He found out somehow that though we live quietly I have a considerable fortune besides Corycombe. . . ."

Captain Aldrich's grin vanished and he groaned. "You do? Lilian, you don't think I . . . ?"

"Of course not!"

"But everyone else will believe . . ."

"Let them."

"I ought not . . ."

Lilian stamped her foot. "Desmond, if you think you can honourably withdraw an offer of marriage simply because I happen to be quite wealthy, I shall never forgive you."

"I don't dare!" He pulled her close. Over her head he winked at Emily and Mariette. "I can see I'm going to hitch myself to a shrew and live beneath the cat's paw."

"Shall you mind?" she asked saucily.

"Provided you don't decide to wear the breeches, not in the least." He bowed his head to kiss her. She put her arms around his neck and raised her face.

Mariette seized Emily's hand and dragged her from the room.

"Well!" said Emily as the door closed behind them. "I never thought to see Mama behave so."

"Nor I," Mariette agreed. What changes love had wrought in the once sedate, proper widow!

When they reached the front hall, they found lurking there all the indoor servants except the lowliest scullery maid. Blount stepped forward.

"Her ladyship, miss?" he enquired, his lined face anxious.

"Unless it is rung for sooner," said Mariette loudly, "you may serve champagne with luncheon."

Through the servants' respectfully hushed huzzas cut Miss Thorne's acid voice. "Champagne!" She stood in the drawing-room doorway like a witch in a fairytale. "Just who do you think you are, Miss Bertrand, to give orders in Lady Lilian's house?"

The servants vanished. Mariette, taken aback, was about to acknowledge with chagrin that she had no right whatsoever to issue orders to the butler. But Emily spoke first.

"It is a celebration, ma'am," she explained eagerly, "and it will be more fun if it is a surprise."

"A celebration!"

"Mama is engaged to be married to Captain Aldrich."

"To Captain Aldrich? Humph! And what has Lord Wareham to say to that?"

"Nothing," said Lilian quietly. Her arm linked with the captain's, she had come up unnoticed. "Pray wish me happy, Cousin Tabitha."

"I am sure I hope you will be happy," said Miss Thorne in a tone expressive of her expectations to the contrary. "But to dismiss a gentleman of the nobility in favour of . . ." She faltered to a halt before Lilian's steely gaze.

"You must be relieved not to have to stay to observe my wedded bliss. When I am married I shall no longer be obliged to have a companion so you may in good conscience go to keep house for your brother, as I know you have long wished. In fact, I should not dream of delaying you until the wedding. Benson shall leave today to bear Mr. Thorne news of your coming, and my carriage shall be at your disposal as soon as you are packed."

Miss Thorne's mouth dropped open and two fiery spots stained her sharp cheekbones. Then she drew herself up again and snapped, "I fear you will bitterly regret this start, Lilian. What your father the marquis will say I dread to think. I wash my hands of you." She stalked past them and up the stairs.

Lilian laughed softly and ruefully. "At last! Desmond, you will not turn tail if Papa is a trifle choleric to begin with? He will come around in the end."

"I daresay you can wind him about your little finger. I'll be sorry to vex the man who helped me to my present position, but you shall not be rid of me so easily."

She cupped his cheek with a loving hand, which he took and kissed. Restored to gaiety, she cried, "Did I hear the word champagne? Blount, we shall drink it now, in the drawing room. And a glass of port to everyone in the servants' hall to drink to the captain's health."

"And yours, my lady." Blount appeared from nowhere in the fashion of all good butlers. "Allow me, on behalf of myself and the entire staff, to wish your ladyship very happy."

"I am, Blount, I am! Champagne is not nearly celebration enough." Suddenly thoughtful, she led the way into the drawing room. "I know, I shall give a ball!"

Chapter 14

"A ball!" Mariette and Emily spoke at the same moment, in the same startled tone.

Captain Aldrich gazed fondly on his betrothed. "A ball?"

"A ball. I shall hire the best assembly room in Plymouth and invite the neighbours and your Navy friends, Desmond, and both our families. We shall need new gowns, girls."

"You mean I may go, Mama? I am not too young?"

"How could I celebrate my betrothal without my dear daughter?"

Emily ran to kiss her mother, and her new step-papa-to-be into the bargain.

"I cannot ask Uncle George for a ball gown," Mariette said wistfully. "He has given me so much lately. Will it serve if I sew a bit of lace and some ribbons onto one of the new dresses I'm making?"

"Oh, if you ladies are going to prattle of clothes, I'm off," said the captain.

Lilian reached for his hand. "Don't go, I need you. Mariette, my dear, you heard Captain Aldrich's dismay when he heard of my fortune. It is clearly my duty to ease his trouble by spending it, so I hope you will assist by accepting the gift of a gown."

The captain laughed. In some confusion, Mariette stammered, "Indeed, I cannot. . . ."

"But you absolutely must look your best for my ball. You

are the only one of my friends whose support I know I can rely upon."

"Malcolm is on our side," her betrothed assured her. "I'd not have had the nerve to offer without his approval."

"But Malcolm may not be able to come to the ball. Please, Mariette?"

"Oh, how can I resist when you make it sound as if I shall be doing you a favour? A ball! I can scarcely believe it." Even if Malcolm did not come, she resolved to enjoy what might very well be the only ball she would ever attend.

Surely he would tear himself from the joys of Town to celebrate his only sister's betrothal to his friend!

"Splendid," said Lilian. "Now let me see, when shall it be? There should be a full moon for safe travelling."

"Ten days," said the weatherwise captain.

"That is far too soon."

"If you wait another month, we shall be celebrating our wedding. You don't think I mean to wait, do you?"

They gazed into each other's eyes, and Mariette feared they were going to fall to kissing again. Fortunately Blount came in with the champagne. After everyone had toasted everyone else, Lilian returned to business.

"Ten days! Desmond, I shall have to leave you to find a suitable place. Besides the ball room, we shall need a supper room, ladies' withdrawing room, and several chambers for those who live at a distance. Mariette, can you go with us to Plymouth this afternoon? Most of my dresses are made in London but I have heard there is a modiste in Plymouth, a French emigrée, who is very capable. This evening, Emily, we must write invitations. Oh, how vexing of Cousin Tabitha to make me send her away just when I need her!"

At that they all laughed, though Mariette could not help feeling just a little sorry for the woman who had lost her place in so delightful a household through her own censorious spleen. Still, Miss Thorne did not find it delightful, so perhaps she would be happier with her brother.

*   *   *

The Maison Duhamel was very different from the dark little shop of the seamstress who had made Mariette's riding habit. Madame Duhamel's customers entered a large, airy, mirrored apartment draped with beautiful materials. Gilt chairs surrounded small tables whereon rested the latest fashion plates from London—and from Paris itself.

None of Madame's clients ventured to question the presence of the French plates. And if some of Madame's silks and laces had a French look to them, Madame was far too discreet to boast of the fact. England had been at war with France for close to two decades, but where ladies' modes were concerned, Paris still reigned supreme.

Smugglers brought cognac and claret across the Channel for the gentlemen; why not fashions for their wives and daughters?

Lady Lilian Farrar, her daughter, and her young friend were greeted with urbane complacency by Madame Duhamel herself. A dark, slender woman perhaps a year or two older than Lilian, she wore a black silk gown of the utmost plainness and the utmost elegance.

"Milady honours my humble establishment," she said in nearly accentless English, curtsying. "It will be a pleasure to dress three ladies so lovely."

Though, as she studied them, her professional gratification appeared to be quite sincere, Mariette thought she caught a gleam of malicious curiosity in her eyes. Perhaps the burgundy-red riding habit Mariette considered so smart aroused Madame's scornful interest. She must wonder why anyone so obviously tonnish as Lilian was visiting her shop with a dowdy provincial.

Lilian explained their needs. Madame went off to look for suitable materials while the ladies sat down to study the fashion plates. Emily was much taken with a violet satin gown ornately beruffled around the hem, the bodice embroidered with seed pearls.

"I think not, dearest," said her mother. "See, that is a French plate. I have heard that the Emperor likes his court to be elaborately dressed, but we shall stay with the simpler

English fashions—though, to be sure, even those came originally from France."

"But they are English now, like Mariette. No, I should not care to wear anything Napoleon likes when it was he who shot off my step-papa's arm."

Lilian smiled as she set aside the Parisian plates. "Very right. Besides, you are far too young for anything but white to be proper."

Emily pouted a little, but the gown finally chosen delighted her: a white dress of exquisite simplicity, falling straight to the ankles from a very high waist, with a tunic of silver Urlinger's net and a white shawl embroidered in silver. In her hair she would wear a wreath of white rosebuds.

"You will look like a fairy princess," Mariette assured her.

Madame advised Lilian to wear celestial blue, to match her eyes. Assenting, Lilian blushed. Mariette guessed her blue eyes had been the subject of more than one compliment from Captain Aldrich.

Turning to Mariette, Madame said, "White is *de rigueur* for young ladies, but mademoiselle is not just come from the schoolroom, I think? The colour of mademoiselle's habit is most becoming. For a ball, a more vivid red, perhaps?"

Crimson zephyr, soft and silky, Madame suggested. A tunic of white gauze, spangled with gold—embroidered with gold, milady preferred? But of course, milady had excellent taste. A tracery of gold embroidery on the tunic, nothing vulgarly ornate. White rosebuds in the hair, perhaps, to match Mademoiselle Farrar's? And a crimson cashmere shawl, for after all, it was February still.

"May I, Lilian?" Mariette asked with bated breath. "Ought I not to wear white?"

"No, you are old enough to wear colours, my dear, and I believe crimson will suit you very well."

Madame's assistants escorted the ladies up to small fitting rooms on the first floor. Stripped to her shabby chemise, Mariette stood raising and lowering her arms to order while the girl measured every inch of her.

She faced a window overlooking a small, walled court-yard with a wing of the house on one side. On a line strung across the court hung several dresses, airing or drying. Mariette was inspecting these with desultory interest when a door in the back wall opened. Around it appeared a man's hat which turned from side to side as if the wearer was peering cautiously around. Apparently all was safe, for he popped in, hastily shut the door behind him, and took off his hat to wipe his forehead.

Mariette at once recognized Lord Wareham's groom, tall and thin, his long, narrow face apprehensive. Clapping his hat back on his head, he scurried across the cobbles towards the house and out of her view.

Odd! For a moment she feared the baron had sent his man to make mischief for Lilian. However, he could not know her whereabouts since they had come to Plymouth on the spur of the moment. Maybe the groom had a sweetheart in the house, though Mariette failed to imagine any female taking up with such an unprepossessing character.

Measurements taken, the ladies descended to the waiting barouche to repair to the Duke of Cornwall Hotel, where Captain Aldrich had invited them to take tea. On the way, Mariette mentioned seeing Lord Wareham's groom, and his furtive behaviour.

"Perhaps he was there in connection with a debt," Lilian surmised. "I know Lord Wareham is deeply in debt, and I have heard Madame Duhamel keeps a gaming house, so what is more likely than that he owes her more than he can pay?"

Emily's eyes grew round. "A gaming house, Mama?"

"A place for gentlemen to gamble," her mother elucidated, frowning. "Not on the dressmaking premises, and it is a private club, quite respectable, I believe, but perhaps we ought not to patronize her."

"Just this once," Mariette pointed out, fearful for her glorious crimson gown, "because we have no time to go elsewhere."

She was relieved when Lilian agreed that it was too late to

seek out a different modiste. All the same, she could not help wondering whether Madame's club was where Ralph had been gambling recently. "Deep play," Mr. Bolger said. Ralph had won to begin with, but already his winnings were lost. Would they let him go on playing when all his ready cash was gone? Might he end up, like Lord Wareham, deep in debt to Madame?

Mariette remembered the fleeting gleam of malice in the Frenchwoman's eyes.

Reaching the Duke of Cornwall, they found the captain awaiting them, pleased with himself: the hotel's assembly room, the best in Plymouth, was available for the betrothal ball. They went to inspect it, and the other accommodations, and Lilian gaily pronounced herself satisfied.

As they returned through the passage, they came face to face with Ralph.

"Hallo, Mariette!" he said. "What on earth are you doing here?" Then he noticed who she was with. Flushing, he stood aside to let them pass.

"I'll speak to you later, Ralph." She was going to move on, but Lilian laid a hand on her arm.

"This gentleman is your cousin, is he not? Will you not present him?"

Grateful for her friendly gesture, Mariette performed the introductions. Lilian promptly invited Ralph to the ball. While he was stammering out a confused and flattered acceptance, Mariette happened to glance at Captain Aldrich.

The captain took a dim view of the invitation. In fact, the captain clearly viewed Ralph with extreme disfavour.

Ralph did not know Captain Aldrich, or so he had said when Mariette mentioned his name at home. Therefore Lord Malcolm must have told the captain about Ralph. What had he said to lead to such deep disapproval?

She had thought his opinion of Ralph less black after their meeting at the manor, but it must once have been black indeed to influence the easy-going captain to such an extent. Perhaps that was why he had left Devon so abruptly: seeing Mariette and Ralph together had forcibly reminded him of the connection, and his fondness . . . his friendship for Mariette had not survived the reminder.

The hollow in her heart swiftly filled with anger. What right had he to condemn her cousin? She could not really be in love with a man as quick to pass judgment as Miss Thorne!

So why was she so miserable?

She forced herself to smile as they parted from Ralph, forced herself to listen to Emily's chatter over the tea. Emmie, with great indignation, told Captain Aldrich about the Parisian fashion plates at Madame Duhamel's, the lace which her mama suspected came from Brussels or Valenciennes. The captain listened intently, though Mariette was not sure whether he was genuinely interested or was humouring his daughter-to-be.

At any rate, when she finished her peroration he did not pursue the subject but said genially, "Are you ladies going to tell me all about your gowns?"

"No." Lilian shook her head. "You would find it tedious, I make no doubt, and, more important, it would lessen their impact on the night."

He laughed and squeezed her hand, and they all went on to talk about supper arrangements for the ball.

The following morning Mariette went to Corycombe to help write invitations. The delivery of the local ones brought a stream of visitors, ostensibly to felicitate Lady Lilian on her betrothal, actually to appease curiosity about the unknown sailor she was to marry.

Lilian begged Mariette to come often to help her entertain the callers. As a result, Mariette made the acquaintance of every young gentleman for miles around, many of whom were flatteringly attentive. Her self-confidence in company steadily increased. She began to think she could scarcely help but enjoy the ball whether Malcolm attended or not.

Lord Radford, Lilian's eldest brother, who lived in Dorset, wrote to say he and his lady would not miss the occasion for the world. They would bring their son and a married daughter with her husband. An uncle and two cousins accepted the invitations. Lilian was not to be cast off by her family. Still, she was on tenterhooks until a letter came from the marchioness.

"Mama says Papa was excessively put out," she confided to Mariette, "but she has prevailed upon him to give us his blessing. They will come to the wedding, though not to the ball, which is just as well for Papa tends rather to overawe ordinary mortals."

Then a brief note arrived from Malcolm.

Emily gave Mariette the news. "Uncle Malcolm says he will attend if he has to ride day and night, but he may have to return to Town at once. The Season will be just beginning, you know, and I daresay he will have invitations to dozens of balls."

Mariette only cared about one ball. He would be there. She'd show him she was a lady worthy of his regard, and at the same time that she did not care a snap whether he stayed or left again the next day.

Now her only worry was whether he would ask her to dance—and how she was to bear it if he didn't.

To Malcolm, cooling his heels in London, time passed with painful slowness. After an initial consultation with his immediate superior, he attended a meeting with two of the Lords of the Admiralty. Nothing was decided as to the propriety of putting Admiral Gault under surveillance like any common suspected criminal.

The Rear-Admiral was brother to Lord Dulwich, a gentleman of high influence in the Government. No one was prepared to risk offending the earl.

Day after day, Malcolm's enquiries were met with excuses for delay.

The amusements of Town quickly palled. The ladies seemed jaded and oversophisticated; his club was full of lamentable bores; playing cards reminded him of Ralph Riddlesworth; dancing made him wish Mariette was his partner; a ride in Hyde Park failed to bear comparison with a gallop on Dartmoor.

The very air was black with coal-smoke. How had he survived city life for so long?

When he married Mariette, he'd bring her up to London for a month or two each spring if she wished. After all, he wanted to show her off to the Beau Monde. But they would live in the country—he was sure she'd choose to live near her uncle.

By then her confounded cousin would be hanged, transported, or fled to France. Bah. It was no use making plans. She'd never marry him after that, Malcolm thought gloomily.

Lilian's letter arrived, announcing her betrothal to Captain Aldrich and begging him to come to her ball. The ball, she said, was as much to introduce Mariette to local society and to the family as to celebrate. However, she had not told Mariette, in case Malcolm proved fickle. If so, at least the poor girl would have memories of a festive night, as well as an increased acquaintance among her neighbours.

Malcolm redoubled his efforts to obtain a decision from the Admiralty, without success. In the end, he told his superior he was going down to Devon for family reasons, whether he was permitted to set a watch on Admiral Gault or not.

The evening before he had to leave to reach Plymouth in time for the ball, he was told to act as he thought best. The responsibility was his, and if things went wrong, his would be the blame.

Speeding westward, he was furious. Not that he minded shouldering the blame, if it came to that. His father's influence in the Government outweighed Lord Dulwich's, and in any case he did not much care what the Government thought of him. He was furious because he could have spent all that time with Mariette, digging himself so deep into her heart that even Riddlesworth's arrest would not oust him.

A lame post-horse, a road blocked by an overturned stage coach, one mishap after another slowed his journey. He was too late to go to Corycombe before the ball. Arriving at the Duke of Cornwall at the same time as the first guests, he was directed up to a chamber where he washed and changed into his evening clothes. By the time Padgett pronounced him fit to appear in public, the strains of the first dance echoed up the stairs.

He stared at himself in the looking-glass. His new waistcoat was embroidered with Tudor roses, crimson and white. Would she like it? Would she even notice with half a hundred admiring swains seeking to stand up with her? Surely she would not promise all her dances before he even arrived!

He hurried down.

Lilian and Des led the first set, compensating in perfect harmony for the missing arm, without a false motion. Opposite them were Emily and her uncle Radford, stout and good-natured. The couple facing the door where Malcolm stood were his niece, Radford's daughter, and Des's brother. A family group, then; he recognized his nephew Edward with his back to the door. But who was Edward's partner? A dark, elegant stranger who moved with lively grace to the centre of the set to turn about with the other three ladies. . . .

No stranger. Mariette. As she returned to Edward's side, her eyes met Malcolm's. Her face lit up, her eyes brightened, her lips parted—and the next moment she laid her hand on Edward's arm and smiled up at him.

She was his partner. She could not break the pattern of the dance to greet Malcolm. But did she have to smile at Edward in that damnably coquettish way?

At last the dance ended. Amid the greetings of his family and his hearty congratulations to the betrothed couple, Malcolm lost his chance to speak to Mariette. When next he saw her, she was dancing up with a handsome young fellow in a shockingly ill-cut evening coat and a lopsided neckcloth. Apparently unaware of her partner's sartorial shortcomings, she talked and laughed with every evidence of enjoyment, flirting with her fan when the figures of the dance allowed.

The rest of the ball was agony. When Mariette was not dancing, she was surrounded by a positive mob of admirers begging for a dance. Every now and then she would disappear for a quarter of an hour. Trying to persuade himself she had simply gone to tidy her hair, Malcolm nonetheless suffered miserable pangs of jealousy as he wondered whether she was being kissed in some dark corner.

As hostess, Lilian, on the arm of her betrothed, mingled with her guests and did not dance again, but Malcolm did his duty by both his nieces and his female cousin. When at last he managed to stand up with Mariette, she smiled and chattered nonsense just as she had with all her other partners. Eyes shining, cheeks flushed, she laughingly admired his waistcoat.

"What a coincidence," she cried. "You see I am wearing the Tudor rose pendant Ralph gave me."

"No coincidence," he vowed, and she laughed again.

She was beautiful and she was maddening and he wanted to drag her away to one of those dark corners and kiss her until she promised to marry him.

Never before had he regretted being a gentleman.

The moment the set ended he was reft from her by her mob. Disconsolate, he wandered about exchanging a few words here and there with friends, family, acquaintances.

He came across a little old man clad in green satin and tarnished lace in the style of the last century. To his astonishment he recognized George Barwith. Mr. Barwith, his eyes bright behind gleaming new spectacles, obviously had no notion who Malcolm was, so he reintroduced himself. For a while they sat together, both contemplating Mariette's slender form, graceful movements, and animated face, but with very different feelings. Her uncle was enraptured to see her enjoying herself with other young people. Malcolm, were he not a gentleman, would happily have taken a horsewhip to every doltish yokel who had the effrontery to touch her hand.

Restless, he moved on. It was his own fault. He had persuaded Lilian to teach Mariette how to go on in Society. He failed to foresee that the unspoiled, courageous, loyal girl he had fallen in love with might turn into a dashing diamond and a heartless flirt.

Malcolm stayed at the Duke of Cornwall for what was left of the night after the ball. Disappointed in love, he resolved to devote his full attention to his work, so he had arranged to meet Des in the morning to discuss how to proceed.

The captain was shown up to his chamber at an abominably early hour. "Can't manage without your eight hours sleep?" he jeered as Malcolm scowled at him from the shelter of his bed. "You landlubbers wouldn't last a week on a ship at sea in rough weather."

"I've no intention of trying." He slitted his eyes against the grey light which flooded in when his friend threw back the curtains. "Go away. Come back later."

"I've told 'em to bring breakfast up in ten minutes." Des positively sparkled with exuberant energy. "If I get to my desk early enough I'll be able to ride over to Corycombe this afternoon. Here's your dressing-gown. Wasn't that a splendid ball? Lilian was splendid. I can't believe my luck."

Malcolm grunted and dragged himself out of bed. "Let's get down to business, if we must," he said sourly, pulling on his dressing-gown.

The inn servants brought in a folding table, followed by a laden tray. Over eggs, bacon, beefsteaks, and ale, Malcolm described his frustrating consultations at the Admiralty.

Des pounced on the salient point. "So in fact we may do as we want? Splendid, simply splendid! I've rather been doing that anyway while you were gone," he added, without noticeable guilt.

"The devil you have! Any luck?"

"Gad yes! Wait till you hear this. Gault has a mistress, a Frenchwoman. . . ."

"French!"

"An emigrée, been in England fifteen years, in Plymouth

ten, but a lot of those people who fled the Revolution prefer a Boney Emperor to a Fat King Louis. She . . ."

"True, though by no means all."

"Do stop interrupting, there's a good chap, or we'll be here all day. Madame Duhamel is a modish dressmaker. Lilian took Emily and Miss Bertrand to her to get their gowns for the ball and . . ."

"Very modish," Malcolm interrupted again, recalling Mariette's elegance.

"*Very* modish," Des echoed. "Emmie told me she has new fashion plates from Paris, and possibly French materials as well. I'm going to like having a daughter."

"I daresay. Smuggled?"

"Oh, undoubtedly."

"And she's the admiral's mistress, hm? But where does the sphinx seal come in?"

"Madame has more than one string to her bow. Besides the dressmaking she owns a private club, a gaming hell, frequented by none other than Sir Ralph Riddlesworth."

Malcolm groaned. Against the evidence of the seal, he had hoped that Mariette's cousin was not involved, but the connection was undeniable. "Gault, boasting of his importance perhaps, whispers his secrets in Madame's pretty ear—one assumes she is attractive, though no longer young. She passes on the news to Riddlesworth, in exchange for smuggled goods. And he deals with the smugglers, presumably through an intermediary with a Devonshire accent."

"A servant or a tenant, maybe, who quite likely has no notion he's mixed up in anything more sinister than smuggling. It hangs together."

"Enough to hang the pair of them together, I expect, but I'd like to find more evidence if we can. We'd best search Madame's premises."

"Shop or hell?" Des took out his silver turnip watch and consulted it.

"Both. Shop first since she may have bullies guarding her club."

"Let's lay our plans later. I must be off."

"All right. I'll go on to Corycombe when I'm dressed and I'll see you there this afternoon." He hesitated, embarrassed. "I don't know if I've made it clear, old fellow, how deuced glad I am you're marrying Lilian."

"So am I." Des grinned, shook his hand heartily, and went off whistling a merry hornpipe.

He left Malcolm desperately trying to convince himself he did not care if Mariette's cousin was a traitor, since her changed character had made him cease to love her.

Chapter 15

Roused at an ungodly hour by the captain, Malcolm arrived at Corycombe well before noon. Taking his coat and hat, Charles announced that only Miss Emily was down as yet, and she was to be found in the breakfast room. Malcolm joined her.

"I am so glad you have come back, Uncle Malcolm," she said, pushing aside a half-eaten, strawberry-jammed muffin. "You will not go straight back to London, will you?"

"No, I'll stay at least a week, I expect." He thought she looked strained. Though she liked Des, the loss of her mother's full attention must be difficult to bear. "How did you enjoy your first ball?" he asked to cheer her up.

Her blue eyes widened apprehensively. "You won't tell Mama?"

Oh Lord, never say one of those doltish yokels had gone beyond the line with Emmie while he was moping over Mariette! "I can't promise," he said. "Did someone attempt familiarities?"

"Familiarities?"

"Try to kiss you."

"Oh no, nothing like that."

He breathed again. "Then what is troubling you, Emmie?"

"I shall tell you, but *pray* do not tell Mama. It's just that I did *not* enjoy the ball, and she would be horridly disappointed when she went to so much trouble to make it perfect. It was fun dancing with Cousin Edward and with you, because I know you both quite well, and I didn't mind dancing with Uncle Radford, because he is so jolly and kind. But . . .''

"But?"

"There were so many people!" she burst out. "I couldn't think of anything to say to anyone and it was perfectly horrid, so in the end I went and hid in the ladies' withdrawing room. I only came out to speak to Mama now and then so she would believe I was enjoying myself. But the worst thing is, when I am old enough she will want me to go to London and have a Season and go to balls *all the time,* and I cannot bear it!" Tears streaming down her face, she sniffed piteously.

Malcolm took her hand. "My dear child, the whole point is that you are *not* old enough. You have had very little experience of meeting strangers. I shouldn't be surprised if you get a good deal more practise in future, for Des is a sociable fellow and won't let your mama shut herself away here. In two or three years time, you will be much more grown-up. You'll be able to converse with anyone at all, even Prinny."

"The Prince of Wales?" She stared at him, teardrops trembling on her lashes. "Do you really think so? That is what Mariette said, too."

Something twisted painfully inside him. "She did?"

"Yes, last night. She kept coming to see me in the ladies' room, to talk to me so I would not be lonely. Without her, it would have been much, much horrider."

He had misjudged her. Though she was a flirt, she was not heartless. Though she was no longer unspoiled, she was still loyal, at least to his bashful little niece.

"I'll ride over to Bell-Tor Manor this afternoon," he decided.

Mariette looked around the drawing room with qualified satisfaction. The woodwork gleamed; the Turkey carpet was rusty red instead of dingy brown; the curtains were

faded blue instead of grimy grey, and only close scrutiny
would reveal that the hems were frayed too badly to be
turned. Bowls of early daffodils distracted attention from
the worn seat-covers, some of them ready to split.

Three of the seat-covers were concealed beneath gentlemen she had danced with last night, and a fourth dancing
partner shared the hearthrug with Ragamuffin. He held out
chilled hands to the flames for it was a damp, raw day outside, which made it the more flattering that they had all
called on her.

She'd willingly exchange the lot of them for Lord Malcolm.

Still, it was kind of them to come, so she did her best to
entertain them. She laughed at their insipid jokes, did her
best to blush at their laboured compliments, listened breathless and admiring to tedious tales of daring deeds on the
hunting field—some of them all too familiar, for one of her
visitors was young Mr. Bolger.

Her thoughts wandered. If only one or two ladies would
call, both to leaven the conversation and to show she was
accepted by local society, not merely admired by callow
youths.

Did Lord Malcolm admire her? Her attempt to flirt with
him at the ball had proved less than successful. She hoped it
was because he was tired from his journey. At least he had
seen that she was much sought after, that she had not lan-
guished away during his absence.

She was quite capable of enjoying herself without him.
Look at all these gentlemen so anxious to amuse her.

"I wouldn't have minded cracking my head," the Hon-
ourable Jack Phillips wound up his story, "if I'd had you,
Miss Bertrand, to soothe my fevered brow and hold my
hand."

"I am sure your mama is a much better nurse than I, sir."

"But not half so pretty."

Mariette smiled at him. He really was doing his best. It
wasn't his fault he had no imagination and no gift with
words.

"A pretty girl don't want to waste her time nursing a clunch like you." Freddy Browne turned from the fire. "She'd rather be dancing . . . I say, Eden!"

Startled, they all looked towards the door. Lord Malcolm stood there, a faint, sardonic smile on his lips.

"Good afternoon, Miss Bertrand, gentlemen. I trust I don't intrude."

Ragamuffin jumped up and ran to greet him.

"Of course not, Lord Malcolm," said Mariette gaily. "There is always room for one more." She meant to be welcoming, but even as she spoke she knew she sounded as if she were boasting of the number of her beaux.

Lord Malcolm bowed silently and took a seat.

"If you ask me," cried Mr. Phillips, "there's a dashed sight too much competition already. No offense, my lord, but what's a fellow to do when he gives his heart to the prettiest girl in the county and half a dozen other fellows want a share of hers?"

"My heart is indivisible, Mr. Phillips," Mariette said, laughing. "I cannot give it away piecemeal."

"I should rather think not," said Mr. Bolger indignantly. "Sounds dashed painful."

"Give the whole thing to me, Miss Bertrand," Mr. Browne suggested. "I'll take deuced good care of it, I swear."

"You can't trust Freddy," piped up the last of the four, a would-be dandy who had been eyeing Lord Malcolm's waistcoat with admiring envy. "Why, I lent him my studs for the ball and I'll be damned . . . dashed if the nodcock hasn't gone and lost them. He'd only go and lose your heart if you gave it to him."

"I don't believe anyone but I can lose my heart," Mariette protested.

The nonsense continued for a few more minutes. Lord Malcolm, fondling Ragamuffin's ears, said nothing but his expression became more and more sardonic. The others grew uneasy and started muttering about not outstaying their welcome. Mariette did not try to keep them. Flirting with those four at once was all very well, but to flirt with Malcolm she wanted to be alone with him.

At last they all bowed themselves out, having begged for and received permission to call again. With a teasing smile she turned to Lord Malcolm.

"Do you, too, wish for a share in my heart?" she asked archly, although he already possessed the whole.

"No!" He sprang to his feet. "I'll be damned if I do! And I cannot stay, since you have no chaperon. Good day to you, ma'am."

And without another word he stalked from the room.

Mariette started to rise, holding out pleading hands, then slumped back into her chair. She bit her lip as tears rose to her eyes.

She ought to have guessed he was in no mood for joking. He had wanted to talk to her seriously, to explain his absence perhaps. Now he was offended, she would never know.

But from the moment he arrived he had looked askance at her little court. He disapproved of her receiving her admirers, although she had never been alone with any one of them. Once again anger came to her rescue. He had no right to object. If she chose to take one of those silly boys at his word and inveigle him into marriage, Lord Malcolm had nothing to say in the matter.

Unfortunately, he was still the only man she wanted to marry.

Everything was going wrong.

Riding up the rocky path towards Bell Tor, Malcolm reined in Incognita and glanced back. A horseman and a carriage were just arriving at the manor.

The rider looked like his nephew Edward, a nice lad Mariette's age, a cut above the four he had interrupted—and eldest son of the heir to a marquis. The vehicle was a smart phaeton of distinctive build driven by a tall, well-built gentleman. Malcolm recognized the phaeton from Town, and he had seen Lord Liscombe at the ball, though he had not known he lived in this part of the country. The earl was a distinguished bachelor in his early thirties, a worthy rival. God send he was merely paying a courtesy call.

Everything was going wrong. Malcolm urged the mare on up the hill, past the heaped boulders of the tor. It began to rain as they galloped along a faint moorland track, startling a herd of wild ponies into flight.

He had absolutely no excuse for snapping at Mariette, still less for marching out without another word. No chaperon, forsooth! Admittedly, Ragamuffin was an unreliable chaperon, but they could have called in a servant to prevent his kissing those delectable lips.

The fact was, the offer of a share in her heart was simply too painful to bear.

She was joking, of course, but the joke put him on a level with those rustic rattlepates. Not that there was anything wrong in her flirting with them—he'd seen far more forward behaviour from well-born, well-bred coquettes accepted by the Ton. It was just a shock to see *her* behave thus. She had been so free of any artifice.

Nor was he jealous of the four youths. Mariette could not possibly care for such callow, corkbrained gabies. She was an intelligent woman, a woman who required more of a man than admiration of her beauty.

God, she was beautiful. As he pictured her laughing face, her slender, supple body, the muscles in his legs clenched and Incognita's stride faltered.

He slowed the confused mare to a canter, leaning forward to stroke her wet neck in apology. Mariette deserved an apology, too. Should he turn back to Bell-Tor Manor and beg her forgiveness for his churlish behaviour?

Edward and Liscombe were there. Besides, he'd have to explain that he wanted all of her heart, not a share, and the time for an avowal was not yet come. Not until he had dealt with her triple-damned cousin.

Des would be waiting for him, to make their plans. He rode back to Corycombe.

Three days passed while one of the captain's trusted men ingratiated himself with Madame Duhamel's maidservant. The girl was the only person to spend the night at the shop, for Madame was no common shopkeeper to sleep over her business.

Three days—on the second Mariette called at Corycombe. She treated Malcolm with a wariness he acknowledged to be deserved. It was no less hurtful for that.

Three days—on the third Malcolm received from the Cornish magistrate, William Penhallow, another sphinx-sealed letter. This one mentioned a possible invasion of Portugal.

The spilling of secrets must not be allowed to continue. Ralph Riddlesworth had to be stopped. All too soon, Malcolm would discover whether Mariette could forgive him for a far worse injury than marching out of her drawing room in a totally unreasonable huff.

On the fourth evening, as church clocks all over Plymouth struck ten, Petty Officer Clark led Malcolm and Des along a dark alley. "The seamstresses allus works till six," he said in a hoarse whisper, "and often enough till eight. Not later acos Madam says they make too many mistakes next day. Leastwise, 'lessn there's a vallyble order to be got out in a hurry, which there ain't tonight,"

"A kind mistress," Des murmured sarcastically.

"There's worse, cap'n, sir, accordin' of Sukey, what's the cook-maid. She's left the alley door unlocked. I'll keep her snug in the kitchen while you're about your business, cap'n."

"Not too snug, Tom! You're on the King's business."

"Now would I, sir?" The sailor sounded injured. "She'll have a bite o' supper for me, and I'll play me fife. Likes a bit o' music, does Sukey, and it'll stop her hearing owt o' your doings. Keep mum, now. Here we be."

They slipped through the door in the wall into a small, cobblestoned courtyard. To their right was the wall of the next house, ahead the three-story main part of the shop, to the left a two-story wing with a light shining in a ground-floor window at the alley end. "The kitchen," breathed Tom Clark.

Des and Malcolm flattened themselves against the wall while the sailor knocked on a door in the centre of the wing. Sukey came to let him in, candle in hand. Giggling, she closed the door and a moment later the light reappeared in the kitchen window.

Malcolm tried the latch. The door swung open and he and Des slipped through. They turned right in a narrow passage.

Clark had explained the plan of the house, which the maid had shown him over. On their left was a storeroom where all the valuable bales of materials were locked up at night. Above was the long workshop where most of the sewing was done. This was also locked at night as it contained work in progress.

In the main house, the topmost floor held a dining parlour for the seamstresses, who had a hot dinner deducted from their wages, and storage space for odds and ends. The first floor was divided into several small fitting-rooms. Most of the ground floor was devoted to the showroom, with one fitting-room for elderly or stout ladies unable to tackle stairs, and Madame's office.

"The which she don't lock," Tom Clark had reported, "being as she goes to the bank every day and takes the rest home, so there ain't no blunt about."

It was too easy. Malcolm did not expect to find anything.

His outstretched hand met the door to the showroom. He felt for the latch. A hinge creaked, but no louder than the groan of old timbers settling. Des closed the door silently behind them and Malcolm opened a panel of their dark lantern.

The beam gleamed on silk and satin draperies, gilt chairs, pier-glasses, windowpanes backed by outside shutters. In one corner it lit on a female figure and Malcolm stopped breathing—momentarily. A manikin, elegantly dressed!

Des nudged him. "Over there," he whispered.

Skirting the small tables, they crossed the long room and

entered Madame's office. Here all was businesslike: shelves of account books, a drawing table with sketches of gowns pinned to it, and a large walnut bureau.

In the keyhole of the fold-down front of the bureau was a small brass key. Carelessness? Design? Or was there simply nothing in the desk of interest to anyone but its owner?

Malcolm turned the key and frowned as the desk failed to open to his tug.

"I expect you locked it," Des said, grinning.

He had. Letting down the flap disclosed pigeon-holes and little drawers galore, innocently filled with pencils, pens, unmade quills, a penknife, ink, paper, sealing wafers, all the predictable paraphernalia.

Des reached past Malcolm. From beneath a neat stack of blotting-paper he abstracted a folded sheet of letter-paper.

It bore no direction, but a slight grubbiness at the creases suggested it had been delivered, not just written. He turned it over. The seal, already slit, was stamped with a clear image of an Egyptian sphinx.

"Too easy," he grunted. "It was sticking out a good half inch."

"Much too easy," Malcolm agreed, taking it and unfolding it.

Dated yesterday. No salutation, no signature. "We must meet," he read. The hand was the same as that of the treasonous letters. "Not the club. There's an untenanted house on the River Plym, near Crabtree." Detailed directions followed, then: "Thursday at eight thirty. Do not fail."

"Thursday," Des muttered. "Tide's high at nine or thereabouts. Down the river by rowboat, meet the smugglers' lugger in the Cattewater, and off to France?"

"That's what we're supposed to think. It may be true, too. If they try to use the same smuggler I daresay we'll be hearing about it from Justice Penwarren. Here, memorize these directions; it's best if we both know the way. Then I'll put it back."

"Just as it was?"

"No, just enough difference so they can be certain we found it."

Malcolm's guess as to the purpose of the letter was virtually confirmed when Tom Waite joined them in the back room of a nearby tavern an hour later. The sailor's round, weather-tanned face was disgruntled.

"What, Tom, didn't your Sukey let you have your way with her?" Des mocked him.

"King's business, cap'n!" he said indignantly. "I di'n't try for more'n a kiss and a bit of a squeeze. No, 'tain't that, sir, 'tis much worser. I'm afeard the rig's blown."

"Blown?" Malcolm said. Clark looked at him with curiosity. He hadn't been told who his captain's companion was. Dressed in nondescript, ill-fitted clothes, Malcolm didn't look in the least like a marquis's son, still less a bit of a dandy. Few would note him now, fewer still recognize him if they saw him tomorrow figged out in his best. "Who blew it?" he asked.

"Sukey. Quite innocent-like, sir, I don't want to get her in trouble. Not that sort nor any," he added, frowning at the captain. "Seems Madame don't mind her having a fellow calling, long as he's respectable. Sukey told her 'bout me, and 'bout me coming tonight, and worstest, 'bout me being a petty officer in the Navy."

"So they know we're after them," Des said, looking at Malcolm.

Malcolm grinned. "As I supposed, the letter was left for us. How fortunate that I put it back crooked to show we had read it, or they might not bother to set the trap!"

Lord Malcolm was always out when Mariette called at Corycombe. Though Emily complained that he was never in, Mariette felt sure he was avoiding her in particular.

She did not blame him. Mistaking his sentiments, she had been so dreadfully forward as to ask whether he wanted a share of her heart. She had driven him away, ruined their friendship just when she most needed a friend's advice.

An unshockable, worldly-wise friend—she could not consult Lilian about Ralph's desperate predicament.

Ralph refused to talk to her about his troubles. He was in over his head, he said. Every penny she possessed could not save him. She offered to give back her rose pendant. With scorn he rejected the trumpery trifle.

"Your sphinx ring?" she asked. He had taken it out of her workbox once or twice but always put it back. "The Tudor signet?"

"Even that. Keep it. One day you may want it to remember me by."

Terrified, she begged him to go to Uncle George.

"No! A fine figure I should cut involving an old dodderer in my downfall. I'd as soon let *you* mix yourself up in it. Swear you won't tell Uncle George or I'll leave now and you'll never see me again."

Mariette was forced to promise. He rode off anyway, but came back later paler and more subdued than ever.

She recalled all too clearly the hints of deep play at Madame Duhamel's hell, of Lord Wareham running so deep into debt he tried to force Lilian to marry him. Had Ralph been threatened with violence as an example to others unable to pay? Or was he contemplating doing away with himself?

Sometimes his words seemed to her to indicate one dreadful alternative, sometimes the other. Sometimes she almost managed to convince herself he was just being melodramatic. Such shocking things could not happen in quiet Devon!

Yet Ralph grew more and more wretched.

At last, late one afternoon, Mariette decided she had to beg Lord Malcolm to advise her, whatever his opinion of her. He was far too kind, too generous-spirited to reject a plea for help. If Jim Groom took a note over to Corycombe first thing in the morning, asking Lord Malcolm to call at the manor at his earliest convenience, surely he would come tomorrow.

She sat down at her little writing table, rarely used, for

who had she to write to? The right words refused to come. Her first attempt sounded presumptuous, the second servile, the third too vague to be taken seriously. She was starting on the fourth when Ralph came into the sitting room, waving a sheet of paper.

"My last chance," he announced with a sort of feverish despair mingled with insouciant optimism. "Tonight will make or break me!"

"What is it?" she demanded. "What's happening tonight?"

"I'll be going out after dinner."

"Where to? What for? Ralph, you must tell me!"

"Don't fuss, Mariette. There's nothing you can do to help this time and if there was I'd be damned if I'd let you after the mull you made of the highwayman business."

"I got your ring back."

"True, and I'll wear it tonight." Stuffing the paper into his pocket, he rummaged in her work-box, retrieved the signet, and put it on. "I'll need all the luck I can get. I shan't pledge it, don't fret. It's too late for that."

"But Ralph, what . . . ?"

"I wish I hadn't told you anything," he said sulkily, and strode out.

Mariette glanced at the clock on the mantelpiece. Nearly dinner-time and far too late to send for Lord Malcolm. She would have to follow Ralph herself.

No sidesaddle tonight. She still had the highwayman costume, neatly packed up by Jenny when she left Corycombe, all except the shot-riddled breeches. Those she had replaced with a more recently outgrown pair of Ralph's. They were too long in the leg and too wide in the waist, as she had discovered on her only moorland gallop since then, but they would serve.

The pistol had been lost on the moor, but its pair was in the gunroom. This time she loaded it. If someone threatened Ralph she would not have to rely upon bluff.

Dinner was a strained meal, though Uncle George appeared to notice nothing amiss. Afterwards, Ralph gave her such an affectionate kiss on the cheek she thought she would cry.

"Don't fret," he said again. "I shall come about."

He went off towards the stables and she raced upstairs to change her clothes. No abigail to ask questions, thank heaven, and by now Jim Groom was in the kitchen eating his supper. Ralph would not risk riding over the moor in the dark, nor even going too fast along the potholed lane. There was only one way out of the Bell Brook valley so she should be able to catch up easily.

He would try to send her home but she'd refuse to go. With so much at stake he could not afford to turn back to escort her.

She turned from the looking-glass after tucking up her hair under the chapeau-bras. Ragamuffin! He sat there grinning, tail swishing on the floor, obviously certain of a good run.

He had almost ruined everything last time. "Stay!" she said firmly. Ignoring his hurt look, she hurried to the door and slipped through. As it clicked shut, she heard the scrabble of claws, followed by a salvo of barks. She prayed no one would hear and let him out until she was well away.

Down to the stables. Ralph had left a lantern burning. By its light, as Sparrow whickered a welcome, she saw a crumpled paper on the floor. She picked it up and smoothed it.

"If you wish to recoup your fortunes, you may wager on tick—one more time only—at a house near Crabtree." Crabtree! Mariette knew the village, on the way to Plymouth. She perused the detailed directions to the house. "Be there by half past eight o'clock tonight," the letter concluded.

Folding it, she pushed it deep into her topcoat pocket and went to fetch Sparrow's saddle. Now she knew where Ralph was going, she need not try to catch up with him but she did not want to fall too far behind.

Ralph was quite addlepated enough to believe he had a chance of winning, she thought as she buckled the girth strap and eased the bit into the gelding's mouth. Madame

Duhamel's motive in drawing him still further into debt was impossible to guess. Why had she granted him credit in the first place? Her letter indicated she knew his only hope of redeeming his vowels was to win.

Surely she did not take pleasure in driving young men to suicide?

Mariette shivered. Leading Sparrow from his stall, she mounted and set off into the starlit night.

Chapter 16

By starlight reflected from the black waters of the Plym, Mariette tied Sparrow's bridle to a sapling just off the river-bank path. Rubbing his nose, she fed him a lump of sugar, then convulsively hugged him. She felt very much alone as she set off towards the dark bulk of the house.

What had once been a lawn sloping down to the river was now a hummocky meadow. Mariette steered clear of the exposed area, creeping through overgrown shrubbery which snatched at her clothes and rustled mysteriously though the night was still. A branch knocked off her hat. She caught it, muttering an expletive that would have shocked Lilian to the core.

A briar caught in her hair. By the time she had disentangled it, half the pins had fallen out and her hair was tumbling down her back. With another oath, she jammed the hat on her head and hurried on.

As she neared the house, a gentleman's residence somewhat smaller than Bell-Tor Manor, she noticed a faint light behind curtains at one corner. French doors flanked by two windows; perhaps with her ear against the glass she'd be able to hear what was going on inside.

Between her and the lit room were a stretch of rough grass and a terrace—no cover except for two large stone urns at the top of the steps. Yet why on earth should anyone be watching?

Her precautions were really rather silly. Nonetheless,

dashing across the grass and up the steps, she cowered by one of the urns for what seemed an age before she had the nerve to go on.

From here she could see the French doors were set in a bay projecting some four feet from the side of the house. On tiptoe she approached. Not a sound escaped from the room beyond. She tried the door-handle.

To her surprise the door was not locked. The curtains hung across the bay, separating it from the room and leaving plenty of space for an eavesdropper.

Fate was on her side, and however momentary that fickle favour, she could not refuse the invitation. She discarded her hat, shrugged out of the bulky topcoat, sat down on the flagstones and removed her riding boots. Heart in mouth, she slipped in.

Still no sound of voices! Holding her breath, she crept between two dust-sheeted chairs, parted the curtains an eighth of an inch, and peeped through. More furniture shrouded in holland covers; an open door in the opposite wall, in the lefthand corner from her vantage point; to her right . . .

Ralph sat at a card-table, looking sulky, his legs stretched out beneath it. Just as she caught sight of him he pulled his watch from its fob and grumbled loudly, "Where the devil are they?"

Somewhere in the house a clock chimed the half hour. In the open doorway a man appeared. Lamplight glinted on the pistol in his hand.

Mariette bit her lip to stop her gasp. She wanted to know what was going on before she intervened. A moment later she bit her lip still harder as the man moved into the room and the light reached his face.

Lord Malcolm! And Captain Aldrich followed him in. Mariette's head spun.

Ralph jumped up, overturning his chair.

"Don't move!" said Lord Malcolm sharply. "The game is up, Riddlesworth. We know you have been spying for France. We've intercepted your letters, sealed with your sphinx signet."

"B-but . . ." Ralph stammered, glancing down at his hand in utter disbelief.

"Hardly a common emblem, is it? There's no way out." His voice was full of contempt. "You ought to hang. However, for your cousin's sake we shall let you flee abroad, where your treachery cannot harm your country."

"What the deuce?" cried Captain Aldrich. "We can't let the traitor go!"

"But I didn't . . . I'm not . . . I haven't . . ." Ralph squawked.

For her sake! Mariette was about to step forth and sort out their baconbrained male idiocies when a new voice, deadly calm, interrupted.

"Drop your weapons or I shoot."

Lord Wareham? Mariette would know that hateful voice anywhere. Icy fear filled her veins as Malcolm's and the captain's pistols thudded to the floor. They turned towards her and she saw their startled, dismayed faces. Ralph was aghast and totally bewildered.

The baron advanced into the room from her extreme left—he must have entered through a door outside her angle of view. He stopped half turned away from her, a pistol in each hand, their unwavering barrels aimed at the men.

Mariette felt for her gun.

"Regrettably," said Lord Wareham, "I mean to shoot anyway. Oh, not you, Riddlesworth," he added, a sneer in his tone, as Ralph took an involuntary step backwards. "You're nothing but a pawn. I shan't waste a shot on you."

She had left the pistol in the pocket of her topcoat. On silent, stockinged feet she scuttled out to the terrace to retrieve it.

Behind her, Malcolm announced grimly, "You cannot escape. The house is surrounded."

A moment's silence, while she found the pocket and disentangled the weapon.

"If that's true," Lord Wareham said, and he sounded just a trifle shaken, "it makes no difference. I shall hang whether you die or not, and sending the gallant captain to meet his reward will be a positive pleasure. Business first, however. Do you know, Eden, I never guessed you were a spycatcher? Nothing personal, I assure you, but should I get away I daresay there might be some reward for putting you out of the picture."

As he raised his right hand, Mariette charged through the curtains. "Stop!" she shouted. "Stop or I'll fire."

The baron swung round. Two shots cracked out. A burning agony seared through Mariette's arm and her pistol fell from strengthless hands.

Lord Wareham rushed towards her, past her, shoving her aside. Losing her balance she crumpled to the floor. A shrill whistle rang in her ears. Through the spots dancing before her eyes she saw Captain Aldrich dash after the baron, Ralph at his heels. Then Malcolm's horrified face filled her universe.

The ringing in her ears faded but his voice came from a vast distance and she could not quite make out the words.

She had to explain. "Ralph . . . lost the sphinx to . . . to Lord . . . Wareham, a year . . . ago," she whispered. She could not see him now, but his hands clutched hers. Though her arm was on fire, she was clammily cold. One more effort: "Sparrow . . ."

"Is Miss Bertrand really fit to receive us?" Des asked as he rode at Malcolm's side over the crest of Wicken's Down.

They had returned late last night from escorting Wareham and Madame Duhamel to London. Nothing was going to stop Malcolm from seeing Mariette today.

Fortunately he was able to say, "She was downstairs yesterday when Lilian and Emily called on her. Emmie said she looks pale and interesting as she did when she first came to Corycombe, but her message says she is more like to die of curiosity than anything else."

Des laughed. Malcolm failed to summon up more than a faint smile.

Her only concern before she swooned had been to excul-

pate her cousin, he thought gloomily for the hundredth
time. She was as loyal and courageous as ever. Loyal to Sir
Ralph Riddlesworth. Courageous in his defence.

They had grown up together, but they were not related by
blood. She had mothered him, but they were of an age. Did
she care for him because he needed her, or did she love him
as a woman loves a man? She was not blind to his faults, his
weakness for gambling, his refusal to take responsibility for
his own mistakes. The more reason she might find to devote
her life to protecting him from himself.

Malcolm swallowed a sigh and turned his attention to
guiding Incognita down the steep slope between the fra-
grant, gaudy masses of yellow gorse.

As they approached the manor, a landau accompanied by
two horsemen drove off down the valley and disappeared
among the greening trees. In the stable yard, Riddlesworth
was talking to Jim Groom. He swung round at the sound of
hooves.

"I say, my lord, are you come to enlighten us?" he asked
eagerly.

At least the lad did not hold a grudge, as he had every
right to, Malcolm admitted reluctantly. "Yes," he said, "if
Miss Bertrand is well enough?"

"She's in fine twig, considering. Bolger and Phillips just
brought their sisters to call but I wouldn't let them stay
long."

"They don't know what happened?"

"Only that she was hurt in an accident. That was bound
to get about since we took her to the inn at Crabtree." He
greeted the captain, holding his horse as he dismounted,
then ushered the visitors into the house.

Malcolm suddenly had to know how things stood between the cousins before he saw Mariette. "I'd like a word
with you, Riddlesworth," he said. "Des, do you mind going
ahead? Tell her we're on our way."

Des glanced at him, in turn surprised, comprehending,
quizzical. He nodded and went on.

"You don't still think I did it?" Riddlesworth demanded in alarm.

"No." If there was a delicate way to phrase what was a deuced impertinent question, it did not come to mind. "I simply wish to ask whether you have an understanding with your cousin."

"Understanding?" He looked puzzled, then aghast. "You mean am I going to marry her? Good gad no! That is, devil take it, I'm deuced fond of Mariette but a fellow don't want a wife who's always ordering a fellow about." His expression changed to one of enlightenment. "Daresay she don't order you about," he observed sapiently.

His face hot, Malcolm strode ahead towards the drawing room, Sir Ralph ambling along behind him. Hope raised its head. Sir Ralph's feelings were no guide to Mariette's, but after all, in the end she had not risked her life to save her cousin's. It was Malcolm whom Wareham had been about to shoot when she burst into the room, terrifyingly foolhardy, superbly brave, utterly adorable.

Fending off Ragamuffin's exuberant welcome allowed him to regain his composure. He nearly lost it again when he looked up to find Mariette smiling at him. Pale and interesting indeed! Though she reclined on a sofa, her arm in a sling, she was blooming, wild roses in her cheeks, dark eyes brilliant. Her loveliness took his breath away.

And she smiled at him! Of course, she did not yet understand that his slow-wittedness had nearly got her killed.

"How is your arm?" he asked, shuddering inside at the memory of his terror as he tried to find where she had been wounded.

"It aches like the very d—like anything," she said frankly. "Captain Aldrich says you are going to tell us *everything*."

"Not to be repeated beyond these four walls," he warned. "It all started with a quasi-patriotic smuggler who mistrusted a letter he was paid to take to France. The Admiralty sent me to investigate."

"I knew you were not just a fribble, in spite of the waistcoats," cried Mariette, and the corners of her mouth quirked as she glanced at his Tudor rose midriff.

Rather exotic for morning wear even for him, but he'd had it made to please her and he was glad he'd worn it today.

Mariette was quite ready to take it as a compliment. Through all the pain and lassitude of her injury, one memory had sustained her: Malcolm's voice announcing his willingness to let a supposed traitor go free for her sake. For her sake he had risked disgrace or worse. What could it mean but that he loved her?

She listened, fascinated and admiring, as he explained about the use and misuse of the sphinx seal. Taking a small object from his pocket, he tossed it to Ralph.

"Here, you ought to have my copy. The other was found on Wareham and will be used in evidence against him. Believe it or not, it never dawned on me that what I could do, so could someone else. If I had not been so sure you were the traitor, we'd not have been taken by surprise and Miss Bertrand would not have been shot."

He sounded so downcast, Mariette hurried to say remorsefully, "I should have mentioned you were not the first person to win the ring from Ralph. I was too proud. You see, when I redeemed it from Lord Wareham, he treated me like a worm. A *squashed* worm. It's all very well laughing, but I did not like to think about it, still less to talk of it."

"Most understandable," said the captain, his lips twitching.

"What I don't understand," Ralph put in, "is why the devil you thought I knew any naval secrets."

"Blame Wareham for that, too," said Malcolm. "Obviously he used your seal originally with an eye to deflecting suspicion from himself should aught go amiss. He told us he learned from a certain highly placed naval officer, by way of Madame Duhamel, that Aldrich was hunting for spies."

Mariette interrupted. "I heard him say he did not realize *you* were after him. How clever not to give yourself away!"

Malcolm grinned and bowed ironically. "Thank you,

ma'am. Unaware of my position, Wareham's first hope of escape was to persuade my sister to marry him, thus obviating the need for money which led him into treason in the first place. However, he then discovered his letters had actually been intercepted. Thus he had to have a scapegoat. He introduced you to Madame's gaming house, did he not, Riddlesworth?"

"Yes." Ralph gave Mariette a guilty look. "I didn't tell you because I knew you disliked him."

"Loathed him!"

Malcolm smiled at her. "Most discerning of you. The club provided a damning link with the high officer—whose embroilment, incidentally, brought about my involuntary departure to London—as well as a link with Madame, his m—er, hm."

"His mistr—? Oh!" Mariette thought of Lilian's lessons and blushed.

"Precisely. She arranged for your cousin to win at cards at first, to encourage him, and then to lose, to be given credit and then to be denied credit. At last he was offered one last chance to recoup."

"If I lost again," said Ralph sombrely, "I was going to take the king's shilling."

"Enlist in the army?" Recalling her fear of a far worse fate, Mariette decided it was best not mentioned. "You dropped the letter in the stables. That's how I found the house."

"I could wish you had not, since you'd not have been injured," Malcolm said unsteadily, his gaze fixed on hers, "but on the other hand I'd now be dead. If I haven't yet attempted to express my gratitude it's because . . ."

"Oh, fustian," she exclaimed, thoroughly embarrassed. "Do go on with the story."

"As you wish, for now." His look made Mariette glow all over. "Madame was growing nervous, and ready to flee to France. Also, by that time Des had cut Wareham out with Lilian, humiliating him. Before leaving the country, he wanted revenge. If he had simply relied upon the letter in

Madame's desk to lure Des to the house, he might have succeeded, though we did guess at a trap and surround the place with sailors. His downfall was that he gilded the lily."

"He what?" said Ralph blankly.

"He lured you to the house, too, as bait, as a decoy. Miss Bertrand followed, and the rest is history."

Ralph was still bursting with questions. "Your turn, Des," said Lord Malcolm laconically. As the captain took over from him, he leaned towards Mariette, and murmured, "Excuse me for a few minutes, I want a word with your uncle," and slipped out of the room.

Mariette's heart sang. Surely, surely, she did not mistake his meaning!

As expected, Malcolm found Mr. Barwith in the front hall, tapping away at a piece of sandstone which now bore a respectable resemblance to a badger. Mr. Barwith was considerably sprucer, too, though he still bore a faint patina of red dust.

At the sound of Malcolm's footsteps, he looked round and beamed. "Ah, the young man who suggested my purchasing spectacles, is it not? My dear sir, you can have no notion of the difference they have made. I was even able to read to Mariette while she was confined to her bed."

"I am prodigious glad to hear it, sir. It is about Miss Bertrand I wish to speak to you."

"Is it, now!" His eyes twinkled behind the new spectacles. "Perhaps we ought to go into the library. All those books I have not been able to read these twenty years, now restored to me." With a happy sigh he led the way.

Impressed by the library, Malcolm began to understand the importance of books in his beloved's lonely life. Her books and her gallops on the moor—he'd deprive her of neither, he vowed, whatever they cost in money or in social acceptance.

"I want to marry your niece, sir," he said bluntly. "As a fifth son I am not wealthy, but my father will increase my allowance on my marriage and I shall be able to support her in comfort." He might even persuade his father to buy

Wareham's forfeited estate for him, he thought. Mariette would want to live near her uncle and cousin. At least she'd never have to hang on Riddlesworth's sleeve.

"My brother left her something," said Mr. Barwith to his surprise, "and her mother smuggled some jewellery out of France."

"Any little bit she can call her own will be welcome."

The elderly gentleman pursed his lips thoughtfully. "It's not exactly a little bit," he said. "To tell the truth, I cannot remember the lawyer's precise figures. Twenty-five or thirty thousand in the funds, I believe, and jewellery amounting to sixty or eighty thousand pounds, though that will have changed, the way prices have risen. It is in a bank vault somewhere in London. No doubt the lawyer will know."

"No doubt," Malcolm agreed faintly. "Does Mariette know of this?"

"Not from me. I don't spend half my income and I'm happy to give her whatever she asks for. You see, when she came to the manor the lawyer suggested she was too young to understand and the figures would only confuse her. I daresay she is old enough now to be told?"

"Quite old enough." Malcolm laughed. "And I supposed I should be rescuing her from the life of a poor relation!"

"I don't consider Mariette a poor relation!" said Mr. Barwith, offended.

"I know you don't, sir. I was thinking of when Riddlesworth inherits Bell-Tor Manor."

"Ralph inherit the manor? I am not quite a doddering dotard, young man. My nephew would bring the estate to wrack and ruin in no time."

"But he is your nearest relative, is he not?"

"Bell-Tor is not entailed. My will bequeaths an adequate income to Ralph and the estate to Mariette, who will care for it and its people." He looked away, blinking, and said shyly, "I hope you will spend some time here when you are married?"

"My dear sir, we shall make our home here if you wish. Mariette would not choose to be parted from you."

"I fear despite his income you will always have Ralph sponging on you."

"Every family has a few sponging relations." His situation suddenly sank in. Intent upon offering for a penniless bride, instead he was offered a fortune, and an estate into the bargain. He burst into irrepressible laughter.

In the passage outside the library, Mariette heard Malcolm's laughter and wondered at it. He sounded less amused than almost hysterical. Her heart sank. What was wrong? She nerved herself to open the door and go in, Ragamuffin at her heels.

Uncle George gazed with benign tolerance upon Lord Malcolm, who sprang to his feet and came to meet her.

"What is so funny?" she asked.

"It's not really funny," he said soberly, looking down at her with an odd expression. "I requested your uncle's permission to ask you to be my wife, hoping to save you from poverty. Now I find you are a great heiress."

"Am I?" she said, baffled, and added wistfully, "Does that mean you don't wish to marry me after all?"

The teasing light she loved came into his eyes. "Aldrich was persuaded to overlook Lilian's fortune, was he not? I daresay you might persuade me to do likewise."

"Might I?" Heart singing again, she fluttered her eyelashes flirtatiously. "How?"

"How about a kiss to begin with?"

Flinging her uninjured arm about his neck, she obliged. His lips were warm and firm, his body hard against hers as he held her close. His kiss became insistent, demanding. Mariette clung to him as a wave of shuddering warmth flooded from her mouth to her toes and back to the centre of her being. The pain of her wound went away, the world was lost; the only reality was his touch, his . . .

"Woof?"

"Ahem!"

Reluctantly she pulled away from him. With one gentle hand he smoothed back a disarranged lock of her hair. His other arm stayed about her waist as they turned to face her uncle.

"I beg your pardon, sir," Malcolm said, a trifle breathless though not nearly so breathless as Mariette felt. "Your niece is most persuasive. Miss Bertrand," he gazed down at her, his eyes warm and smiling but not teasing at all now, "I love you very, very dearly. Will you do me the honour of accepting my hand in marriage?"

"Oh yes, my dear lord! I have loved you forever and thought you'd never ask. Only," she had to say it, "I cannot help hoping I shan't be shot again."

With a rueful laugh he swept her up in his arms and sat down with her on his lap. "I shall quit the spy business instantly," he promised. "I know as long as I'm involved I shall not be able to keep my adventurous darling out of it. And I don't want to keep you out of any part of my life, Mariette. I'm not sure I shall ever bring myself to let you out of my arms, now I have you safe."

Such an avowal deserved another kiss—and won one. When breathing became essential, Malcolm said severely, "I trust you don't mean to continue to address me as my lord?"

"No, Malcolm." A thought struck her. "I shall be Lady Mariette! Or Lady Eden?"

"Lady Malcolm."

"Truly?" She giggled. "How odd. I trust you don't mean to address me as Lady Malcolm?"

"I rather fancy I shall call you beloved. Or perhaps sweetheart, or dearest love, or possibly even snugglepuss."

"I shall like that," said Mariette dreamily and kissed him again.

"Ahem!"

She had forgotten Uncle George. Tactful or abstracted, he had been most forbearing while they cuddled and whispered sweet nothings. Ragamuffin had apparently given up in disgust. He sprawled on the hearthrug, asleep.

"I have been thinking," announced Uncle George, "about what to give you for a wedding gift. You will have the funds to buy all you need so I shall make you a statue.

Not sandstone; good, enduring granite. But what animal would you prefer?"

"A sphinx," Mariette said promptly, "since it was a sphinx which brought us together."

Malcolm looked appalled. "A *small* sphinx," he pleaded, "but all the same, if you don't object, sir, we shan't postpone the wedding until it's finished!"

ZEBRA REGENCIES
ARE THE
TALK OF THE TON!

A REFORMED RAKE (4499, $3.99)

by Jeanne Savery

After governess Harriet Cole helped her young charge flee to France—and the designs of a despicable suitor, more trouble soon arrived in the person of a London rake. Sir Frederick Carrington insisted on providing safe escort back to England. Harriet deemed Carrington more dangerous than any band of brigands, but secretly relished matching wits with him. But after being taken in his arms for a tender kiss, she found herself wondering—*could* a lady find love with an irresistible rogue?

A SCANDALOUS PROPOSAL (4504, $4.99)

by Teresa DesJardien

After only two weeks into the London season, Lady Pamela Premington has already received her first offer of marriage. If only it hadn't come from the *ton's* most notorious rake, Lord Marchmont. Pamela had already set her sights on the distinguished Lieutenant Penford, who had the heroism and honor that made him the ideal match. Now she had to keep from falling under the spell of the seductive Lord so she could pursue the man more worthy of her love. Or was he?

A LADY'S CHAMPION (4535, $3.99)

by Janice Bennett

Miss Daphne, art mistress of the Selwood Academy for Young Ladies, greeted the notion of ghosts haunting the academy with skepticism. However, to avoid rumors frightening off students, she found herself turning to Mr. Adrian Carstairs, sent by her uncle to be her "protector" against the "ghosts." Although, Daphne would accept no interference in her life, she *would* accept aid in exposing any spectral spirits. What she never expected was for Adrian to expose the secret wishes of her hidden heart . . .

CHARITY'S GAMBIT (4537, $3.99)

by Marcy Stewart

Charity Abercrombie reluctantly embarks on a London season in hopes of making a suitable match. However she cannot forget the mysterious Dominic Castille—and the kiss they shared—when he fell from a tree as she strolled through the woods. Charity does not know that the dark and dashing captain harbors a dangerous secret that will ensnare them both in its web—leaving Charity to risk certain ruin and losing the man she so passionately loves . . .

Taylor-made Romance from Zebra Books

WHISPERED KISSES   (0-8217-3830-5, $4.99/$5.99)
Beautiful Texas heiress Laura Leigh Webster never imagined
that her biggest worry on her African safari would be the handsome Jace Elliot, her tour guide. Laura's guardian, Lord Chad-
wick Hamilton, warns her of Jace's dangerous past; she simply
cannot resist the lure of his strong arms and the passion of his
Whispered Kisses.

KISS OF THE NIGHT WIND   (0-8217-5279-0, $5.99/$6.99)
Carrie Sue Strover thought she was leaving trouble behind her
when she deserted her brother's outlaw gang to live her life as
schoolmarm Carolyn Starns. On her journey, her stagecoach
was attacked and she was rescued by handsome T.J. Rogue. T.J.
plots to have Carrie lead him to her brother's cohorts who mur-
dered his family. T.J., however, soon succumbs to the beautiful
runaway's charms and loving caresses.

FORTUNE'S FLAMES   (0-8217-3825-9, $4.99/$5.99)
Impatient to begin her journey back home to New Orleans,
beautiful Maren James was furious when Captain Hawk delayed
the voyage by searching for stowaways. Impatience gave way
to uncontrollable desire once the handsome captain searched
her cabin. He was looking for illegal passengers; what he found
was wild passion with a woman he knew was unlike all those
he had known before!

PASSIONS WILD AND FREE   (0-8217-5275-8, $5.99/$6.99)
After seeing her family and home destroyed by the cruel and
hateful Epson gang, Randee Hollis swore revenge. She knew
she found the perfect man to help her—gunslinger Marsh
Logan. Not only strong and brave, Marsh had the ebony hair
and light blue eyes to make Randee forget her hate and seek
the love and passion that only he could give her.

*Available wherever paperbacks are sold, or order direct from the
Publisher. Send cover price plus 50¢ per copy for mailing and
handling to Penguin USA, P.O. Box 999, c/o Dept. 17109,
Bergenfield, NJ 07621. Residents of New York and Tennessee
must include sales tax. DO NOT SEND CASH.*